ASSASSINS AT OSPREYS

When one of detective novelist Antonia Darcy's admiring readers becomes too friendly, Antonia and her husband, Hugh, think at first it's just a bit of a bore, but when they pay a visit to Beatrice Ardleigh and her live-in companion Ingrid they begin to suspect something more sinister is going on. Is the lovely Bee really an invalid? Where does Ingrid go during her mysterious outings? Why has the master of Ospreys decided to change his will and leave his fortune not to his nephew, but to Beatrice Ardleigh? Antonia and Hugh try to prevent a murder, but find themselves investigating a gruesome death...

ASSASSINS AT OSPREYS

by

R. T. Raichev

Dales Large Print Books
Long Preston, North Yorkshire,
BD23 4ND, England.

British Library Cataloguing in Publication Data.

Raichev, R. T.
    Assassins at Ospreys.

    A catalogue record of this book is
    available from the British Library

    ISBN   978-0-7505-2970-9

First published in Great Britain 2008 by Constable,
an imprint of Constable & Robinson Ltd.

Copyright © R. T. Raichev 2008

Cover illustration by arrangement with
Constable & Robinson Ltd.

Published in Large Print 2008 by arrangement with
Constable & Robinson Ltd.

Magna Large Print is an imprint of Library Magna Books Ltd.

Printed and bound in Great Britain by
T.J. (International) Ltd., Cornwall, PL28 8RW

For Elizabeth,
who introduced me to Ce Soir Je T'Aime.

Also
for Kate,
who let me read the letter.

Author's Note

This is a work of fiction. All the characters are imaginary and bear no relation to any living person.

R.T. R.

Contents

1

The Maids

The two women sat at the very end of the first row, quite close to the platform, and Antonia couldn't say precisely which one she had noticed first. She convinced herself that it had been the one with hair like burnished gold because she was the only member of the audience who was in a wheelchair. The woman wore an extremely smart-looking cream and blue silk dress, a diamond necklace and clips, too elegant for such a minor literary event, really, and she clutched Antonia's latest book in her hands. A bunch of red roses lay across her lap. But it might have been the other, the dark one – on account of the fact that, as far as Antonia could see, she was the only person in the auditorium wearing black gloves. It was a very warm day in early June, the air conditioning in the hall wasn't working properly, and to wear any kind of gloves, no matter how fine the material, was to draw attention and invite speculation as to the reason. (Didn't sartorial quirks sometimes hint at deeper eccentricities of character?)

'Goldilocks and Cerberus' was how Antonia's husband dubbed them when she described them to him later, though by the time they paid their first visit to Millbrook House, the two nicknames had been largely forgotten.

The annual literary festival was taking place at Hay-on-Wye. Antonia was on a panel of crime writers who were addressing a small audience of about sixty. For the past twenty minutes they had been talking about various aspects of their trade. Antonia's eyes kept straying towards the two women.

They were probably in their forties, but the Goldilocks' vivacious expression, round doll-like eyes and smooth radiant face made her appear much younger. The Cerberus' hair was closely cropped and she wore a severely cut black suit. She had an air of seniority about her. Her complexion was wax-like and she had a curiously blank stare. Her gloved hands were busy, adjusting and readjusting the blanket across Goldilocks' knees. She touched Goldilocks' bare arm with the back of her hand as though to convince herself that her friend was not running a temperature, or was not too hot. She pulled a thermos flask out of her bag and motioned Goldilocks to have a drink. These attentions were accepted as though Goldilocks were used to them, but every now and then she gave the distinct impres-

10

sion she could do without them. Goldilocks' gaze did not leave the platform and it seemed to be fixed on Antonia. When their eyes eventually met, Goldilocks smiled and nodded and twiddled the fingers of her right hand in greeting. The red roses, Antonia suspected – and in a way rather dreaded – were for her. Goldilocks was clearly an aficionado.

The crime writers discussed subjects such as whether or not they could spot potential criminals, the ethics of employing real life murders as 'copy', what happened when good women fell in with crooked men ('How about vice versa?' a male member of the audience cried, raising a laugh), murder and class, whether all the strategies of deception had been exhausted, the question of implausible motives, the legacy of Agatha Christie (the 'Curse of Christie', the youngest member of the panel, a floppy-haired, truculent-looking Scot, called it), and what exactly constituted 'cheating' in detective stories – *did* readers really care?

It was all very entertaining and light-hearted. A good time seemed to be had by all. At one point the audience were invited to ask questions. The event culminated in a signing session when fans had the opportunity to meet their favourite author.

'What lovely roses... Thank you very much,' Antonia said.

'Your latest book. I would be very happy if you inscribed it for me,' Goldilocks breathed. 'I am looking forward to reading it terribly... My name is Beatrice. Beatrice Ardleigh.' Her voice was high, girlish, slightly clipped.

There had been about twelve people waiting for Antonia. Beatrice Ardleigh had appeared last. She had been wheeled up to her table by the taciturn Cerberus, whose name, it turned out, was Ingrid. Beatrice went on to describe Antonia's previous book as 'sublime'. The plot had been 'devilishly clever', 'darkly comical' and 'stupefyingly ingenious', the clueing 'superb'. *She had never guessed the murderer.* Besides – she adored it when characters displayed such high levels of literacy and erudition.

'Thank you very much,' Antonia said again. She shifted uncomfortably in her seat. She always felt extremely foolish in the face of extravagant compliments.

'Ingrid says it's all a trick – that it can all be done with a dictionary of quotations,' Beatrice continued. 'Surely that's not how *you* do it? Ingrid hates it when characters swap lines of poetry "like in a game of ping-pong", but I think it's such fun... Do you like poetry?'

'I do.' Antonia picked up her pen. 'Shall I write – "To Beatrice"?'

'"To Bee"... *Please*. That's what my best

friends call me.'

Antonia wrote obligingly on the flyleaf, *To Bee – With my very best wishes. Antonia Darcy.*

'Would you cross out your name and write it in your own hand? The way writers do it? *Thank* you. It means so much to me.'

'Thank you very much,' Antonia said for the third time, with an air of finality, she hoped. She went on smiling but leant back in her chair. She was encouraged to see Ingrid's grip on the wheelchair handles tighten, but Beatrice Ardleigh said, 'A moment, darling... Ingrid doesn't care much for detective stories, I am afraid.'

'Well, some people don't.' Antonia managed a light-hearted shrug.

'Not the tricksy whodunit type, no,' Ingrid said. She smiled only with her lips – her eyes remained expressionless, Antonia noticed. 'All that insufferably cosy amateurish atmosphere of "let's sit down and puzzle it out". Denouements that hinge on seemingly irrelevant details placed in Chapter 1.'

'Darling!' Beatrice protested. 'That's part of the fun! It's called fair play.'

'I am sorry, but tricksy whodunits irritate me to screaming point.' That means she doesn't like my books, Antonia thought. She saw Beatrice mouth at her, *Pay no attention.*

'Same as church music and Dickens' novels, which I *used* to love,' Ingrid went on.

13

'I used to have a dog named Pip.'

Both women were terribly well spoken, though Ingrid's voice was deep and gravelly. They brought to mind Cheltenham Ladies' College, or even Benenden. There was something almost parodically Pathe-like about their diction. Were they actresses? Speech therapists? Bridge hostesses? (Did bridge hostesses still exist?)

'Not every crime has a punishment, every mystery a solution and every story an ending,' Ingrid declared somewhat inconsequentially.

'Ingrid prefers excursions into the – how shall I put it? The darker reaches of the human psyche. Don't you, my sweet?' Beatrice said. 'It's affected the way she looks at things. Honestly. For example, she says – shall I tell Miss Darcy?'

'Tell her what?' Ingrid said absently. Her attention seemed to be distracted by a woman and a little girl and her eyes followed them as they walked across the hall towards the exit.

'Ingrid says I sometimes do things which I have no recollection of having done. She suggests I have fugues.'

'I never said you had fugues.' Ingrid was still looking in the direction of the exit.

'All right. I did do *something*.' Beatrice heaved a histrionic sigh. 'But it happened only *once* and that was so *silly*.'

'I like Patricia Highsmith,' Ingrid said suddenly. 'Now there's a highly original writer who never allowed her books to become calcified by cliché.'

'Some of them are very good,' Antonia agreed. 'Not the later ones though.'

'As a matter of fact I *particularly* like the later ones.'

That she was saying this only to be awkward, Antonia had no doubt. How could anyone like ponderous, plotless confections like *Found in the Street?* Calcified by cliché. That was not a bad phrase. Mysteries without out a solution, stories without an end. Was Ingrid a mighty metaphysician, obsessively searching for meaning, solace and peace in the wake of some dreadful personal tragedy? Did she write poetry of the more obscure kind? *Conventions shield us from the shivering void–* Really, Antonia thought, the silly ideas that come into my head.

Beatrice was speaking. 'Patricia Highsmith always wrote about psychotic aesthetes and alternative lives, didn't she? About people assuming different identities and doing all sorts of truly appalling things to other people, like – like smashing their skulls with ashtrays and forcing lethal doses of sleeping pills down their throats and – and holding their heads under water?'

'There is *much* more to Patricia Highsmith than that, Bee,' Ingrid said. 'And when you say "psychotic aesthetes", you mean Ripley, right? Well, he is the only one.'

'I am sure he isn't the only one,' Beatrice said stubbornly.

How intensely tedious this was becoming. Antonia stole a glance at her watch.

'One must be very unhappy to want to be somebody else, don't you think?' Beatrice appealed to Antonia.

'Well, yes – I suppose so.'

'Or very disturbed.' Ingrid gave a short laugh. She put her hand on Beatrice's shoulder.

'There are people apparently who suffer from a multiple personality disorder without being aware of it! Isn't that fascinating? I have tried to imagine what it must be like–'

'Shall we go, Bee?'

The way Ingrid kept saying 'Bee' – somehow it ceased to be a woman's nickname or a diminutive; it didn't bring to mind the insect either, rather it became an incantation – a sorceress's formula. At once Antonia castigated herself for her fanciful thoughts. The lack of air, she decided. She wanted to leave the hall, stretch her legs, have tea, phone Hugh. She glanced towards her bag. She hadn't left her mobile at home again, had she?

'Now don't laugh at me, but I thought about writing a story about someone who is in fact *two people* – I am sure it's been done hundreds of times! Dear me. The way I go on. We have lived in such isolation, Miss Darcy – we have become a bit peculiar. A little – cracked?' Beatrice Ardleigh laughed, a tinkling girlish laugh, as though to indicate this was not to be taken too seriously. 'I realize it each time we go out and meet people. I do hope you aren't finding us too objectionable? We have the silliest and pettiest of spats sometimes. I bet people think us quite mad!'

Antonia gave another polite smile. She was wondering what to do. Shouldn't she simply rise, apologize and say she had an important engagement? 'Where do you live?' she heard herself ask instead.

'Oxfordshire. Wallingford. It's a pleasant enough place but quite dreary. It's our first visit to Hay-on-Wye and I am loving every moment of it. I find the smell of new books intoxicating!' Beatrice shut and opened her eyes in a show of ecstasy. Her bosom rose and fell. The finest perfumes of Arabia might have been paraded for her inspection. Everything about her was heightened, exaggerated – dress, words, gestures. *Is* that Kinky Friedman? Over there – look!' She pointed excitedly. 'The tall man with the drooping moustache and the desert boots? Or is it one of the Village People? I heard they were here – they have written a joint memoir, haven't they?'

'I am afraid I have no idea,' Antonia said.

'Apparently–' Beatrice went on in a loud whisper, choking with silent laughter, 'Apparently, Kinky Friedman thought Hay-on-Wye a *sandwich*, when he first heard about it! I've read two of his books. *Not* my cup of tea at all, but I read all the time. I would read *anything*. I suppose I am what you'd call "chronically literary" – the kind of person who, when the rhododendrons are in bloom, will amble round Kew Gardens reading the labels on the trees!' Suddenly she became serious. 'Reading is my life. I used to feel quite apocalyptic about things, human existence in general, but books saved my life. My sanity. If I didn't read, I might have turned into a monster. Honestly.'

For some reason Ingrid looked extremely tense now, very much on edge – just as a cat is supposed to be minutes before a devastating earthquake, Antonia thought. Was Ingrid afraid that Beatrice was saying too much – giving away too much? Beatrice was voluble in a way that suggested a degree of instability. Was her interest in multiple personality disorder of any significance? The two women seemed totally incompatible in terms of sociability, but then Beatrice hinted at things one shouldn't really be talking about in front of total strangers.

Aloud Antonia said, 'Yes. Reading is the most wonderful of panaceas.'

18

Did people think of their favourite authors as of close friends? Antonia admired a number of writers but, if she ever were to meet them, she wouldn't dream of talking to them about, say, her failed first marriage and how she nearly suffered a nervous breakdown as a result, or how she left her librarian job at the Military Club to do full-time writing, or about her second husband selling his Sussex farm and moving in with her in Hampstead. Certainly not on first meeting them!

'There's a speculative glint in your eye.' Beatrice leant forward. 'Shall I tell you what I think? I think you are going to put us in your next book.'

'I never do that kind of thing,' Antonia said with a smile, not entirely truthfully, because, somewhere at the back of her mind, she had already been considering the two women from a writer's point of view, as potential characters.

Beatrice, she had decided, looked like some rich man's wife, spoilt, affected, annoyingly child-like, and yes, a little cracked, the result no doubt of long years spent in a wheelchair, but there was no evidence of a Mr Ardleigh – none of her rings was a wedding one. Ingrid too was peculiar, even a bit creepy, with her garb of woe, black gloves that brought to mind Victorian undertakers, and mother-hen solicitousness, yet, it was not taken separately, but collectively, *as an ensemble piece*, in relation to one another, that the two women became really interesting. They appealed to her sense of anomaly. They stimulated her Gothic imagination. (For some time Antonia had wanted to write a detective story with Gothic overtones.)

Some kind of strange symbiosis seemed to have been at work. *Les bonnes*, or the maids – as Antonia whimsically dubbed them in her mind – couldn't have been more different, yet there was an odd likeness between them – it was something subtle, elusive, indefinable – blink and it was gone. That was what happened when two people had lived together a long time. Antonia had observed the phenomenon with husbands and wives.

What was the nature of their relationship? Ingrid was more than a mere carer, of that Antonia was certain, but she didn't think they were a 'couple', not in the Sapphic sense of the word. Somehow one could always tell if people were lovers. Ingrid was treating Beatrice as though she were her daughter – her little girl. Yes. That was where the oddity came from. The glances Ingrid cast upon Beatrice were a blend of intense devotion and concern. She had kept her hand on Beatrice's shoulder. It was a possessive kind of gesture, but it also looked like a restraining one.

Antonia indulged in some lurid hypotheses. The two women shared a dark secret. They had committed murder together – in the manner perhaps of Genet's *Les Bonnes?* They had killed Beatrice's rich old aunt or rich old uncle. (That would explain Bee's fascination with murder mysteries.) Could Bee's paralysis be hysterical in origin? Guilt-induced? No – she had broken her back in an accident that had occurred as they had been trying to escape justice. It was Ingrid who had been driving. They had changed their identities – were leading alternative lives. Or it might be something completely different. Ageing actresses living in isolation – ancient rivalries rearing up their ugly heads – no, not another *Baby Jane* plot! She could do better than that, surely. Maybe there was a man at the back of it somewhere, for whose affections they fought – their family doctor perhaps – or the boy who did their garden?

'It's getting terribly late, Bee,' Antonia heard Ingrid say.

'Late for what, darling? I am not at all tempted to go outside. It's hot and horrid and utter ghastly drears outside,' Beatrice said petulantly. 'You don't want me to get sunstroke, do you?'

'I've got your hat here.'

'I hate that hat! It makes me look middle-aged.'

'We haven't seen all the bookshops,' Ingrid said patiently. 'That's one reason we came, isn't it? To see the bookshops.'

'I am fed up with bookshops. Our house looks like a bookshop full of tiresome old tomes. It's much more fun here, talking to Miss Darcy. *I've thought of something.*' Suddenly Beatrice reached out for Antonia's hand and held it tight. 'You must say yes. Promise you will say yes.'

'Yes to what?' Antonia glanced round nervously to see if there were any witnesses to this spectacle. Her eyes met the gleeful gaze of one of her fellow crime writers, the floppy-haired Scot, whose edgy hard-drinking characters she had never been able to take to her heart.

'Would you allow us to give you tea? It would be such a great pleasure,' Beatrice Ardleigh said. 'Honestly. We'll have a *proper* conversation. There are hundreds of questions I want to ask you.'

'Isn't it going to be too much for you? Won't you – get tired?'

'Oh, rubbish. I am not as bad as you probably think. Watch–' To Antonia's utter astonishment, Beatrice rose to her feet, stepped away from the wheelchair and held up her hands. *'Voilà.* I couldn't walk for quite a bit, but I am fine now. I allow myself to be perambulated about in this horrid chair *only* because Ingrid fusses so. She thinks I might stumble and collapse and die, don't you, my sweet?'

'It used to amuse you,' Ingrid said.

'I suppose it did – everybody so kind and solicitous – elderly gentlemen offering their services – special public lavatories and so on – but no more. It's a bore.' Beatrice resumed her seat. 'Please, say yes, Miss Darcy. Do let's have tea together.'

Ingrid's face looked like thunder. Ingrid was clearly not wild about the idea of entertaining to tea a detective story writer of dubious merit, but Beatrice had already started saying that they had discovered a wonderful old-world tea-place, just round the corner, where they served the *best cream teas imaginable*.

In the end Antonia accepted. *Les bonnes* exercised a morbid fascination over her. She was curious about them. If somebody had told her at that point that by agreeing to have tea with Beatrice Ardleigh and Ingrid Delmar, she was setting in motion a chain of events that would end in her husband's bringing about a man's death by merely leaving his tobacco pouch behind, she wouldn't have believed it.

But that was what happened.

2

Death-Watch

They talked about death of course, or rather he did; it was inevitable in the circumstances that he should talk about death. He quoted the Bible – *A vile disease has beset me and I will never get up from the place where I lie.* He dwelt on his impending end. He had no fear and, now that she had come, no regrets. ('Thank you, thank you, dear Bee,' he reiterated.) God hadn't brought about a miraculous healing, God hadn't shrivelled up the tumours, *but* He had granted him that one wish, that he should see her. Who was he to question God's wisdom? God was good. Now he could die in peace.

Ralph Renshawe rambled on. He had made all the arrangements for his own funeral. He had interviewed the undertakers and ordered his coffin. (A plain one, made of unvarnished pine.) He had chosen the hymns and seen to the printing of the service sheets. (*O Deus, ego amo te* and suchlike.) He informed her what was going to happen to Ospreys. (The National Trust was going to take over, apparently.) Ospreys was in a state of disrepair – it was falling apart, but he didn't think it mattered a hoot – not even if it were to sink into the ground like the House of Usher. (Only the other month a garden urn had been torn off its Coade stone pedestal and stolen. He wished the whole bloody place could be dismantled.)

He referred to his vast fortune in dismissive terms. (He couldn't take it with him and, even if he could, money would be of little use to him where he was going.) He groaned and grumbled about his nephew Robin. (Morally bankrupt – a terrible disappointment.) Listening to readings from St Thomas à Kempis on tape had been a great comfort. (A man calling himself a saint must be so disciplined that he is able to control his thoughts from evil. It was not enough merely to smile blandly, as some thought.) He kept asking what month it was. (Was it really *November*? Already?)

She was bored to tears but she let him talk. In fact she encouraged him. He was getting quite breathless now. He had started gasping. She liked that.

He talked about the awful things men did to those they professed to love, about guilt, redemption, atonement, about forgiveness and simple human kindness. He meant him and her of course.

'Thank you, Bee. Thank you for coming. Thank you for being here,' he whispered.

His eyes shut. He had tired himself. He was fading fast, that was what the nurse had said. The chemotherapy had made him lose all his hair as well as his lashes and eyebrows. His face was smooth, epicene; it looked neither female nor male. It was the colour of parchment; distorted, swollen, barely human. He felt nauseous and faint all the time and he had constant ringing in his ears. She could hardly contain her satisfied smile.

The bloodless lips were moving once more. 'I became a Catholic the very same day the test results came. I used to disapprove of everything they stood for. I mean the Catholic Church. I used to mock them. I used to say there was nothing to it but superstition, empty rituals, trickery and buggery. Yet, inexplicably, it was into a Catholic church that I stumbled that day– I fell to my knees and bowed my head low–'

A priest visited him every day at Ospreys. It was somebody who had been recommended by Ralph Renshawe's nephew, the infamous Robin. The nurse had let that slip out and then had begged her anxiously not to tell Mr Renshawe. The nurse, it seemed, had a soft spot for Master Robin.

She had bumped into the priest at the front door. Father Lillie-Lysander, some such name. She didn't think much of him. He was plump and sleek; he looked worldly, self-important, insincere. That had been her overwhelming impression. He had hardly glanced at her, either out of fear that her golden hair might lead him into temptation or because he wasn't interested in women – probably the latter.

'I cried. I couldn't help myself. I thought I'd drown in tears. I wasn't pitying myself,' Ralph went on. 'I was thinking of you, Bee. I didn't care that I had only a short time to live. I honestly didn't. I decided to write to you, to find you. I made up my mind I wouldn't leave this world before I'd sought your forgiveness. I thought about that other unfortunate woman too – what was her name?'

'Ingrid,' she said after a pause. There was a strange expression on her face.

'Ingrid? Dear Lord. Terrible thing to happen.'

'Apocalyptic,' she said.

'I was to blame. All my fault. I wrecked your lives–' He broke off. 'It was such a warm night when it happened – the kind of night songs are written about. *Starry, starry night,*' he sang out in a thin reedy voice. The next moment he started coughing.

'Every so often I shut my eyes and recreate the episode in my mind,' she said. 'I rewind it, as though it were a film. I run it through again and again. Then I freeze the frame and look at it carefully. I examine every detail–'

She was interrupted by a scream coming

from outside and she turned her head sharply towards the french windows. Rooks. Rooks were circling above the vast, over-grown garden. She could see the wishing well and parts of the old stone wall with its deep arched embrasures, crumbling into ruin. When the National Trust took over, all that would change, she imagined. Ospreys would be open to the public. Or maybe the National Trust was going to keep things as they were? Some people liked the idea of picturesque decay.

'It was 4th May,' he whispered. 'That's when it happened.'

'It was twenty minutes to midnight. There was the smell of lilacs in the air. The car windows were open. The radio was on. They were playing "Clair de Lune". There was a moon – like a friendly face, smiling down at me. Lots of stars. I was full of hope. I felt ecstatic, yet serene. For the first time I had peace of mind. I was leaving my old life behind. I was thinking of my little golden-haired girl–'

'Lilacs, yes … I remember the lilacs… The sweetest, the most intoxicating of smells, I always think, though not as intoxicating as your scent, Bee.' The skeletal hand stirred and she froze, clenching her teeth, imagin-ing he was about to touch her. 'Ce Soir Je T'Aime. You still use it, I can tell. I haven't entirely lost my sense of smell. We were talking – laughing. I'd said something that made you laugh. Then that other car appeared. It kept coming closer. I saw it as though in slow motion, wasn't that odd? Am I being fanciful?'

'You were drunk.'

'The crash... I felt nothing. It felt like running into masses of cotton wool. I heard you moan, but when I flicked my lighter, you smiled at me. You said you didn't think you were too badly hurt, only you couldn't move your legs... I was without a scratch on me. You asked me to check on the other car. That other woman – Ingrid – was clutching at her stomach. She didn't make a sound – just looked at me. Her eyes – merciful God – I'll never forget those eyes. She held out her right hand when she saw me – as though asking why–'

'She was pregnant.'

'I had no idea. I learnt later. Her hand looked as though she had dipped it in blood – it was a birthmark of some sort–' Ralph Renshawe broke off. 'It was I who should have died. Or suffered some terrible mutilation. Only I didn't. Father Lillie-Lysander says there was a reason to it, a higher purpose, why I didn't die in the crash.'

'You got off lightly.'

'I got a fine. I had Biretta & Baal on my side – legal luminaries – crooks. I chose them carefully. I should have been sent to jail but wasn't. Should have rotted in jail. My picture was in the papers. People recognized me and kept staring at me wherever I went, or so I imagined. I was annoyed by the attention. I imagined everybody disapproved, which of course they must have done. Your father wrote to me. He assumed I would take care of you. That, he suggested, was the decent thing to do, the act of a gentleman, but the mere idea filled me with horror.'

'Daddy was a fool.'

'I didn't fancy at all the idea of being tied down to an invalid.'

'You disappeared.'

'I left England. Covered my tracks. I was afraid of some sort of retribution, I think. For quite a while I kept looking over my shoulder. For quite a while I was convinced that that woman – Ingrid – would come after me. Or that she'd hire someone to bump me off. I can only imagine what you went through – what it was like.'

'Apocalyptic,' she said. 'Hell on earth.'

'I am so sorry. Day after day, week after week, year after year, lying in that bed. Were you in a lot of pain?'

'I was. Terrible pain.' She thought she heard the nurse hovering outside the door and raised her voice. 'My whole personality has changed as a result. People have the wrong idea of what I am really like. Everybody is convinced I am of a happy disposition – light-hearted, easy-going, frivolous, girlish. People comment on my *joie de vivre*. On my insatiable zest for life. They compliment me on my appearance. They ask me how I have managed to look so well, so healthy. The other day somebody called me a "good sport". I seem to strike everybody as balanced and normal, but the truth is that I am all bitter and twisted inside. There is a monster lurking behind the mask.'

'I am so glad that you have recovered, my dear, so glad. You have hardly changed at all. You look the same. The same pretty face. God is good. We must put all our trust in God.' Most of her words had clearly been lost on him. A drop of saliva appeared at the corner of his mouth. He was drooling, like an idiot. He looked delirious. His hearing, like the rest of him, had been greatly reduced.

Had the nurse heard her? The nurse had struck her as the kind that eavesdropped at keyholes. It might be useful – if she were ever to change her mind and revert to what she still thought of as Plan A. It was good to know she might still kill him and get away with it. She smiled – she might have been a character in one of Antonia Darcy's detective novels!

He was speaking. 'I had no idea where you were. I had the letter sent to your old

31

address. Thank God you got it... Thank God... I don't know what I'd have done if you hadn't got in touch... Are your parents...?'

'Dead,' she said.

'I am sorry. Your father thought I'd make you an excellent husband.'

'Daddy was a fool.'

'Father Lillie-Lysander tells me that I have been forgiven but I am not certain. Not certain at all. I made so many people un-happy... I went on wrecking lives... You... That other woman, Ingrid.' Ralph Renshawe's rheumy eyes had started filling with tears. 'Judith – my late wife. Poor Judith. I gave her such a hard time. I married Judith soon after I arrived in Calgary – sweet girl – rather plain but incredibly rich – an heiress. I married her for her money and we moved to Florida. We had no children. A good thing too. Judith should have left her fortune to someone else – to a home for cats – she adored cats – or to her charities. Judith was a saint. I deserve nothing – nothing at all. She left all her money to me instead. Her fabulous fortune. Can you imagine?'

'Fool,' she said.

'I did a lot of things I shouldn't have done, Bee. Before I got ill, I kept a mistress,' he went on. 'She was extremely upset when I told her to leave. She had started seeing herself as the "Mistress of Ospreys", I suppose. She threatened to kill me. She said she couldn't live without me. She was a passionate, hot-blooded creature. She followed her instincts, never her mind. Her appetites were more than a match for mine. She originated from the Subcontinent, but was quite taken with our English ways. She changed her accent; her speech assumed the numinous purity of Home County intonation, which was a bit of a bore. Perhaps she was after my money, I don't know. Are you cold?' He suddenly looked at her gloved hands and sighed. 'I am always cold. They say that the merest chill might be fatal.'

He shut his eyes. He had wearied himself. He was dying slowly, by degrees; each minute brought him closer to the grave. In a funny way that was what had saved his life. Seeing him in this pitiable state had made her change her mind. I like that, she remembered thinking. She must try to stretch this out for as long as possible.

Killing him would have been too easy – an act of mercy really, and mercy was not something she was prepared to give him. A speedy death? Oh no. This was better. Much better. Much more – enjoyable.

Her eyes narrowed and she ran her tongue across her lips.

Yes. Infinitely more satisfying.

3

A Connoisseur's Case

It had been a mysterious, rather oppressive kind of afternoon, all the familiar landmarks outside engulfed by an old-fashioned smog, either unrecognizable or completely vanished. Intrigued by the alien look of things, rather like characters out of Chesterton, Antonia and Hugh Payne decided to go for a short walk on Hampstead Heath. They heard the ghostly ringing of a church bell, disembodied yellowish lights flickered in the air and they appeared to be wading knee-deep in candyfloss. But for the unpleasant squishing of wet grass beneath their feet, Major Payne said, they might have been in some abandoned ancient land high above the clouds – in Valhalla itself! Neither of them could see the ground and they had to feel their way with their rolled-up umbrellas held out before them, blind-man fashion.

When they returned home, they sat down to tea and crumpets before a blazing fire. The curtains were drawn across the windows and all the table lamps in the sitting room were on. The Rockingham teapot gleamed.

'How about a game of Scrabble? And a brandy, I think.' Major Payne crossed to the sideboard while Antonia took out the Scrabble.

'No brandy for me, thank you.' Antonia opened the Scrabble board and shook the green bag of letters.

'This time,' he said, 'I intend to beat you.'

'I intend to beat *you*. No Shakespearean words,' she reminded him.

It was a quarter to six and they had been playing for twenty minutes when the telephone rang.

'Damn,' Payne said. 'Just when–'

'I will get it.' Antonia rose.

Major Payne listened with half an ear to her part of the conversation while trying to think of a good word that could be formed with a P, a Q, an O, an I, an A, a G and an N. He took a sip of brandy Pin. Pig. Gin. Nip. Gap. He wouldn't get much, dammit. Such rotten letters. Nog? Pan? Peanuts? Nap? Pans? He pulled at his lower lip. Well, he could have 'quoin', he supposed – but he would have to pinch Antonia's U first. *Could* he replace it with his P? No – she was bound to notice, she always did. Antonia, like all professional wordsmiths, took Scrabble too seriously. Earlier on they had argued over the meaning of 'zori'. He thought it meant a skunk-like beast out of Africa while Antonia insisted it was a Japanese straw sandal. The dictionary would have provided a solution, but he had no idea where the damned thing had gone.

He saw Antonia put down the receiver. There was a puzzled expression on her face. 'How very odd,' she said. 'Do you remember me telling you about that woman in the wheelchair I met last June? In Hay-on-Wye?'

'I do remember. I had some clever name for her. What was it? Snow White?'

'Goldilocks. That was her on the phone. Her name is Beatrice Ardleigh.'

Major Payne leant back in his chair. 'Some rigmarole about whether or not to answer a letter from an old flame of hers? She is on the horns of a dilemma? She needs your advice desperately?' He welcomed the interruption – he had been losing badly and he was not a particularly gracious loser.

'She doesn't need my advice "desperately". And if the man is an old flame of hers, she didn't say. It was all rather garbled. She received the letter last month. It was from somebody she used to know a very long time ago. The letter came to her as a shock – um – because of something the man had done to her. Something like that. She'd never expected to hear from him. She'd thought he was dead. She said she didn't know what to do.'

Payne cocked an eyebrow. 'And you do? Or would, as soon as you'd read the letter?'

'Well, she believes I am endowed with perfect knowledge and understanding of human nature. She credits me with one of those laser-sharp criminologist minds – as well as with Ariadne's penchant for un-ravelling.' Antonia gave a little smile.

'My dear sweet girl. If I didn't know you better, I might have imagined that you were finding this kind of attention flattering.'

'I am not the least bit flattered. Actually I suspect Beatrice is using this letter as a pre-text to get me to visit her – as a kind of bait. She's been trying to get me to visit her, I've told you. She's probably making the situation sound much more intriguing and mysterious than it is. I think she is bored and lonely. In many ways she is rather irritating. She lives in Wallingford. She said you could come too.'

'Jolly kind of her. Writers do attract nut-cases.' Payne shook his head. 'I can't believe you let her have your phone number.'

'She gave me tea. It would have been impossibly rude to refuse.'

'You could have given her a wrong number.'

'She wore a Jacques Azagury dress,' Antonia murmured reminiscently. 'I would love a dress like that.'

Payne's eyes had strayed towards the Scrabble board. 'I don't suppose you realize that "funeral" is also "real fun"? All you do is rearrange the letters – thus.'

'What were these things called? Not anagrams?'

'*Anti*grams.'

'United – untied?'

'Yes ... Man's laughter – manslaughter.'

'Beatrice said it was a very peculiar letter and that it might give me an idea for a novel,' Antonia went on. 'She made it sound like some special treat. It was a perfectly extra-ordinary, *frightfully* delicate kind of situation and she was baffled. *Honestly, my dear, it's like the start of one of your fiendish puzzles*.'

'Golly, does she talk like that?'

'She does. This man – the author of the letter – I think she called him Ralph – *Rafe* – was at death's door – his departure from this world was imminent – his last wish was to see her. It was like something out of a book. Quite extraordinary.' Antonia paused. 'She was about to tell me more, but then – then a very curious thing happened. She suddenly changed tack. Someone came into the room. I am sure I heard a door open somewhere in the background. Beatrice gave a little gasp – then started talking fast – in a much louder voice. You know, when someone starts put-ting on an act?'

'Go on.'

'She laughed and said, "Actually, my dear, it is all a dreary muddle. I don't know the man from Adam. I have no idea what he is on about. I think it's some lunatic." Or it was all a mistake – he was taking her for someone else – wouldn't that be tiresome?'

Major Payne frowned. 'You think she changed her story because of whoever entered the room?'

'Yes... For some reason Beatrice didn't want the person who entered the room to know about the exact contents of the letter she had received.'

'It must have been the girlfriend, don't you think?' Payne stroked his jaw with a forefinger. 'The masterful Matron with the Medusa gaze? She who transfixed you like a butterfly on a board?'

'She didn't take to me, true, but I don't think she was Bee's girlfriend. I think Bee likes men. Bee kept shooting coy glances at the men while we were having tea. All the presentable-looking men seemed to be with their wives, but that didn't deter Bee. She kept giving little smiles and lowering her eyelashes. I daresay her attentions were reciprocated.'

'Some men actually find the idea of a woman in a wheelchair tremendously exciting – a positive thrill.'

'Don't be disgusting, Hugh.'

'It's all to do with *control*, or so I have read. The idea that the woman is entirely at their mercy.'

'It was probably Ingrid who entered the

room, yes… They live by themselves. That was what I was given to understand. At least they did back in June. They are so different. I've been trying to imagine what it is like, the two of them living together.'

'The opposite of sugar and spice? Something – not very nice? Creepy clotted claustrophobia? Perhaps there is no such person as "Ingrid". Perhaps the "Ingrid" you met was Bee's husband in drag?' Major Payne mused, arranging idly the word 'drag' with Scrabble letters. 'Some couples are into role-playing, you know. The purpose would be – in the vulgar parlance – to spice up a casserole that might have become too bland. I bet Ingrid was suspiciously tall, hulking and blue-jawed and smoked cheroots?'

'She was nothing of the sort. Nobody smokes cheroots nowadays.'

'A chap at the Military Club does.'

'Ingrid was dressed in sombre black – black suit and black gloves. There was an air of tragedy hanging about her.'

'She might have been in mourning for her youth.' Payne yawned. 'Like the woman in Chekhov. Some contretemps took place when you went to have tea with them, I think you said?'

'Oh dear, yes. Ingrid put two lumps of sugar into Beatrice's tea instead of one and Beatrice refused to drink it. She was sitting beside a potted palm and she poured the tea into it. At which Ingrid threw a tantrum and went and sat at another table, by herself. She rejoined us several minutes later and acted as though nothing had happened. Actually, we managed to have quite an interesting talk about TM–'

'Ah.' Payne gave a grave nod. 'Tsunami madness. One of the most dangerous forms of mental disorder. The most extreme?'

'Don't you ever get tired of saying silly things? TM stands for "transcendental meditation". Beatrice explained that practising TM had enabled her brain to fall deep into a state of rest. TM was the only thing that had succeeded in soothing her tormented soul. Something called "mantra mellow" comes into it. Bee and Ingrid agreed that TM worked, but then – then they had another squabble.'

'This is becoming addictive.'

'Beatrice started telling me a story. Apparently not long before her father died, he had what Beatrice called a "second vision". Her father woke up in the middle of the night and saw his dead wife – Beatrice's mother – standing beside his bed, looking down at him as though in great disapproval. He told her to go away and stay away. He then went back to sleep. Ingrid said, "Wasn't that rather unkind?" Bee's eyes filled with tears and she said, what a horrid thing to say. Her father had been frightfully upset by the

41

experience and he died only three days later. Ingrid pointed out he *couldn't* have been frightfully upset – he wouldn't have been able to go back to sleep if he had been "frightfully upset". She mimicked Beatrice's high voice, which only made matters worse.'

'How fascinating.' Payne produced his pipe and tobacco pouch. 'Or do I mean, how ridiculous?'

'Another curious thing happened earlier on. A woman with a child passed by – the little girl was crying. Ingrid reacted in a rather peculiar way. Her eyes opened wide. She looked startled – shocked. As though – I don't know.'

'As though she felt certain the woman was abducting the child?' Payne suggested.

'Yes... But Ingrid also gave the distinct impression that she knew the child. Her eyes were on the little girl. That's what made the whole thing so odd.' Antonia paused. 'She looked very tense. She seemed to want to follow them, but decided against it. Her face was the picture of misery and frustration.'

For a couple of moments Major Payne smoked in silence. Leaning back in his chair he watched the blue smoke rings as they chased each other up to the ceiling. 'I think, my love,' he remarked at last, 'that of all the cases we have investigated, none is more fantastical than this. It presents us with an irresistible mixture of the absurd, the inexplicable and the menacing. The case is marked by a pervading sense of *strangeness*.'

'There is no case as such, Hugh. Nothing's actually *happened*.'

'Nothing that *we* know of. A lot may have been happening behind the scenes. Well, I think we should avail ourselves of Mistress Ardleigh's kind invitation and pay her a visit. Ring her up and make her happy.'

As Antonia dialled Beatrice Ardleigh's phone number, she felt her heart beating fast. What if it was Ingrid who answered? I am afraid of Ingrid, she admitted to herself. I am scared to death by her – those black gloves! Eventually the receiver was lifted – but it was a man's voice that answered.

'Bee is having a rest. She's just put her feet up. Would you like to call again later, or can I take a message?' Antonia had the fleeting impression of somebody bluff, solid, genial and imperturbably placid. 'Who? Antonia Darcy? *Of course.* I am so sorry. Bee was talking to you a moment ago. Yes? Yes? With your husband? But of course. Splendid! I'm terribly glad. It means so much to her. She'd be delighted. She is a great fan of yours. And of course she wants you to see the letter.' He cleared his throat. 'When can you come? Saturday? No, not this Saturday... Let me look at the diary... How about next week – Saturday the 24th? Splendid. Say, half past three? We'll give you tea. Splendid.

I do look forward to meeting you.'

Putting down the receiver, Antonia turned round. 'That was a man. He said they would be delighted to have us to tea. He didn't introduce himself. So Beatrice does have a man in the house.'

'Her butler?' Payne suggested. 'All my aunts have butlers but only one is happy with hers.'

'The man sounded extremely familiar. He referred to her as "Bee" and kept saying "splendid" – would a butler say "splendid"?'

Payne said that anything was possible in this egalitarian day and age. Butlers were not what they used to be. Butlers were no longer deferential. This one might even be having an affair with his mistress – that would explain why he was taking liberties with diminutives and was generally acting beyond his station.

'The man sounded like a husband. Beatrice might have got married, don't you think?'

'She might have,' Payne agreed. He puffed at his pipe. 'Perhaps the man who spoke to you was none other than the incredible Ingrid *en travesti* – in her masculine role. Which means that Ingrid has now succeeded in luring us to a house where identities shift and melt and savage punishments are a daily affair–'

'What have you done with the board?' Antonia cried. 'We never finished the game, did we? I realize I could have had "incarnadine"!'

'We said no Shakespeare words. Blood on your mind already?' Payne joked.

4

Malice Aforethought

The ground was frozen and crunched under her feet. The sky was a forbidding shade of grey. Rooks, stiff and black, croaked and circled low above the house. For a moment she had imagined they were ospreys – otherwise why call the house Ospreys? People did give country houses silly names. Clouds – Nunspardon – Charleston – Ham House – Owlpen Manor! She stopped, her hands thrust deep in the pockets of her mink coat, the cashmere scarf the colour of crushed raspberries covering her blonde head, and watched the rooks for a couple of moments. They had been perched on the turrets but had heard her coming. Creatures of ill omen, harbingers of doom, or so it had been said – could they really sense death, someone about to die?

Ralph had bought Ospreys from a Sir Marcus Laud, who had been eager to sell. It was easy to see why. A faint smell, as from a sick animal, emanated from the crumbling plaster. No one in their right mind would want to live in a place like that. The House of Usher, Ralph had called it. Something in that. She could well imagine children coming over on Hallowe'en with lighted pumpkins and marching round Ospreys, chanting spells that invoked evil spirits. One whole wall was covered in ivy. *Creeping ivy hides the ruin it feeds upon.* (Cowper?) There was smoke coming out of only one of the six chimneys. Most of the rooms were not in use, that was what the nurse had told her.

The walk from the bus stop had taken only five minutes. Thank God for that. It was another bleak, dark, dispiriting day. The air was raw and she felt chilled to the bone. Five minutes if she walked briskly. If she dawdled, ten, even fifteen. She had timed her journey carefully during her very first visit. She had also drawn a plan of Ralph's part of the house – the french windows – the terrace – and, for good measure, she had added the wishing well too – it was in a direct line from the windows. She didn't know precisely why she did that. She had been in an odd mood that day. She had made it look like one of those diagrams one found in old-fashioned detective stories.

X *marks the spot. This is where the body was found.* Antonia Darcy probably knew all about house plans. Modern detective stories weren't likely to have house plans in them, but then Antonia Darcy didn't exactly write 'modern' detective stories. Well, writers who did not trust their descriptive powers resorted to diagrams. As a matter of fact she had the sheet with the diagram in her pocket at that very moment. How funny. It wasn't as though she would ever *need* it. Sometimes she did do things, she had to admit, which were not entirely rational…

Progress was slow today. So slippery – that damned ice! Her shoes needed new soles, or maybe she needed new shoes? It would have been much faster if she had been driving. Once upon a time, a million years ago, she had been able to drive – she'd had a cherry-red racer – she had *enjoyed* driving. No longer. The mere thought of getting into a car and sitting behind the steering wheel made her start shaking.

Again she passed the priest. She looked at her watch: four o'clock. Her coming and his going always seemed to coincide. Today Father Lillie-Lysander was wearing a tall astrakhan hat and was smoking a cigar. His dog collar was invisible under a scarf of some shimmering silver pattern and he wore grey gloves. He was carrying a small black leather bag. He looked prosperous – nothing like a priest – he brought to mind a banker or a *rentier*. He had a somewhat furtive air about him and she wondered as to the reason. (Weren't priests allowed to smoke cigars?) This time he acknowledged her with a distant nod; for a moment his eyes rested upon her speculatively.

The front door opened before she reached it. 'Good afternoon, Beatrice,' the young nurse greeted her cheerfully and she gasped at the sight of her breath coming out of her mouth in swirls. 'So cold, isn't it? I hadn't realized. Much colder than yesterday. The ground's frozen.' Nurse Wilkes – stating the obvious as usual. 'That's a nice scarf... Ralph's expecting you. He kept asking me to look out for you.'

Pale face, pink lipstick, dark nail varnish, gold stud in the nose. *And* she was chewing gum. As annoying a habit as the use of the first names. 'Ralph' – 'Beatrice' – they weren't exactly Nurse Wilkes' contemporaries or friends, were they? What was private medical care coming to? Had the stately matron type gone for ever? She was conservative about that sort of thing. Incongruously, Nurse Wilkes was holding what looked like a half-finished jumper and knitting needles.

'Come in, come in. It's freezing!' Nurse Wilkes cried.

'How is he?'

Well, Ralph had had a seizure the night before but had recovered. For a man in his condition he was doing remarkably well. Nurse Wilkes spoke with relentless good cheer. She led the way in. 'He's been much better since you started coming. Isn't that wonderful?'

Ralph's room was on the ground floor, just across the octagonal marble hall with the armour and the angels. He had been in an upstairs room to start with, but had been moved downstairs because it made things *so* much easier for her, the nurse said as she pushed the door open.

She took off her scarf. The nurse spoke in a very loud voice. 'It's Beatrice, Ralph. Beatrice is here. I'll leave you alone now.'

She looked at the french windows. She could see the flight of crumbling steps and had a clear view of the terribly overgrown lawn. Ralph sat slumped between several pillows. His eyes were shut. He looked worse, she noted with quiet satisfaction, contrary to what the nurse had said – much worse. He blinked several times. 'What? Who is it?' His voice was softer and thinner than before. 'Wilkes?'

'It's me–'

'Bee? Oh, my dear. You've come again.'

'I said I would.'

She sat on the edge of the chair beside the bed. It was her third visit. She'd come the day before and she hoped to come again tomorrow – and the day after. She felt her spirits soaring. She was enjoying herself so much! She resisted the impulse to rub her hands. She glanced round. If anything the room looked more Spartan than before; it was like a monk's cell. The crucifix above the bed was slightly askew. Did they dust it? She felt the urge to laugh aloud at the thought of a feather duster being run ticklishly over Our Saviour.

There was a photograph propped up against one of the medicine bottles on the bedside table, which hadn't been there before. *Ralph and Bee at the Colosseum, April 1975*. It was his writing at the bottom, faint and jumbled, as it had been in the letter. He had written it recently. He had been thinking about the past, clearly. In the photograph he looked dashing in a white suit – handsome – not unlike Cary Grant in his prime – nothing like the ragged scarecrow in the bed.

'D'you remember the Colosseum, Bee? You look so lovely there with your golden hair,' he said.

'I look grumpy. Why do I look grumpy?'

'Don't you remember the ice-cream cone? Some ice-cream dripped on your dress... You've hardly changed at all... If only we could turn the clock back...'

If only they could... April 1975... She felt a shiver run down her spine. That was only a month before the accident. She knew why she remembered it so well. She had been to her gynaecologist for a check. Once more she saw Dr Fallowell's smiling face. No problems at all. Everything was going to be fine. *Excellent progress. This is better than I*

51

expected. You are going to have a healthy baby.

She had conceived her plan as soon as she read Ralph Renshawe's letter. She hadn't hesitated one second. She had neither deliberated nor prevaricated. The idea had come into her head fully formed. *Double revenge.* Two birds with one stone. She had set herself some conditions. One, Ralph had to know he was being murdered, therefore it had to be done slowly and methodically. Two, no ambiguities. The murder had to be made obvious – the police mustn't waste their time thinking that it might have been an accident or suicide. Three, the killer's identity had to be plain and unequivocal, so that it led to an immediate arrest...

Well, she had changed her mind the moment she had laid eyes on him. She had abandoned the plan. This was better – watching him dying slowly, by degrees – savouring every moment of it.

She regarded him dispassionately. He looked worse today. He was disintegrating before her very eyes! They had tried some alternative remedy – in a half-hearted kind of way, she gathered – he had been dehydrated and fed nothing but raw carrots and walnuts for a month, something like that – there wasn't the slightest evidence it had done him any good.

A doctor apparently came every now and then, but these were little more than courtesy calls. They could do nothing more for him. He was given morphine injections, to keep the pain at bay, to ease his suffering. The way his head lolled and his mouth gaped! Urgh. He was no longer of this world. She hadn't expected him to be so ill on first reading the letter. *I am at death's door.* Well, she had suspected him of exaggerating the gravity of his condition, of employing melodramatic phrases to gain her sympathy.

'Would you like tea – coffee? Cake? All you need to do is press that buzzer,' Ralph Renshawe said. 'Wilkes will bring it.'

'No, thank you... Honestly... I am all right.' The idea of sipping coffee or eating cake in this room of death filled her with revulsion.

He said he was feeling better now for seeing her. He tried to smile, struggled up. 'You aren't cold, are you? My hands are like ice.'

'I am afraid I can't stay long,' she said abruptly. The idea that her arrival might have made him feel better, that her presence might have the effect of a positive stimulant, irritated her. 'I need to get back promptly today – or they'll wonder what's become of me.'

'Who's they? If you don't mind me asking.'

'My husband,' she said. 'I am married now.'

'Married? I am so glad... I didn't mean to pry... I feared I – I might have ruined your life.' His breathing was again becoming extremely laboured.

He feared he *might* have ruined her life.

53

She remained silent and still, but her hands clenched into fists. Fury rose inside her – the sudden urge to attack him – to batter at his face with her fists. She wanted to push him off the bed and kick him till she smashed every bone in his body. Suddenly she felt extremely hot. She broke out into a sweat. She took off her gloves.

You don't understand. You did ruin my life. You destroyed me. That's why I am here.

'You have forgiven me, haven't you, Bee?' His voice was barely audible. He was peering at her. He sounded extremely anxious. 'Really forgiven me?' He looked like an ancient tortoise – the way he pushed his head forward. He was only – what? Sixty – sixty-one? The illness had made him look a hundred.

She stared down at her hands. *I haven't forgiven you. You fool. You think you know me but you don't. You don't understand a thing. I could tear you apart with my bare hands. The only reason you are still alive is because it gives me such great joy to watch you die.*

Suddenly Ralph Renshawe's eyes grew wider with incredulity and fear. He had seen something. A memory had stirred at the back of his mind and that was followed by a shocking realization. His eyes darted towards the buzzer. Then something equally curious happened. He gave a little sigh; he sank back and a tight little smile appeared on his bluish lips.

She was not aware of the changes in his expression; she had been looking at the crucifix on the wall once more, at the pathetic, broken figure of the Christ. Stick-like arms and legs, tiny *cache-sex*, dolorous, rolled-up eyes, agonized mouth. Her lip curled scornfully. Orthodox religions filled her with contempt. Christianity she deemed particularly bogus. How could *anyone* accept the idea of a benign all-loving, all-caring, all-powerful Creator?

An all-loving Creator wouldn't have allowed her little girl to perish.

5

Portrait of a Marriage

'Conundrums, conundrums. How boring life would be without them. Why did the parsley sink into the butter?' Major Payne murmured. 'Do you remember that Sherlock Holmes story? Was it something to do with the *depth?* What is your favourite conundrum?'

'What name Achilles assumed when he hid himself among women.'

'You aren't by any chance thinking about the mystery man at Millbrook House?'

Antonia frowned. 'I probably am...'

It was the following week, Saturday afternoon, as arranged, and they were driving across Berkshire in the direction of Wallingford. The day was bright and clear, but extremely cold. The countryside stretched out on either side of the road – it had been bronze and copper and lemon and greenish-white, also gold, but there had been several frosts and the colours were fading fast.

Payne went on to say he didn't know of many writers who allowed themselves to be befriended by their fans.

'Some writers actually marry their fans,' said Antonia.

'No, they don't.'

'They do. Daphne du Maurier married Commander Browning after he wrote to her a fan letter concerning *The Loving Spirit*. And didn't you marry me soon after you told me how much you admired my first novel?'

'Golly, so I did. *Touché!*'

The Thames Valley. Must be pleasant in spring and summer, but in autumn and winter it was cold and dank. Beatrice Ardleigh's house – Millbrook – was right on the road at the end of the town. It was a Queen Anne house in excellent condition. Payne nodded with approval as he took off his driving gloves. He wondered aloud how Beatrice and Ingrid – or for that matter the mystery man – could put up with the traffic right on the road. Earlier on in the car he had speculated as to the possibility of them walking in on some extraordinary *ménage à trois*. Was the man perhaps married to *both* women? Did Antonia know what 'troilism' meant? Perhaps the man would turn out to be a polygamous Mussulman?

'There's hardly any traffic here,' Antonia observed and she then pointed to the slightly sinister holly trees that grew up to the top windows and shielded most of the front. 'I am sure these muffle any noise there might be.'

'This could work either way...' Major Payne lowered his voice. 'No one would hear screams for help coming from inside the house. Just a thought.'

He rang the doorbell.

The man who opened the front door didn't look like anybody's idea of a polygamous Mussulman – nor was he Ingrid in drag. Introducing himself as Leonard Colville, he shook hands with them and invited them in. He was middle-aged, with grizzled hair sleeked back; early or mid-fifties, at a guess. He was broad and heavily built, with intensely blue eyes and a cheerful, round, somewhat comic pink face. He might have been a not particularly effectual Tory cabinet minister of the better class, of the kind one last saw in the early '90s – or a Father Christmas in mufti, Payne decided. He looked as though he had just taken off his beard and was taking it easy with a glass of port. He was wearing an ancient tweed jacket with leather patches, a silk scarf around his neck, twill trousers and highly polished brogues.

He stood beaming at them. 'Delighted to meet you. I am Bee's husband. We got married only last month.'

'Congratulations,' Payne said.

'Haven't got used to my new status yet. Bee calls it my "promotion". Ha-ha. We were talking about it just now. This way. Bee is thrilled. Absolutely thrilled. Your visit means a lot to her.'

The room which they entered was at the back and the french windows looked out on the garden and the flat water-meadows beyond, sloping down to where presumably the river lay. It was an extremely comfortable room, cosy in an old-fashioned kind of way, and at the moment it was flooded by the wine-coloured autumn sun. Quiet air of genteel well-being. *Gemütlichkeit*. Major Payne couldn't quite explain why he had thought of the German word. There were large billowing armchairs, an equally large sofa covered in white quilted chintz, bowls of chrysanthemums, a faded tapestry on one of the walls. A cedar-wood fire crackled under the mahogany chimneypiece. The *Telegraph*, with a half-completed crossword, lay on the low coffee table, next to a Polaroid camera and a pack of cards. They had been playing Patience Poker, Colville said in a low voice, making it sound rather daring.

Beatrice Ardleigh sat in an armchair beside the fireplace, her legs invisible underneath a blanket of a tartan design. Her hands were clasped on her lap and she was biting her lower lip. If anything she looked younger than when Antonia had first seen her five months before. Her face glowed. Her golden hair seemed freshly coiffed and it shimmered each time sparks flew upwards. Her eyes were open wide. She had the innocent look Antonia remembered – untouched by experience, absurdly virginal. She brought to mind a little girl who was about to receive a long-awaited present.

'Here they are,' Beatrice's husband announced, having opened the door with something of a theatrical flourish.

Antonia glanced nervously about but there was no sign of Ingrid.

Beatrice started hoisting herself up, but Colville raised his hand. She assumed an expression of comic deprecation as though to say, *fuss*, *fuss*, then, leaning back, she silently held her hands out towards Antonia who was compelled to bend over and kiss her. Beatrice's face was flawless like luminous china, her eyelashes were lightly mascara-ed and she wore pendant earrings and a necklace of some Oriental design. She had a fine cashmere shawl around her shoulders. Antonia saw copies of her two books on the small table by Beatrice's side.

'I can't tell you how happy I am. I'd given up hope. Honestly,' Beatrice whispered, clutching at the tips of Antonia's fingers, and for an emotional moment it looked as though she was going to burst into tears. 'Is that really you?'

'Yes, it's me,' Antonia said, feeling a little foolish.

'I can't believe it. Antonia Darcy, here, at

my house! I thought you were avoiding me. I convinced myself you hated me.'

'Not a bit of it,' Antonia said in light-hearted tones. 'I've been extremely busy with my new novel. I don't think it's turning out at all well.'

'I refuse to believe that,' Beatrice Ardleigh declared firmly.

'This is my husband Hugh.'

'How do you do. *Wonderful* meeting you,' Beatrice Ardleigh breathed, and she proffered her hand in a somewhat affected gesture, as though she expected him to raise it to his lips. 'Have you been married long? Oh dear – do forgive me! Not the done thing, asking questions like that. I have marriage on my mind. Len and I got married only last month.'

'So we heard. Congratulations,' Antonia said. She didn't like the way Beatrice was looking at Hugh.

'We haven't been married long ourselves,' Payne said.

'*Really?*' Beatrice Ardleigh tilted her head a little to the left. 'You too? What a coincidence. Did you hear that, Len? Newlyweds, like us!'

She was flirting with Hugh, Antonia thought.

'Not exactly newly-weds. For both of us it's our second.'

'I've never been married before. Nobody

believes me when I tell them. It seems I look the much-married type. Do sit down – please! The sofa – it's more comfortable than it looks. So cold, isn't it? Or is it just me?' Beatrice shivered and pulled the shawl around her shoulders. 'Len darling – feel my hands!' She stretched them towards Colville in a helpless gesture.

He gripped her fingers and frowned. 'That's not right.' He crossed purposefully over to the fireplace. He had given his wife a glance of such ardour and devotion that Antonia wouldn't have been surprised if, instead of merely fortifying it with an extra log, he had walked straight into the fire and allowed himself to be consumed by flames, burnt as an offering of warmth to his beloved.

Beatrice Ardleigh gave a blissful sigh. A moment later Colville was sitting on a stool by her side – he brought to mind a friendly, rather civilized sort of bear – and once more they held hands. He was clearly in the throes of post-nuptial euphoria. His face was turned up towards his wife's and it had become crimson. Marrying Bee, he said, was the best thing that had happened to him. He had known her all his life – he had been secretly in love with her ever since he had been a boy of seventeen and she a girl of fourteen. He had been too shy, too gauche – a great lumbering fool – while she

– she had been perfection personified – a young goddess–

'Stop talking rot!' Beatrice slapped his cheek playfully. 'I was nothing of the kind. All right, I was extremely pretty,' she conceded with a self-deprecating moue. 'I suppose I had this wayward appeal. Men went instantly crazy for me. Could be an awful bore. You know the type of girl that emerges from a birthday cake at a bachelor party? The bunny girl, yes! Well, *that's* what I looked like.'

'Very nice,' Payne murmured.

He had worshipped Bee in secret, Colville went on – he had dreamt about Bee – he had lost his appetite over her – he had become obsessed with her – as a matter of fact, he had stalked her and taken secret photos of her as she had walked in the street–

'Darling! Honestly! This is too terrible. What would these good people think? I have married my stalker!' Beatrice shuddered in mock-horror. She kept trying to catch Payne's eye, or so Antonia imagined.

Colville had never dared ask her out – he had thought he would die if she refused him. When he had finally mustered up enough courage, it had been too late – she had said there was somebody else. Well, he had then married a woman he hadn't loved. He had grown-up children. He and his wife had separated two years before. As soon as his divorce was made absolute, he got in touch with Beatrice. She had been sweet and kind and understanding. He had felt so encouraged that later that same day, he had proposed – and been accepted.

'Len can't get enough of me now,' Beatrice said with the air of one sharing some great secret. 'He's like a giddy teenager. He always carries one of my handkerchiefs. Next to his heart. It's drenched in my favourite scent.'

Payne arched a brow. (A fetish? By Jove, she keeps staring at me.)

'Ce Soir Je T'Aime,' Colville murmured, holding his wife's hand to his lips. That, Antonia decided, must be the name of the scent and not an extravagant declaration of love.

'*Such* an old silly... Len's been taking photos of me too.' Beatrice pointed to the Polaroid camera and for some reason giggled and lowered her eyes.

Antonia looked towards the fire. (Do we want to know all this?)

Payne drew his forefinger along his jaw. (Naughty pictures?)

'Photography is something of a hobby of mine.' Colville cleared his throat. He looked embarrassed.

'I don't deserve such devotion. I honestly don't. Thirty years ago I treated Len appallingly. I was terrible. I was spoilt, you see. Daddy was possessed of plentiful capital.

That was the trouble. Inherited wealth,' Beatrice mouthed. 'It's a curse.'

'Nothing wrong with being used to the best things in life,' Colville said – somewhat fatuously, Antonia thought. Beatrice, she felt sure now, was making sheep's eyes at Hugh.

'Daddy talked about his "bankers" the way other people talk about their bank manager,' Beatrice went on. 'Daddy gave me *everything* I wanted. I remember succumbing to the unholy attractions of hand-stitched shoes and Italian handbags! Once I said I wanted a Venus dress–'

'What *is* a Venus dress?' Payne asked with a twinkle.

Did he really want to know? And why did he have to twinkle? Antonia was suddenly very annoyed.

'A dress the colour of burnt crimson, Hugh. I had seen a picture of the planet Venus, you see – in a magazine. Have you seen the planet Venus?'

'No,' he admitted.

'I adored the colour. Well, Daddy got the dress specially made. Oh, I was an acquisitive, beastly creature.' Beatrice shook her head. 'I got my Cartier diamond-encrusted watch when I was fourteen. I lost it in St Moritz. We went skiing to all those places. Salzburg-Innsbruck-Villach-Graz. I can still recite these in my sleep, like the names of saints. We always stayed at the best hotels – the kind that charges like – like–'

'Like the Light Brigade?' Payne suggested.

Antonia gave him a sidelong glance. Beatrice laughed exuberantly, then turned to Colville. 'Darling, did you hear that?'

Their host gave a strained, dutiful kind of smile. Antonia imagined she saw a shadow of annoyance pass across his face – or was she projecting her own feelings on him?

'The *luxe* – I have always had an agonized craving for the *luxe.*' Beatrice sighed. 'Daddy adored me. Daddy spoilt me. Well, my mother died when I was five, you see, so I remained his little girl. Oh well. I still love expensive baubles. I tend to spend like a drunken sailor. I bought a Lulu Guinness bag only the other day, would you believe it? *In the shape of a flowerpot.* I won't say how much I gave for it. I am a terrible person. Of course I was *much* worse when I was young.'

'You are being too hard on yourself,' Colville grumbled.

'No, darling, I am not.'

'Yes, you are.'

'I am *not*. I was insensitive, wilful, demanding, selfish and deceitful.'

Beatrice had spoken with great relish, as though such self-flagellation was giving her inordinate pleasure. Something American about her crucifying candour. What a manipulative bitch, Antonia thought. She seemed to say things like that so that she

66

could be contradicted. She was looking at Hugh again! Really, Antonia thought, feeling ridiculously upset, we shouldn't have come.

'Well, I was punished for it.' Beatrice glanced down at her knees. 'Nearly thirty years of unmitigated misery. I do believe in divine retribution.'

'Don't say that.' Colville reached out and squeezed her hand. *'Don't you ever say that.'*

'Darling Len. I don't deserve you.' For a moment they sat gazing into each other's eyes, then Beatrice gave a laugh and pulled her hand away.

'We must stop! Honestly! We can't possibly assume that our *histoire* is of any great interest to anyone but us! Recounting our ardours and endurances like that. So embarrassing. What must our visitors be *thinking?*' Beatrice waved her hands. 'There are few things more tedious than self-obsessed newly-weds. Middle-aged romances are a particular bore. It must strike you as grotesque, the way we've been going on. No, don't deny it! You are much too beautifully mannered to say it, I know... Len, we are getting peckish. Do you think you could...?'

'Tea? Splendid idea.' Colville rose obediently to his feet.

'Thank you, darling. I keep expecting Ingrid to wheel in the tea, I am so used to it.' Beatrice reached out for the pearl-inlaid cigarette box on the table and took out a

67

gold-tipped cigarette with a languorous femme-fatale-ish gesture. 'I keep forgetting things are different now. Would you like a cigarette? Antonia? No? Wise girl. It's a filthy habit. Where's the...?' She looked helplessly round. 'Hugh, I don't suppose you happen to have a light? I am sure you are a smoker. I do believe I caught a whiff of some superior blend emanating from you.'

'You are absolutely right,' Payne said, crossing to her. 'I smoke a pipe.'

Antonia pursed her lips. She had seen Beatrice place one of the two books on top of the matchbox with a casual gesture, thus ensuring the matches were hidden from view. Such flagrant falsity. Antonia watched her husband produce his lighter and flick it. As he held it for her, Beatrice put her two fingers on his hand.

'*Thank* you, Hugh,' she breathed. One might be excused for thinking he'd saved her life, Antonia thought grimly.

'Turkish cigarettes?' Payne was sniffing the air.

'I see you are something of a connoisseur. Smell divine, don't they?'

'Where is Ingrid? Doesn't Ingrid live here any more?' Antonia asked in a loud voice.

I am jealous, she thought. Oh my God, I am jealous. What a dreadful feeling this is.

6

The Enigmatic Mr Lushington

So the golden-haired Bee Ardleigh had had had the devil's own luck. Amazing things *did* happen to some people. Poor Robin. What a blow the news would be to him. He didn't feel particularly sorry for his friend, rather he felt strange excitement bubbling up inside him and that was mingled with a sense of anticipation. He couldn't quite say why...

Father Lillie-Lysander shut his eyes and a little moan escaped his lips. He had had a vision of two meteors of living flame colliding and fusing into one enormous golden ball of fire. Was that it? Was it – *starting?*

He sat in his study, cross-legged, swathed in a rather sumptuous apple-green dressing gown with frogged lapels. On the round table by his side was a glass of Chartreuse, also apple-green in colour, which every now and then he raised to his lips. Not many people drank Chartreuse these days, but Father Lillie-Lysander was not like other people. He prided himself on being, in a great number of ways, unique.

Next to the glass with the Chartreuse lay

his round, silver-framed reading glasses and a syringe. A minute earlier he had injected himself with morphine – he had stolen the ampoule from Ralph Renshawe's bedside table – and was waiting for it to take effect.

Papaver somniferum. Juice of poppies. Three grains would be fatal, but he was taking a 'recreational' dose. Like the opium eaters in the nineteenth century. Being of an obsessive mind, Lillie-Lysander had read all about it. On the floor beside his chair lay that month's bank statement, where he had dropped it, also a letter from his bank manager. He had expected some such development. He was overdrawn. It was the second time in six months.

The week before he had won five thousand pounds at the Midas, the privately run casino situated in London's Park Lane – only to lose it, again at the Midas, some forty-five minutes later. The Midas was Father Lillie-Lysander's secret haunt. He went there every Friday night, wearing a dinner jacket, a red carnation in his buttonhole, and a false moustache. He had a penchant for the absurdly histrionic, for high-camp masquerades, for subterfuge and noms de plume, for mind games and twilight dealings. Ambiguities of every kind delighted him. At the casino he was known as 'Lushington', which, as it happened, was his mother's maiden name. (At school, inevitably, he had been known as 'Lily'.)

He had bumped into Robin Renshawe two months previously at one of the gaming tables at the Midas. The two hadn't met since their schooldays. At Antleforth – or 'Antlers', as Robin kept calling it – Robin had enjoyed universal adulation thanks to his languid good looks, sporting prowess and dangerous kind of wit – also for the skill with which he could tear a pack of cards in two.

They hadn't been friends to start with; if anything, Lillie-Lysander had been a little afraid of Robin, but they had discovered common ground in their love for the theatre. They had appeared in every school play together. Contrary to expectations and much to his classmates' disappointment, Lillie-Lysander had refused to play women's roles, plumping instead for the slippered pantaloon/stuffed shirt character part. He had raised great laughs as Pooh-Bah and Polonius while Robin had been Nanki-Poo and Hamlet. Then they had appeared in *The Master Cracksman* – he had been a somewhat plump Bunny to Robin's dashing Raffles. And finally, in their last year, Robin had played an exceedingly sinister Mephistopheles to his susceptible Dr Faustus.

'I always knew you had a weakness for heavy betting,' Robin had said, a smile on his thin handsome face, and it felt as though they had parted only the other day. 'Or are you here to deliver the last rites to a fellow member who is about to blow his brains out? I did hear the ugly rumour that you'd become a priest – it's not true, is it?'

'It is true.'

'Like Father Canteloupe!' Robin gasped in mock-horror and covered his eyes. 'Remember Father Canteloupe?'

'Nothing like Father Canteloupe.'

'Chaps here do get desperate, if only occasionally – not as much as in Monte, where at one time apparently they could never tell if the popping sounds were gunshots or produced by the uncorking of champagne bottles. The terrace at the back is a favourite spot. It's known as "terror terrace", isn't that *silly?*'

Lillie-Lysander had laughed.

'I wonder if I could employ your services, old boy. My uncle is on his way out and he needs a father confessor badly. No, I'm not joking. I've been commissioned to find a priest. Incidentally, that's the cleverest moustache I've seen in a long while. Not mass-produced, I trust?'

'No. I had it specially made.'

At school Robin Renshawe had been his hero. Lillie-Lysander had admired Robin's cleverness and droll sense of humour, his air of sarcastic knowingness, his cool manner, the ease with which Robin always managed to bluff his way through the trickiest of situations. Had lust, as St Augustine put it so dramatically, stormed confusedly within him? He was not sure. No, he didn't think so. He had always had a low sex drive and that, coupled with his extreme fastidiousness, he considered a blessing.

Take no care for the flesh in its desires. St Augustine knew all about that kind of thing. Well, yes, quite. Now that he had turned forty, any vestige of desire he might have had for either man or woman had completely disappeared. Like Christ he had remained a virgin – the thought never failed to amuse him; he regarded that as another instance of his uniqueness. All of his energies for the past couple of years had been directed into his activities at the Midas. He found himself caring less and less what God made of it all – if indeed there was a God. It was a matter of genes, that was what they said anyway – you either had a God gene or you hadn't... How then did one explain the fact that celebrating Mass in his gold-and-white robe sometimes reduced him to tears? Odd.

Robin had seemed genuinely pleased to see him. 'Such a marvellous stroke of luck, us meeting like that. I was thinking about you only this morning. They say there's no such thing as coincidence. I do believe our paths were *meant* to converge. Come and have a drink... You would be perfect for the job... You aren't a real priest, of course?'

73

'I am.' Lillie-Lysander giggled.

'Good man. Well, it helps to have a mole in the citadel.' Robin had ordered two double whiskies. 'I'd be grateful if you kept me informed about what was going on in the old man's mind.'

(Lillie-Lysander didn't remember having said yes yet.)

'I am not exactly *persona grata* at Ospreys. I must admit I am a trifle apprehensive about my future. My uncle thinks me not only dishonourable but without a trace of finer feeling. I am afraid that things might deteriorate. I want to know what's going on, which way the wind is blowing and so on. As my uncle's father confessor, you will be privy to his innermost thoughts and secrets. You will be his godly anchorman. He's been given only two months at the most. I'll make it worth your while. Can you start tomorrow? It's in Oxfordshire – place called Ospreys.'

'Ospreys? I believe I have heard of it.'

'Excellent. Shall we drink to it?'

(How much money could Robin let him have? *Could* Robin provide him with regular supplies of morphine? Robin had hinted he had suppliers for 'everything' – a tantalizing prospect.)

'Ah.' Father Lillie-Lysander gave a sigh of the deepest satisfaction as he felt himself relax more and more... and more. 'The Holy

Spirit is upon me,' he murmured blasphemously, his lips curved in a ridiculous grin.

The morphine – *Papaver somniferum!* (He made it sound like a benediction.)

At last... At last. (He must speak to Robin... Break the news... What *would* Robin do?)

Strangely enough, Father Lillie-Lysander's last thought before he passed out was of Miss Ardleigh. There was something that wasn't right about her. He was an old thesp and he was ready to swear that that blonde hair of hers–

What a delicious sensation – it felt like being in the centre of a giant centrifuge!

Down-down-down – light as a feather.

7

The Letter

'Ingrid? Do you know Ingrid?' Beatrice appeared surprised.

'I met her in Hay-on-Wye,' Antonia reminded her.

'Of course you did. Sorry, my dear. I've got so much on my mind. Oh, yes, she still lives here, but now that Len's moved in, she's planning to move out.' Beatrice Ardleigh gave a sigh. 'I am so sad. I am *deeply* grateful to her. She did *everything* for me, you see. We've lived together for – what is it? Nearly thirty years? Goodness, that's a terribly long time, isn't it? She never allowed anyone to come near me. Never.'

'Not even your doctor?'

'Dr Aylard found her quite difficult.' Beatrice held her cigarette away from her eyes. 'Once she pushed him out of my room! Well, Ingrid saw me through all my indignities. When I couldn't sit up and had to lie down all the time. When I couldn't go by myself to the loo. It is so easy to be dismissive and say, "Oh, one of those feverish female friendships," I am sure that's what people are saying, but it was so much more than that. Whenever I felt down and wanted to have a little cry, Ingrid sat beside me and held my hand. She read to me. She's particularly good with voices. She sang me to sleep. Honestly. She fed me, mopped my brow, brushed my hair, bathed me, gave me massages. She dealt with all my correspondence–'

'She reads your letters?' Payne interrupted.

'Used to – I mean she did it until recently. Not any more – not since Len's been around. But before that she acted as my secretary. She was also my nurse, nanny – mother, if you like – guardian angel! All rolled up in one! I was Ingrid's baby, her very special little girl. I know this sounds ridiculous and strange, but she lost her child, you see. She was seven months pregnant when it happened. It was going to be a little girl, apparently. Claire.'

'Claire?'

'That was the name Ingrid *intended* to give her little girl. She had been listening to "Clair de Lune" on the radio when the accident happened. She's got all those photos in her room – various little girls – blonde and demure-looking. She said they were her nieces, but, you see, she hasn't got any sisters. Once she was off guard and she said, "That's Claire, my daughter." Some of the photos are actually magazine cuttings.

Photos of fair-haired girls modelling children's clothes.'

'You mean she pretends they are her daughter?' Payne's eyebrow went up. 'She imagines they are her daughter?'

'Yes. *Yes*. She could never get over the loss of her baby. She keeps having conversations with Claire in her head. She sends a monthly cheque to the Convent of the Poor Claires. She keeps listening to "Clair de Lune"–' Beatrice broke off. 'Oh, I know – I *know* – it's totally mad. You poor things – the look on your faces! Well, losing the baby was a most devastating blow for Ingrid. She was quite unable to come to terms with the fact she'd never have another child too. To cut a long story short, I became a – a substitute. I allowed her to mother me. I don't care what people think. Great shame it all has to end like that.'

'She didn't like the idea of you marrying?'

'She didn't. She was distraught. She made a ghastly scene.' Beatrice shut and opened her eyes. 'It was quite frightening. Honestly. She said some truly appalling things to me. She made me cry. I didn't really see why the three of us couldn't be happy together. I honestly didn't. Len said he didn't mind at all; he is an angel... I misjudged the situation completely, it seems. I must be terribly naive. Ingrid took it all rather badly. "You don't really expect me to *cohabit* with you?"

78

How she screamed! She seemed outraged. She made it sound as though I'd come up with some really improper suggestion.'

'You haven't made up?'

'I am afraid not. She's still extremely cut up. She won't speak to Len. Pretends he's not there. She calls him "the interloper". She hates Len. She is very, very cross with me. She keeps saying I betrayed her. She calls it an "act of treachery". She said I was "the most selfish, the most ungrateful, the most unappreciative person who ever lived". She hates me. I did try to explain – to reassure her. I did my best, believe me.' Beatrice's voice shook. 'I made it clear that nothing had changed, but she didn't want to listen. She was beyond reason. I did want to discuss things openly and rationally, the way sensible people do, but she just sat and stared in her inscrutable manner.'

'Where is she?' Antonia asked.

'I have no idea.' Beatrice stubbed out her cigarette and looked at the clock. 'She went out over three hours ago. It's freezing cold outside. Where *does* she go? She has no friends. *Not a single friend*. Can you imagine? She mistrusts people. I do hope she's taken the train to Oxford and gone to the cinema and is not roaming the streets, brooding.'

'Does she go out often?'

'Quite often, yes. Lately, that is. She slips out without a word. And here's an odd thing

– we hear her but *never see her*. She seems to time her exits very carefully. We hear the stairs creak or the front door opening or closing. And she always comes back *after* we have gone to bed. I thought it was my imagination, but then Len noticed it too – and he is not particularly imaginative... Ingrid's exits and entrances invariably take place when Len and I are together, either here, watching something on the box, or in our bedroom. We tend to spend a lot of time in our bedroom.' Beatrice gave a coy smile. 'Call me a stupid fool, but each time Ingrid goes out, I tend to imagine the worst – that she would do something silly. She did say once that the idea of suicide was never too far from her mind.'

The chink of china was heard, the door opened and a beaming Colville wheeled in a trolley laden with tea-things. Four cups, a large silver teapot, a muffin dish, a plate of smoked salmon sandwiches and a chocolate cake.

'She is often troubled by suicidal fantasies,' Beatrice went on. 'I am telling them about Ingrid, darling.'

'Ah. Ingrid.' Colville's smile faded and he shook his head.

'She told me that at times suicide seemed not only frighteningly real but the *only option*. Varied and violent methods of ending her life keep presenting themselves to her–

Darling, would you pour? At first it was the usual stuff – sleeping pills, cyanide, exhaust fumes, but then she said she had started considering slitting her wrists with the blades of a Gillette sensor razor or cutting her throat with an X-Acto knife... Another drop of milk, please... Now that's too much! Honestly!' For a moment Beatrice looked furious. 'I am sorry, Len, but you *know* I don't like my tea drowned in milk. Can I have another cup?'

'Yes, of course, darling. So – so sorry. I didn't mean to–'Colville appeared greatly flustered. 'Here you are. Sorry, darling.' His face had turned red.

'*Thank* you.' Beatrice leant towards Payne. 'What is an X-Acto knife? I've been wondering. Is it an *army* kind of knife? I know you are the right person to ask.'

Payne, however, admitted he had no idea.

'Ingrid once went so far as to try a beam in her room to see if it would be strong enough to support a noose. And on another occasion she considered driving off a cliff.'

'People who talk so much about killing themselves never do it,' Colville said a shade regretfully. 'Did you show Miss Darcy the letter?'

'I haven't yet. I was about to. Would you be an angel and turn on the lights?'

Again Colville did as asked. 'Better hurry up and do it before she comes back.' He glanced at the clock on the mantel. 'Remember what happened the other day?'

'I certainly do.' Beatrice took a sip of tea and grimaced. 'Darling – *sugar*. Why is it that you *always* forget?' She looked at Antonia and said gravely, 'I owe you an apology, Antonia. May I call you Antonia?'

'Of course you may.'

'And you must call me Bee. Well, I have a confession to make, Antonia. I detest fibbing, I really do – but I did tell you a fib the other day when I spoke to you on the phone.'

'About the letter?'

'Yes.' Beatrice picked up one of the two books that lay on the little table beside her. From between its pages she drew out an envelope. 'I meant to tell you the truth – but Ingrid came into the room just then, so I couldn't. I didn't want her to know who the letter was from, so I told you I didn't know the man from Adam.'

'You said his name was Ralph.'

'Yes. Ralph Renshawe.' Beatrice pronounced 'Ralph' over-emphatically as *Rafe*. 'Many years ago he and I were engaged to be married. I was *extremely* young. Practically a child. It turns out he lives at a big house not so very far from here, can you imagine? A place called Ospreys. It's a listed house. There is a wishing well in the back garden that goes back to the seventeenth century, apparently. I read a piece about it in *Homes and Gardens*. We've been practically neighbours all this time and neither of us the wiser! Life is so *strange*. Anyhow. I want you to read the letter. I rely on your wise counsel.' She handed it over to Antonia. Payne moved closer. He thought he detected a slight medicinal smell emanating from the envelope.

The letter was written in a faint, shaky, hardly legible hand. It began:

This is a communication from the past you never expected and almost certainly did not want. I hope you will read it. And before you rip it up and drop it in the bin, I must tell you that I am dying. This is the literal truth: I have been given a month at the most. I do not deserve any sympathy and I do not expect any...

It was not a long letter. Eventually Antonia looked up.

'What do you think?' Beatrice held her hand at her bosom. 'Extraordinary, isn't it?'

Antonia said slowly, 'You and Ralph Renshawe were engaged to be married. He was driving you in his car. There was an accident. It was entirely his fault. He had been drinking. You had a head-on collision with another car. He wasn't hurt but you were. Your injuries were extremely serious. You became paralysed from the waist down. You spent a very long time in hospital.'

'Six months,' Beatrice whispered.

'Ralph visited you only once, then disappeared. You never saw him again. That happened thirty years ago. He went to Nova Scotia, then to Calgary, where he married a very rich woman–'

'He married an oil heiress,' Colville said stiffly. 'There was something about it in the paper – years ago. She must have left him all her money. The price tag put on Ospreys was just over eight million pounds.'

'Len knows all about houses. If you are interested in buying or renting a house, he is your man,' Beatrice said. 'All right, darling, I won't embarrass you, I promise. Oh, how I wish we weren't so worried about money! Sorry, darling!' Colville had harrumphed again. 'Well, nobody believes me when I say we are as poor as the proverbial church mice.'

She really was most indiscreet. Must be a nightmare, being married to her, Antonia thought, shooting a sympathetic glance at Colville.

'I suppose appearances can be jolly deceptive,' Payne murmured, waving his hand round the comfortable room with its crackling cosy fire.

Beatrice laughed exuberantly once more – as though he had made some risqué joke. 'Honestly,' she breathed. 'I am afraid Daddy's money is running out – and poor Len's come an ugly cropper in his business dealings–'

'Bee,' Colville said warningly.

'Well, I admit I am scared,' she declared. 'Honestly! I think I might end up like some sort of an Emma Bovary of the impoverished squirearchy! I know I am being silly.'

Antonia went on, 'Soon after he inherited his late wife's fortune, Ralph Renshawe came back to England and bought Ospreys. He was then diagnosed with cancer. He has been told it is terminal, inoperable. He is dying. He is consumed by guilt. His reason for writing the letter is to beg your forgiveness.'

'It's all so – so operatically melodramatic, isn't it?' Beatrice rolled her eyes. 'I can't imagine Ralph filled to the brim with remorse and shaking in fear of eternal damnation. I simply can't. Thirty years ago he was completely different – hard as nails. Now he mentions God in every sentence he writes.'

'He mentions a priest,' Antonia said.

'Yes. His very own personal padre, it seems.'

'He is a Catholic then?'

'He wasn't a Catholic when I knew him. He wasn't anything. He looked down on all religions. He said there was no God. Do you think there is God, Hugh?'

'Yes,' Payne said. 'Indubitably.'

'When I hear a person of subtle intelligence express such positive views, I feel terribly encouraged. But sometimes I do wonder.' Beatrice gave a mournful sigh.

Payne had been examining the envelope. He tapped the letter with his forefinger. 'Renshawe asks you to visit him. Says it would mean a lot to him if you did.'

'Oh dear, yes. I have no idea what I should do about it. I haven't written back or anything. I thought you might be able to give me some advice. I am in a quandary. Len thinks I shouldn't.'

'You shouldn't,' Colville said. 'Let him rot. He wrecked your life.'

Payne looked at him. 'Did you know him, Colville?'

'I did. Not at all well. Long time ago.' There was a silence but Colville said no more.

'How does Ingrid come into this?' Antonia asked with a frown.

'Well, she came into the room that day.' Beatrice lowered her voice. 'Just as I'd started telling you about the letter. I couldn't possibly give you any details with her in the room. I lost my nerve. Ingrid would flip if she knew that Ralph is not only alive but living just round the corner from here as well. She'd go and – I don't want to think what she might do. I really don't.'

'She'd kill him, that's what she'd do,' said Colville.

'Why should she want to do that?'

'Well, you see, Antonia, I told her that Ralph had left for Nova Scotia, which was true, but I also said he'd died there,' Beatrice started explaining. 'I told her I'd read his obituary in the paper. She seemed frightfully disappointed. She said he'd had an easy escape. So much hatred! It can't be good for her, can it? I read somewhere if you hate too much, you develop cancer. Ingrid still flies into rages at the mere mention of his name! Honestly.'

She loves that word 'honestly', Payne thought. Was there an antigram? He did some quick mental arithmetic. *There was.* Honestly – on the sly! How very interesting.

'I personally don't bear Ralph any grudges. I honestly don't,' Beatrice went on. 'I did suffer, I know. I suffered awfully. My life was turned upside down by the accident, but it's never occurred to me to want to kill him. Not even in my darkest hour.'

'You are easily the nicest person who ever lived,' Colville said.

She shook her head resolutely from side to side. 'No, I am not.'

'Yes, you are.'

No, she is not, Antonia thought. You fool.

'I happen to be well adjusted, that's all. Ingrid is not. Ingrid has always inhabited an agitated universe. Awful things keep happening to her. Let me give you an example. When she was a girl she had a pet owl called

Cassandra and she doted on it, but one day the poor wretched thing swallowed the end of the cord for the window blinds. It was found swinging in the breeze upside-down – hanged! Can you imagine? Ingrid was distraught.'

'I think she killed that bird,' Colville said. 'The way she killed those two bitches.'

'Darling!' Beatrice protested. 'Well, Ingrid *is* volatile. She was diagnosed as manic-depressive well before she lost her baby. She told me all about it. She said she tended to brood for hours on end on something trivial. She was prescribed all sorts of powerful drugs. Demerol? Then of course she had the nervous breakdown and that was – *mega*. They feared for her life. She kept harming herself. She wrote a frightfully disturbing poem called "Madrigals for Mad Girls". She started having delusions. Once she imagined her doctor was Ralph in disguise and she tried to stab him in the eye with the paper knife from his desk. She underwent all sorts of very special treatments and it took her *ages* to recover.'

'She never recovered,' Colville said emphatically. *'Au contraire.'*

'I know she's been particularly horrid to you, darling, but do try to be fair.' Beatrice sighed. 'She still takes anti-depressants – when she remembers, that is. Her room is full of pills. Well, taking care of me seemed to help her. Len is not convinced, but she *did* get better for a while. She put on weight. She started taking an interest in clothes and flowers and things. We went places. That picture on the mantelpiece – Len, would you be so kind? Thank you, darling. Look at us! Just look at us. We are at Cliveden. Doesn't Ingrid look in the pink?'

'She certainly seems different from the time I met her,' Antonia admitted.

The photograph showed a radiant Beatrice in her wheelchair, a mink coat draped around her shoulders, clutching a bottle of Veuve Clicquot, and a plumper, smiling Ingrid, her eyes a little puffy, in a Yum-Yum haircut and encased in a silk magenta-coloured trouser suit with an embroidered front.

'She looks like an ornament the Astors might have brought back from their travels in the Mysterious East,' Payne murmured.

'Yes! Doesn't she just?' Beatrice leant towards Antonia and whispered, *'Your husband says such clever things.'*

Colville's smile, Antonia observed, was beginning to look as if it had been left on his face by an oversight.

Beatrice had become wistful once more. 'We had such good times. All right. She's deteriorated since.'

'Tell them about the bitches,' Colville prompted.

'Ingrid had two dogs,' Beatrice began after a pause. 'A golden retriever and a pit bull – Pip and Taylor – both bitches, as it happens. She had them put down for being "control freaks". She explained the dogs had been putting her under an awful lot of pressure. The funny thing is that Ingrid is something of a control freak herself. You saw her in Hay-on-Wye, Antonia. You noticed the way she acted? I am infinitely grateful to Ingrid, mind, but sometimes it did feel as though she'd injected me with some paralysing fluid. I am probably being fanciful, but every so often I'd get this most peculiar feeling. How can I explain it? As though I'd been cocooned in an undetectable glaze of fixative. Goodness, that does sound weird, doesn't it?'

Payne murmured, 'Perhaps she did inject you with something?'

'I bet she did,' said Colville. 'She gave Bee all sorts of injections – vitamins, painkillers and so on. She had plenty of opportunity to do something to her.'

'Well, there were times when I did feel my power of choice diminishing – my rational judgement about things weakening–' Beatrice broke off. 'My main worry at the moment is that Ingrid might do something terrible to Ralph if somehow she were to learn that he isn't dead but living next door.'

'What's the connection between Ingrid

and Ralph?' Antonia was frowning. 'And how did Ingrid and you meet?'

'Oh, didn't I say? I am hopeless at explaining things. Sorry, my dear. It was the accident. The accident brought us together,' Beatrice said. 'I was in hospital – bedridden. The worst time of my life! Ingrid paid me a visit. She sat beside my bed and stroked my hand. She said she intended to take care of me. It seemed the most natural thing in the world, it honestly did, at least at the time. I knew at once she was looking for a substitute, but that didn't really bother me much.'

'A substitute? What substitute?' Payne looked puzzled.

'For her dead child of course,' said Beatrice. 'She lost her baby, you see. In the accident.'

8

Doppelgänger

Payne stared. 'In the same accident?'

'Yes – she was in the *other* car. The one we collided with. She was seven months pregnant at the time. She survived but she lost her baby. She had a miscarriage.'

'How terrible,' Antonia said.

'Oh, it was. Doesn't bear thinking about!' Beatrice flapped her hands. 'It was the most tragic thing. Poor Ingrid was all alone in the world when it happened. She wasn't married. She hated her parents. She had run away from home. She wasn't in what is known as a "stable relationship" either. A caring, loving, understanding husband or boyfriend might have helped her recover, but that man – Ingrid's boyfriend – the child's father – was no good. He'd never really loved Ingrid.'

'He didn't care about the child?'

'Not one bit, Antonia. Poor Ingrid, on the other hand, wanted a child more than anything else in the world, so she lied to him that she was on the pill. I don't think he ever forgave her for it. Oh, it is all so sordid.

Anyhow, she got pregnant, which had been her intention all along. It made her extremely happy. She started buying things for the baby – clothes, a cot, a pram, various toys.' Beatrice pressed her handkerchief against her lips.

'I don't think you should get upset now, really.' Colville put a protective arm round her shoulders.

Beatrice sniffed. 'She said she'd never been so happy... But then the accident happened and she lost the baby. And then – then she was dealt another blow – the doctors told her she couldn't have any more children. That's when it happened. She said it felt like a wire snapping inside her brain.'

'She swore she'd kill Renshawe, didn't she?' Colville said portentously.

Beatrice didn't answer. She had covered her face with her hands.

There was a pause. 'Ralph was drunk that night, but he isn't the only one to blame.' Beatrice looked from Antonia to Payne, her eyes brimming with tears. 'I haven't told you the whole story. You see, *it was my fault too.*'

'Nonsense,' Colville said robustly. The next moment he looked up. 'Was that the front door?'

'No, it *was* my fault. I was tipsy that night. Not as drunk as Ralph was but tipsy nevertheless. We had been drinking at Baudolino's Bar in Greek Street. We'd had such a marvellous time. Ralph made me laugh. He said such outrageous things! I was very much taken by him, I must admit. How I laughed. I was quite hysterical with it. That's always a bad sign, isn't it?'

'I think Ingrid's back,' Colville said.

Beatrice didn't seem to hear. 'I didn't stop Ralph from driving. I should have done, but didn't. I had actually brought a bottle of champagne with me. We kept drinking from it. I encouraged him to drive fast. If I had been a mature, responsible kind of person, I wouldn't have allowed Ralph to get into the car, but I wasn't. I was intent on having a good time. I wanted to please Ralph. We could have taken a cab. Don't you see? I might have prevented the accident. Only I didn't.'

'Did you ever tell Ingrid that part of the story?' Antonia asked after a pause.

'Goodness, *no*. I gave her a completely different version of events. How I'd begged Ralph not to drive that night. How I had implored him. How I had wept. How I had tried to hide the car keys. I told Ingrid a pack of whoppers. Well, I am as bad as Ralph. I as good as killed Ingrid's baby. What's the matter now, darling?' Beatrice asked irritably as Colville rose abruptly from his seat. 'Where are you going?'

'I'm going to check,' he said in a low voice. 'I think Ingrid's come back.'

Beatrice blinked. *'Come back?'* Her expression changed and she clapped her hand over her mouth. 'Oh my God. The *door*–' She shook her forefinger. 'Look! It's ajar! Oh, Len, why didn't you shut it?' She gesticulated frantically.

Without a word Colville lumbered out of the room.

Beatrice Ardleigh looked at Antonia with wild eyes. 'Do you think she might have heard? Was I shouting? I was shouting, wasn't I? Oh my God.'

'I don't think you were that loud,' Antonia tried to reassure her.

'I was shouting, Antonia. She must have heard every word I said. She knows now that I lied to her.'

The next moment Colville re-entered the room. He stood by the door and leant against the wall. His ruddy face was visibly paler. His eyes had a dazed look. He appeared to have had a shock of some kind.

'Darling, what is it?' Beatrice cried. 'Was it Ingrid?'

He swallowed. Then he gave an awkward laugh and passed his hand across his face. 'It must have been, but it looked nothing like her.' Aware how absurd this sounded, he shook his head.

'What the hell do you mean, Colville?' Major Payne asked.

There was a pause. 'If I didn't know that

at this very moment Bee was here in this very room,' Colville said hoarsely, 'I'd have said it was ... *her*.'

'You thought it was me? What – what are you talking about?' Suddenly Beatrice looked terrified.

'It was your doppelgänger, Bee. Your double. I saw your double going up the stairs.' He swallowed. 'She even *smelled* like you. She smelled of Ce Soir Je T'Aime.'

9

Partners in Crime

Father Lillie-Lysander had 'gone off' at five in the afternoon. It was over two hours later that he came to. He found he was lying across his bed, spread-eagled, still wearing his sumptuous dressing gown. He had no recollection of going into his bedroom, but he must have done. It was dark now. He had missed the twilight – he liked the twilight. *An atmosphere of tenebrous deliquescence.* That was how Baron Corvo would have put it.

He remained lying with his eyes open. He had a special feeling for twilight. He got a thrill out of it. Well, he seemed to be one of those men who – how did it go? – rebelled against the light and knew not the way thereof, nor abided in the paths thereof.

Suddenly he laughed. He had remembered a joke Robin had made concerning the long black cassock favoured by Jesuits, about one of its rather peculiar features – the sleeve-like strip of material attached to each shoulder – the so-called wings. These curious appendages, Robin had said, are a vestigial legacy of the days when the Holy

Fathers had four arms and could distribute the Body of Christ in two directions at once.

Lillie-Lysander wondered idly what his bishop's reaction might be if he went to him and made a full confession – about the way he felt, the thoughts he had, the things he did. Would the old fool call for an exorcism? For public defrocking? The bishop would probably have him flogged if he could! He might even be inspired to write a sermon on the subject.

Be vigilant, my brethren (Lillie-Lysander improvised). *These cunning, crafty and artful creatures manage to pass themselves off as men of God, but they are only wolves in sheep's clothing. They preach not the Gospel of Truth but their own diabolical philosophies and counsels. They make the black night their morning and ally themselves with the terrors of the pit. Yes, they feel secure only when surrounded by deep shades of darkness–*

Father Lillie-Lysander rose gingerly from the bed. He felt only the tiniest bit woozy – a trifle swimmy. He had read somewhere that drugs killed brain cells. Surely that was an exaggeration? He was proud of his brain; he wouldn't want to harm it. He should be fine in a couple of minutes. After he had had a cup of coffee and some breakfast – he was feeling ravenous – or did he mean dinner? It *was* morning, wasn't it?

He knew he needed to do something rather

urgently. He needed to speak to somebody – no, not to the bishop. To Robin? Yes. He needed to speak to Robin. Poor Robin. Lillie-Lysander put on his slippers and walked across the room. How funny. He felt light inside, yet it was like wading through treacle.

Lillie-Lysander dialled Robin's number and as soon as he heard Robin's voice, said, 'I am afraid I have some bad news. I don't think you will like it.' His tongue felt thick – but he didn't think he was lisping.

'I will most certainly not like it if it's bad news.'

'Your uncle has sent for his solicitor, Robin.'

'Don't tell me he intends to change his will,' Robin said quietly.

'Well – yes.' Lillie-Lysander was a bit annoyed that Robin had guessed the nature of the problem so quickly, but then Robin must be thinking of little else. 'That is his intention. You are no longer his heir.' Lillie-Lysander kept shutting his eyes and shading them against the electric light with his hand. He felt extremely thirsty.

'I expected something of the sort,' Robin sounded almost casual. 'Who or what will be getting the Hartz millions?'

'You will never guess.'

'Don't tell me it's you, Lily. That might mean I'd have to marry you.'

'No such luck, I fear. I will get my rewards

99

in heaven.' Lillie-Lysander giggled.

'Not Wilkes? I'd definitely marry Wilkes.'

'Not Nurse Wilkes either. I said you'd never guess. Well, he has decided to leave all his money to Beatrice Ardleigh.' Lillie-Lysander paused, expecting an interruption, but there wasn't any. 'Your uncle's solicitor is coming tomorrow morning.'

'Who the fuck is Beatrice Ardleigh?'

'A woman your uncle nearly married thirty years ago. They were in an accident and she lost the power of her legs. She's been calling on him–'

'Good lord. *That* woman. I have heard the story of course. Bee Ardleigh, is how Uncle Ralph refers to her.'

'That's correct.'

'You don't mean she's been perambulating herself to Ospreys in her wheelchair? Are you sure she is not a mere chimera? Perhaps she only exists in my uncle's imagination. I bet my uncle is delusional. That frequently happens to those about to depart.' Robin continued to sound extremely composed. Lillie-Lysander would have preferred him to sigh, groan, even utter some unprintable oath.

'She is real enough, Robin. I did meet her. She seems to have made a complete recovery. She is in fine shape. Her legs are perfectly steady. The only oddity about her, if you'd call it that, was that she wears a wig.'

'You couldn't have misunderstood about the will? Uncle Ralph is less than lucid these days; you said so yourself.'

'He was extremely lucid. He talked about his decision at some length. He still feels guilty about Beatrice Ardleigh and is determined to do something by way of compensating her for the torment and misery he has caused her. His solicitor is coming tomorrow at eleven.'

'I think we should meet. I am coming over.'

'Actually, Robin, I am not feeling very well at the moment. I have a bit of a headache. Can't we meet tomorrow morning?'

'Make some coffee. One of your superior brews. I'll be with you in about forty-five minutes.'

Lillie-Lysander lived at Athlone Place in Charterhouse Square while Robin had a tiny flat in Knightsbridge.

Lillie-Lysander started saying something but realized that Robin had rung off. He shook his head and smiled, a slightly twisted smile. *I am coming over.* Robin hadn't asked whether it would be convenient. He had shown scant regard for Lillie-Lysander's headache. Well, Robin always saw things exclusively from his own point of view. It was remarkable how Robin always managed to get his way. Lillie-Lysander's resentment was mixed with admiration.

He had intended to go back to bed and

read from *Don Tarquinio*, a book which he knew by heart and whose author, the enigmatic Baron Corvo, was one of his heroes, but he went to the kitchen instead.

'*Bearing armorials on their tabards, displayed at the prow the double-cross and the high Estense gonfalon,*' Lillie-Lysander quoted aloud, articulating as carefully as he could while at the same time speaking fast and making it sound like a tongue-twister. He wanted to prove to himself that he wasn't really lisping. Robin had a sharp ear and was bound to tease him about it.

His kitchen was a Vermeer oasis of pewter and glass. He put coffee in the percolator. Coffee from the Himalayan hills. The packet bore the Harrods label. Well, he simply *had* to have the best. Some of his smart acquaintances were boycotting Harrods, but he personally didn't disapprove of Mr Al Fayed. Lillie-Lysander couldn't help having affinity with people who did outrageous things and defied the Establishment.

As he turned on the radio, he peered at the clock – not eight yet? It was still dark outside and the lights in the kitchen were on. Was there a storm coming? No, he didn't feel like listening to the radio. It was exactly twelve minutes to eight. Thought For The Day would start any second, and that was the last thing he wanted. He had an aversion to high-minded bores. Liberated ex-nuns and suchlike. The next moment, remembering that it was eight in the *evening*, not in the morning, he laughed, a somewhat high-pitched giggle.

He was getting confused. *Papaver somniferum* was turning out to be more powerful than he expected, but oh the joy and ecstasy supreme before oblivion had taken over! He reached out for the radio once more and found Jazz FM. It was a little-known Cole Porter song they were playing. 'A Shooting-Box in Scotland'. Lillie-Lysander hummed along with the singer:

> *'Having lots of idle leisure,*
> *I pursue a life of pleasure—'*

Actually that wasn't true. He didn't have lots of idle leisure. He did work. He listened to the incredibly boring confessions of mortally ill elderly gentlemen. He then reported to the elderly gentlemen's scapegrace nephews. He could actually run that as a regular service, he supposed. *A double-crossing father confessor seeks employment. Would undertake most delicate and unusual of tasks. No religious scruples—*

Lillie-Lysander felt so light-headed, he wouldn't have been surprised if he had started soaring up to the ceiling. *The Times* lay on the kitchen table. He hadn't been able to so much as glance at it. He put on his reading glasses but the next moment he started recalling how he had pinched the ampoule from Ralph Renshawe's bedside table. He had been tempted. He had always wondered what it would feel like.

The wicked flourish like a green bay tree. Well, yes. Quite. He was in excellent health and brimming with ideas.

Lillie-Lysander kept his eye on the clock, imagining that Robin, true to his inconsiderate nature, would be either late or early, but Robin was as good as his word. Forty-six minutes later his friend was lounging on the sofa, his legs stretched out before him. Robin had taken off his long charcoal-grey coat but left his white muffler fluttering rakishly at his throat. He wore a black Dior jacket, a cashmere roll-neck and slim polished boots. He looked smart in a French, *nouvelle vague* kind of way.

Lillie-Lysander put the small tray with the silver coffeepot and two cups on the round malachite table between them. Robin's foxy face looked merely blank but he must feel far from happy. Well, it had been Robin's intention to spend Christmas in the Seychelles. It was his uncle's money that he had felt sure would pay for it since his uncle would be dead by the end of November, early December at the latest. Robin had probably been envisioning himself bouncing around in speedboats feeding caviar to the fish. Now of course he would have to review his plans.

'*All* his money?' Robin sipped coffee from the delicate eggshell cup with the gold border which Lillie-Lysander had handed him. 'Surely not *all* his money?'

'Every penny of it,' Lillie-Lysander said with ill-concealed relish. 'Those were his exact words.'

'He's lost his mind. Do sit down, Lily. It puts me on edge seeing you hovering about. And would you stop rustling that newspaper?' For the first time Robin was showing signs of emotion.

Lillie-Lysander balanced himself gingerly on one of his little flat-seated heraldic chairs and took a sip of coffee. The chair was part of a set, which he had bought at Christie's. He had been enthralled by the elaborate armorial painting on the chairs' backs. 'You can always contest the will,' he said.

'And who's going to foot my legal bills? Would you? Incidentally, does the lucky slut know about his intentions?'

'No. He hasn't told her yet. He hasn't said so, but I think he intends it to be a surprise.'

'A surprise... What precisely did he say about me?'

'Well, um, he said you have been a disappointment. He said he hoped you would understand why he was doing this–'

'Would I?'

'You were still young and–'

'Young?' Robin gave a rueful smile. 'I will be forty-one soon.'

They were the same age but beside him Robin looked positively boyish, or rather, as the Gallic flavour of his clothes suggested, *comme un garçon*. Did he like *les garçons?* Lillie-Lysander wondered. Robin had courted a baronet's daughter twenty years before, at least that was what he had told him – a girl called Samantha, they had been practically engaged, but she had gone and married someone else who was in politics. Once at the Midas, Lillie-Lysander had seen him arm in arm with two exceptionally good-looking young Spaniards. He had introduced them as his 'neophytes'. On that particular occasion Robin had been rather drunk. But then Lillie-Lysander had also encountered Robin at the gaming table, holding hands with a stunning-looking black girl. The girl had been long-legged, smooth-skinned and pouted a lot. She looked like a model and Robin appeared quite taken with her. Robin had introduced her as Mascot – or had he called her *his* mascot? She had certainly brought him luck that night, Lillie-Lysander remembered.

'Your uncle referred to the money your father left you,' Lillie-Lysander went on. 'He said your father had left you extremely well provided for.'

'My father didn't leave me well provided for. Or if he did, that was a very long time ago.'

'Your uncle said that if you've frittered away your father's money, his decision might be an incentive for you to get a job. He said you had no history of lawful employment. He called you an idler and a waster. He said you were leading a parasitic existence.'

'How well my uncle knows me.' Robin frowned. 'A job would be a bore *and* a bind... So he's serious about disinheriting me?'

'Yes. He is convinced he has made the right decision. He did ask me for my opinion though.' Lillie-Lysander paused. 'I said that this was a very serious matter and he shouldn't rush things. I told him that he should give the matter careful consideration.'

'That was kind of you, Lily, but I don't imagine my uncle was swayed by your views on the subject?'

'No. Actually it made him laugh. This brought on a coughing fit. It nearly killed him–'

'Really?'

'Yes.' Lillie-Lysander was watching Robin carefully. 'Your uncle started gasping – choking. It was ghastly – absolutely ghastly. Nurse Wilkes ran over. Your uncle did look as though he were breathing his last. He recovered eventually, but for a minute or two I was quite worried that I might have killed him.'

Robin loosened his muffler. His face remained expressionless. 'You were worried that you might have killed him. You realize, don't you, that if you had – that if my uncle had died there and then, as a result of your perfectly innocent remark – you would have been talking to a multi-millionaire now?'

Lillie-Lysander inserted a cigar into his cigar holder but did not light it. He sat very still. Something like an electric current had run through his body. He had had a powerful sense of déjà vu. *You would have been talking to a multi-millionaire now.* He had expected Robin to say something like that. Yes. He had the oddest feeling that a curtain had lifted and they were once more on the stage. They were in a play together and he had given Robin a cue...

Lillie-Lysander felt the beginnings of a peculiar elation. He went on speaking, but for some reason he found it hard to concentrate. 'When your uncle recovered, he reminded me that he might die at any moment. He pointed out that careful consideration, as I had put it, would be an extravagant luxury, which he couldn't afford. He was going to see his solicitor tomorrow morning at eleven; he had already made arrangements. Mr Saunders was coming to Ospreys at eleven in the morning.'

'I know old Saunders. Of Saunders, Merrick & Bell. Office in New Bond Street. Tomorrow at eleven, did you say?'

'Tomorrow at eleven.' Lillie-Lysander nodded. He thought it sounded like the title of a play – a Noel Coward pastiche? More like a Francis Durbridge-style thriller, actually. *Tomorrow at Eleven.* There was a menacing ring to it. Did they still do Durbridge? Mainly rep, he imagined. As a matter of fact he and Robin were a bit like the two main characters in Patrick Hamilton's *Rope* – Lillie-Lysander had always wanted to play Brandon, the 'dominant' one. This scene was crucial; it had to be done in an understated, almost perfunctory fashion – not too perfunctory though – over-acting either way would kill it, Lillie-Lysander had no doubt. Well, Robin seemed to have established the right register. Was that how people talked in real life? Well, this *was* real life. How funny.

'This is what I would like you to do, Lily. I would like you to be at Ospreys at ten. Or even a couple of minutes before ten, to give yourself enough time.' Robin put down the coffee cup. 'Do take off your glasses. You can't concentrate with your glasses on. Your pupils are like pinpoints, incidentally.'

Lillie-Lysander took off his glasses. I do everything he tells me, he thought, fascinated. It was like that silly childish game,

Simon Says. There should be a game called Robin Orders. *Robin orders: 'Take off your glasses.'*

'What do you want me to do?' Lillie-Lysander asked and as he did, he was transported back in time once more, to school, to the day he had rigged up a booby-trap over the classroom door minutes before one of the most popular masters had entered. It had been a carefully premeditated exercise in authority-destruction. The bucket had contained red paint. The master had never managed to enjoy the same degree of popularity afterwards. It was Robin who had put Lillie-Lysander up to it. Robin had managed to persuade him without much difficulty. Neither of them had been caught.

Robin had crossed his legs. A little smile was playing on his lips. Lillie-Lysander was aware that he too was smiling, he couldn't say why exactly. Robin knows I am an opium-eater, he thought. 'You won't be disturbed by Wilkes until half past ten, that's when she makes you a cup of tea, is that right? Does Wilkes still knit?'

'I think so. Yes.' For some reason Lillie-Lysander experienced an unpleasant frisson at the thought of Nurse Wilkes' knitting needles.

'I recall the big feather pillows at the foot of my uncle's bed. Are they still there?'

'Yes. There are two pillows – no, three.'

'Have you ever touched them?'

'Well, yes. Once or twice – without thinking.'

'How do they feel – soft? Or are they of the somewhat harder, springier variety?'

'Soft – they are filled with feathers, I think.' A touch of perversity had entered the dialogue – they must be careful. This was a crucial scene. It had to be played straight, in a matter-of-fact manner. Any suggestion of facetiousness or double entendre would be disastrous.

There was a moment's pause, then Robin said quietly, 'You will need to press firmly but make sure you don't bruise his face. Given Uncle Ralph's enfeebled state, it would take less than a minute.'

Lillie-Lysander sat very still, staring before him. *Robin orders: 'Smother my uncle.'* Had he goaded Robin into this? He had certainly exaggerated when he said that Ralph Renshawe had nearly died as a result of his coughing fit, which he, Lillie-Lysander, had brought about. Had he done it on purpose? Had he planted the idea of murder in Robin's mind? Had that been his intention ... all along?

'...take the pillow off his face, plump it up and place it at his feet. Check his wrist. He *will* have expired, but if he hasn't, you may have to repeat the procedure. Make certain his eyes are closed and not glazed and staring. That accomplished, sit beside him as you normally do. Is the chair by the bed comfortable?'

'Not in the least. It's a genuine Empire.'

'Excellent. No danger of you dozing off then. Well, that's where Wilkes should find you. In your dog collar, the rosary clicking between your fingers, your head bowed in prayer. As you hear her enter, look up, execute the sign of the cross over my uncle's body. *Ego te absolvo in nomine Patris.* That's what you say, don't you? Turn to Wilkes – *Mr Renshawe is at peace now. He must have died in his sleep. I have given him his last rites.* Don't forget to bring your little leather bag, will you? What does it contain exactly? I have always wondered.'

'Chalice. Anointing oil. Bible.'

'It's highly unlikely that anyone would insist on a postmortem in the case of a gravely ill cancer patient.' Robin picked up the silver pot and poured himself more coffee. 'You could stay until Saunders comes at eleven and break the sad tidings to him, if you like. Saunders' errand would have been fruitless, or bootless. The status quo would remain undisturbed. There will be no new will and according to the old one, it is Robin Renshawe, nephew of the deceased, who receives the bulk of my uncle's fortune.'

'You are confident of success,' Lillie-

Lysander said in an uninflected voice.

'I don't see how it could go wrong. You are already an integral part of the Ospreys set-up. You have been performing your duties impeccably. You won't incur a blink of suspicion. Not that anyone would ever consider the possibility of foul play.' Robin took a sip of coffee. 'We'll go halves. That's a *lot*, Lily. Judith Hartz II was a rich bitch. We are talking millions. At least twenty. She left it all to Uncle Ralph, though by all accounts he was the husband from hell. That was well before he found God. I can put it in writing, if you like. I am sure you trust me?'

Lillie-Lysander remained silent. Did he trust Robin? Well, no, not entirely, but then that was part of the thrill. (Was he a masochist?)

Robin murmured, 'It wouldn't be as messy as the fox...'

Lillie-Lysander knew at once what he meant. Back at school all those years ago a fox had strayed into the cricket pavilion and he – Lillie-Lysander – had battered it with a cricket bat. Robin had dared him to do it. Robin had suggested Lillie-Lysander was too fastidious, too squeamish, too 'lily-livered'. Well, he had shown him. They had disposed of the fox's body together, by wrapping it in back numbers of the *Catholic Herald* and the *Tablet*, which they had stolen from the school library and placing it inside one of the gardener's green refuse bags.

Robin went on, 'Just imagine your pockets full of lustrous plastic counters – what you could achieve at the Midas if you had that kind of money... You wouldn't have to go back to St Edmund's – *ever*. Or any other similar establishment.'

St Edmund's was the particularly awful minor public school where Lillie-Lysander had taught English for a year. He had despised and detested St Edmund's. The boys had been beastly – they had driven him mad. He had told Robin how he had found himself devising ingenious ways of exterminating them one by one, starting with the leaders. It would have been a kind of *Unman, Wittering and Zigo* in reverse...

Robin's eyes had strayed to the papers on Lillie-Lysander's desk – they slid over to the letter concerning his friend's depleted account. Lillie-Lysander looked down at his unlit cigar in its ornate holder. He was experiencing a rather complex sort of feeling, a curious blend of dread-cum-relish. Soon enough he heard a sigh of commiseration he knew was as *faux* as the copy of the 'original' Dr Crippen's diary he had picked up at a book auction a couple of months back.

'My poor Lily,' Robin said. 'Just *think* of the difference this would make to your finances. Think what it would be like to have lots of idle leisure, to pursue a life of pleasure–'

'"A Shooting-Box in Scotland".' Lillie-Lysander looked up. 'You too heard it?'

'It was on the radio earlier on. I was in the car. So, what do you say?'

In a strange way that was what did it – the fact that they had been listening to the same song at the same time. Not that Lillie-Lysander had ever thought of saying no. *Thou shall not serve alien gods.* Yes, quite.

'I will think about it,' he said.

10

Cul-de-Sac

'Now, why should she want to make herself look like Beatrice?'

'Why indeed, my love. These are deep waters. The Bafflement of the Bogus Blonde. The Puzzle of the Peroxide Peruke. More Chesterton than Conan Doyle, wouldn't you say?' Major Payne put a thoughtful match to his pipe. 'I did tell you we always met unhinged people, didn't I? A prophecy fulfilled.'

'Do we always meet unhinged people?'

'We most certainly do. There's *something* about us. I don't know what it is. We seem to act as a magnet for madmen – and madwomen. Think Dufrette, think Eleanor Merchant, think Colonel Mallard–'

Antonia pointed out that they had never actually *met* Colonel Mallard. Colonel Mallard had been dead for sixty years when they first heard about him.

'But we were told so much about him, we felt we knew him. And now Ingrid Delmar. Glazed of eye, ascending the stairs bizarrely bedecked in a blonde wig, sporting gloves as black as her soul, a moth-eaten mink coat coquettishly draped round her shoulders. A chilling sight. *Out flew the web and floated wide – the curse has come upon me, cried the Lady of Shalott,'* Major Payne recited between puffs. 'Sorry. Couldn't resist it.'

'Ingrid used to burn herself with steam irons claiming it offered her relief from tension. I can't believe Beatrice stuck with her for thirty years.' Antonia shook her head.

'A prophecy fulfilled... Damned good coffee, this. Pour me some more, would you, my love?'

Beatrice had persuaded them to take a thermos flask of black coffee for their journey home – as well as a packet of ham sandwiches wrapped in a moist napkin and two pieces of chocolate orange cake. Beatrice had insisted they needed to keep up their strength. They might have been members of an expedition returning from the North Pole or some such place.

They were sitting inside the car further down the road from Millbrook House. It was a beautiful evening, and a full pale moon glowed in the sky like a silver florin. They had said goodbye to Colville and Beatrice, but for some reason felt reluctant to drive off. It was almost as though they expected something to happen...

Antonia kept glancing back towards the house. The light had come on in a first-floor window and she imagined she caught a glimpse of Ingrid's silhouette outlined momentarily against the curtain. Ingrid appeared to be shaking her head and gesticulating agitatedly. There was something extremely theatrical about the whole set-up, Payne agreed. The unnerved newly-weds downstairs, the loon in the blonde wig upstairs. Beatrice had been strongly opposed to the idea of involving the police... Colville didn't believe Ingrid had heard him when he went out into the hall. Ingrid hadn't so much as glanced in his direction. She had stared straight ahead of her and moved like one in a trance. Surely, that suggested that she had heard Beatrice's admission of guilt and been stunned by it? What would happen when the shock was over?

'Beatrice might be in danger. Colville too,' said Antonia. 'Ingrid hates them both. She wouldn't try to slit their throats as they sleep, would she?'

'Or do a Mrs Danvers, set the house on fire and dance among the flames. Well, let's hope not.'

'At what point does a maniac become a homicidal maniac?'

'Difficult to say, my love. Beatrice's confession tonight might have managed to unzip Ingrid's already shaky grip on sanity.'

'I do think we should inform the police, Hugh.'

'You heard what Beatrice said. *No police.*

Beatrice doesn't want to "snitch" on Ingrid, silly woman.'

'Silly woman,' Antonia agreed with greater emphasis than she intended.

Colville had been confident he could keep the situation under control. Colville said he was capable of taking good care of Beatrice. He said that he wouldn't hesitate to ring 999 the moment he felt Ingrid might be 'up to something'. Colville might be besotted with *la belle* Bee, Payne pointed out, but he wouldn't stand any nonsense from Ingrid. Colville had confided in Payne on parting that he'd be damned if he did.

'That's reassuring,' Antonia said in a doubtful voice. 'I wouldn't dream of sleeping under the same roof as Ingrid – would you?'

'Not for all the tea in China.'

'Where *does* Ingrid go dressed up as Beatrice?' Antonia wondered aloud, looking out into the darkness. 'You heard what Beatrice said. Ingrid's been slipping out without a word quite often lately.'

'I don't imagine she goes for country walks or to the cinema or window-shopping, or merely roams aimlessly.' Major Payne stroked his jaw with his forefinger. 'I think she goes to ... Ospreys.'

'To Ospreys! You mean she knows that Ralph Renshawe lives there?'

'I think she does, yes.'

'How did she learn about it? No, don't tell

me. *She read his letter to Beatrice.* I saw you looking at that envelope.' Antonia paused. 'It's been tampered with, hasn't it?'

'Steamed open. There was smearing around the flap and it felt thicker – glue had been used to reseal it,' Major Payne explained.

He hadn't mentioned the fact in front of Beatrice. Beatrice had been in a state of near-collapse. She had flapped her hands and babbled about ancient beliefs – wasn't it said that encountering your double was a prelude to death? Beatrice had felt so faint, she had lain on the sofa, where she had remained, among the silk cushions, rather picturesquely, looking like an odalisque.

'Here's a theory.' Major Payne cleared his throat. 'Ingrid's love for Beatrice turns to darkest detestation at the news of her friend's nuptials. Ingrid accuses Bee of "betrayal". Renshawe's fate has already been sealed. Ingrid concocts an ingenious scheme. Kill Renshawe and have Beatrice arrested for the murder.'

'Double revenge?'

'Double revenge. Ingrid goes to Ospreys dressed up as Beatrice. Renshawe is delighted. He suspects nothing. It has been thirty years since he saw Beatrice last, besides he is a very ill man, all his faculties greatly diminished. Ingrid lets the nurse and whoever else is at the house take a good look at her. She tells them she is practically a neighbour. She makes sure they learn her name and address – *Beatrice Ardleigh – Millbrook House.'*

'Could she really believe she'd be able to get away with it?'

'I am sure she could. She is crackers. Her brain must be as valuable as a cap full of porridge. She is probably convinced she has been diabolically clever.'

There was a pause. Antonia said, 'You don't suppose she has killed Ralph Renshawe yet?'

'I don't know. She might have.' Payne puffed pensively at his pipe. 'How about checking?'

'Do you mean we should phone Ralph?'

'The matter is too complicated for phoning. Um. I suggest we drive to Ospreys.'

Antonia stared at him. *'Now?'*

'Now. Why not? Ospreys is apparently only five miles from here. It will take us twenty minutes at the most.'

'What shall we say when we get there?'

'We'll ask to speak to Renshawe – if he is still alive, we'll warn him of the danger – we'll tell him that the Beatrice who's been visiting him is in fact Ingrid. If he is not well enough to grant us an audience, we'll have a word with the nurse, the padre or whoever's taking care of him.'

Antonia said, 'If Ingrid has been visiting

121

him, but hasn't killed him yet, it would be interesting to know why... Is it possible that she has forgiven him?'

'I wouldn't have thought it terribly likely – not from what Beatrice told us, but who can say? *Anything* is possible. Ingrid might be biding her time. Or she might not have had the chance to be alone with him.'

'Or she might be getting a kick out of watching him die?'

'She might indeed. May I have some more coffee? Thank you... Of course there's always the chance that we are making complete asses of ourselves,' Payne went on, taking a sip of coffee. 'We might be imagining this whole phantasmagoric imbroglio. Ingrid might turn out to be a fanatical cinephile – she might have been going to the cinema. Or she might have a boyfriend, with whom she holds passionate trysts.'

'Dressed up as Beatrice?'

'Well, Beatrice is the more attractive of the two, so Ingrid might be trying to emulate her–' Payne broke off. 'No, I don't really believe that.'

'You thought Beatrice attractive, didn't you?' Antonia said.

'Good lord. Not in the least. I didn't do or say anything to suggest I did, did I?'

'You kept trying to be funny!'

'My dearest love! I was only breaking the ice.'

'I don't think there was much ice to break.'

'Did I say many funny things?'

'Personally, I didn't think so,' said Antonia, 'but Bee clearly regarded you as the wag and wit of the party.'

He shrugged. 'I couldn't help it if the silly creature rolled round in hysterical merriment at every absurdity I uttered.'

'She fancied you wildly. She made that abundantly clear. I don't think her husband liked it.'

'Golly. I do need to be careful. She's a nightmare.' Payne started the car. 'Though of course not as great a nightmare as Ingrid.'

It took them much longer than they thought to locate Ospreys.

They lost their way twice and had to stop at two pubs to ask for directions. 'It's outside Coulston,' a woman with a pleasant round face, glasses and hair as flat as Cromwell's told them in mellifluous tones. She was nursing a gin and tonic but now she produced a local map and pointed. 'Coulston is a small village – the house isn't marked but it's here, I think.' The woman's husband, a man with an unruly beard, disagreed vehemently. 'No, no, Kate – Ospreys is *here* – on the other side.' He stabbed his forefinger at a spot on the map. They were clearly visitors, strangers to these parts.

One of the locals, a very old woman in a woollen hat embroidered with dancing harlequins, had been sipping what looked like brandy and barley water and examining the advertisements section in the local paper through a magnifying glass, but she looked up when Antonia mentioned Ospreys.

'Ospreys, eh? That house has a bad name... Some millionaire from Florida's dying there now, but it's never been a happy place. Never. The secret house of death they used to call it. Someone got killed there many years ago–'

'Really?'

'Yes. A couple. That was why it remained empty for so long. Most people don't fancy houses like that. Attract weirdos, places like that. An American actress bought it – Moira Montano. Don't think anyone remembers her.' The old woman took a sip of her drink.

'Moira Montano? The name does ring a bell,' Payne said. 'All those cheap horror films in the '50s?'

'That's right. She made oceans of money, heaven knows how, the films were so bad, but that's what they said. She had a pink conservatory added to the house. She bought masses of exotic plants but then she died suddenly. Then Sir Marcus bought it – Sir Marcus Laud, that is – for his new bride. He married this very young girl, you see, but she ran away after about a month, so it was *the death of love*, I suppose.' The old woman sniffed. 'Sir Marcus was heartbroken and he sold the house. One of my nieces was the housekeeper at Ospreys at the time, that's how I know. Then the American gentleman bought it and he brought a fat foreign woman with him.'

'Is his name Ralph Renshawe?' Antonia asked.

'Don't know, dearie. He's no longer for this world, that's all I've been told. A priest visits him. Also a blonde in a mink coat,' the old woman continued. 'Regular as clockwork. People keep seeing her, walking from the bus stop towards the house, talking to herself, laughing and waving her hands in the air.'

'Do they know who she is?' Payne said casually.

'The American gentleman's old flame, somebody said. Some flame!'

'See how easily poor Bee could land in the soup if something were to happen to Renshawe?' Payne said as they left the pub a couple of minutes later.

'That's why poor Bee should go to the police and tell them the whole story before it's too late,' Antonia pointed out.

It had got colder and they walked quickly towards their car.

Twenty minutes later they reached their destination. The village of Coulston seemed to consist of a single street. Although it was only a quarter to nine, not a single living soul was in sight and they didn't see lights in any of the windows either. A phantom village? Antonia experienced a mixture of anxiety and desolation. Then, suddenly, they found themselves outside a pair of cast-iron gates with *Ospreys* written across them. The gates were gaping open. They drove through what looked like a park or a small forest, along a driveway that was unevenly covered in old gravel, potholed and obviously little used.

'We can't just barge in on a total stranger,' Antonia said in a sudden panic.

'Of course we can. In matters of life and death, social niceties cease to have the slightest importance. In the eighteenth century it was considered terribly impolite if a traveller came across a gentleman's seat and ignored it.'

'Do you mean you just drove up to the big house and announced yourself and an upper servant led you to the library and gave you a glass of Madeira and cake?'

'Absolutely. And, at a pinch, they could provide you with a room for the night, complete with a stack of the *Illustrated London News* and a tin of some superior F&M munchies on the bedside table – all the customary adjuncts of civilized slumber.'

'Have you ever seen anyone actually reading the *Illustrated London News?* I haven't,' said Antonia. 'Not even at the Military Club. Isn't that interesting?'

'You are right. Now that you've mentioned it, I don't think I have even seen it sold anywhere. It's one of those strange publications that are mentioned a lot in books—' Payne broke off. 'Good lord. *Not* Victorian Gothic.'

Ospreys loomed before them in sharp, inkblack silhouette, all turrets and spikes against the dark sky. The lancet windows of armorial stained glass were unlit and the house looked rather eerie in the pale moonlight.

Surely, Antonia reflected, they wouldn't turn off all the lights when somebody was as gravely ill as Ralph Renshawe, would they? It wasn't that late either. Had there been a power cut? But, if that were the case, they would use candles or some of the brass-and-wrought-iron gasoliers one associated with this kind of place. Wouldn't a house like Ospreys have its own electricity generator?

Antonia got out of the car first and Payne followed, leaving the headlights on. Antonia gave an involuntary shudder at the sight of their distorted shadows dancing across the avenue. There was not a breath of wind. Intense, uncanny quiet. The house was white with hoar frost. They caught a glimpse of frozen fairylike trees on either side of the drive, their skeletal branches pointing upwards.

'*A haunt of ancient peace*,' Payne whispered.

'There are always legends hanging about these old houses,' said Antonia as though to give herself courage. 'They are not difficult to invent and cost nothing.'

Pipe in mouth, Major Payne walked up to the front door and pressed the bell button.

Antonia stood behind him. They seemed to be passing through the early stages of a cliché-ridden horror film. (The kind Moira Montano had made?) A time-eaten and grotesque mansion with a dark history, long deserted through superstitious fears, tottering to its fall in a retired and desolate part of Oxfordshire. Gaping gates and gloomy gables. A creepy creaking noise, which was probably caused by the frozen trees, but might prove to be something much more sinister... Would the front door turn out to have been left unlocked?

She didn't hear the bell ring and no one answered the door. Major Payne pushed the bell button again.

'Not a single light... What's happened?' Antonia said. 'Where is everybody? They couldn't have suddenly gone away, just like that, could they?'

'They might have. Or they might be dead,' Payne said in a sepulchral voice. 'You heard what the old biddy said – the secret house of death.'

'How many people actually live here?'

'No idea. The letter didn't say. There are bound to be nurses and people.' Payne stomped his feet. 'It's freezing!'

'They said it's going to get warmer tomorrow.'

'Don't you believe it.'

'Shall we go?' Antonia drew back from the door. It was indeed unbearably cold. She had thrust her hands deep into the pockets of her coat. She longed to be back in the safety of the car, sipping hot coffee from the thermos, listening to Vivaldi on the CD player.

She looked up. No stars, only the florin-like moon. No sign of any ospreys flapping their wings... The secret house of death... It might be interesting to find out why it had been given that name – what exactly had taken place – was there any truth in the gruesome story?

Payne pushed the bell once more, then he reached out and rattled the door knocker. He got hold of the door handle–

Antonia said again, 'Let's go.' She felt the beginnings of a sore throat.

'Good lord,' she heard her husband whisper. 'It's open.'

Antonia blinked. 'What? The door is open?'

'Yes... Look... What's this muck?' He stood looking down at his hand. 'The door handle – it's covered in something sticky – like jelly – urgh!'

'I don't believe you,' Antonia said.

He muttered an oath. 'I am not joking—'

Antonia experienced a disconcerting sense of unreality. 'Don't tell me it's blood.'

'I don't know. Golly. It might be blood... Yes... Looks black... Someone seems to have had an accident...'

'Hugh, are you serious?' Her hand had gone up to her heart.

For what seemed a long time he stood as though petrified. Suddenly he laughed. 'No, I'm not. There's no blood. The door is not open.' He turned round and grinned at Antonia. 'Only joking. There's nothing.'

She stood staring at him. 'It isn't funny, Hugh,' she said. 'I can't believe you did this.'

'Sorry, my love,' he said.

She turned round and walked silently back towards the car. He followed sheepishly, stroking his jaw. She got into the back seat and slammed the door.

He tried to talk to her, to cajole her to sit beside him, but she remained silent. He put on the Vivaldi concerto. *'Konzert für Zwei Violinen, Streichorchester und Basso continuo,'* he announced in comically execrable German as he started the car. He was trying to make her laugh.

She pursed her lips and shut her eyes. She decided she wouldn't speak to him. Her thoughts went back to the dark forbidding house they were leaving behind. Had anything happened? What if – what if Ospreys wasn't empty? What if there were people inside – Ralph and the nurse – lying dead, their throats slit? What if Ingrid had killed them?

On an impulse, Antonia took out her mobile phone and dialled 999.

When the police phoned her two hours later, Antonia was sitting in bed alone, reading.

'Yes, madam. We did gain access into the house and checked all the rooms. There is nothing suspicious. Nothing's been disturbed. There is no one in the house. We did check very carefully, yes. Perhaps the people have gone away. We do realize that Mr Renshawe is a very sick man, yes... We'll check the hospitals... Thanks for calling us.'

Though nothing in the policeman's voice suggested it, Antonia couldn't help feeling a little foolish... Well, better safe than sorry.

Where had Ralph and the nurse gone?

11

The Heat of the Day

For once the weather forecasts had got it absolutely right and global warming was blamed for it. The next morning at around half past nine the weather started undergoing a remarkable change. As temperatures rose, the packed ice underfoot cracked, puddles unfroze, icicles melted and slithered down rooftops, frost patterns on windows dissolved. A wave of unseasonable warmth, unknown in the British Isles for at least seventy-five years, was crossing the south – it felt as though someone had left open the door of a gargantuan oven. Scarves and heavy coats were discarded, radiators turned down and then off, windows flew open. The sun had come out and the rooks once more circled over Ospreys, shrieking in great excitement.

Ingrid Delmar stood gazing up at them with eyes that were swollen and red with crying, listening to the rooks' savage chant. Her face was dry now but her tears earlier on had dug rivulets into the Beatrice make-up. The sun looked like some malign,

132

jubilant eye – no, like one of those ill-fated fabulous diamonds people killed to obtain. (As a child she had been enchanted by *The Moonstone* and become quite obsessed with those sinister Brahmins.) She felt the sun's million rays of dazzling brilliant energy beat mercilessly upon the Beatrice wig. She had a headache – a throbbing sensation in her temples, like miniature drums. There was a ringing in her ears, as though she had descended to the very bottom of the ocean. Her whole brain hurt. She would have liked to take it out of her skull and put it through the wash!

She had had a sleepless night. Only at dawn had she managed to doze off. She had had a dream.

She saw herself trapped in the cross-section of some giant frosted wasps' nest, among walls layered with shelves of bluish ice, which her fall seemed to have shattered. It was extremely cold and she was shivering. All round her feet lay the frozen bodies of giant wasps – as big as sparrows. Realization had then come to her – *these were the wasps she had destroyed with cyanide last August.*

It was November but today it felt like August. Freak weather – and they said it would be like that for some time. She regarded this as a portent. She was a great believer in omens and auguries. *Anything could happen in such weather.* Strange days lay ahead, of that Ingrid had no doubt. Strange things were about to happen. She had a picture of herself growing feathers and transmogrifying into a rook, flapping her wings and taking off – flying up, then down, then up again and diving down once more, her sharp beak poised to strike at the treacherous eyes of the enemy.

'Those to whom evil is done,' Ingrid said aloud, 'do evil in return.'

Bee was as guilty as Ralph Renshawe. Bee had ruined her life. But for Bee, Ingrid would have given birth to a healthy child. Her little girl would have been with her now...

She had overheard Bee's confession only moments after entering the hall. Bee had been talking in her highest and silliest voice, her 'society' voice, trying to impress her visitors – that writer woman and her husband. Ingrid hadn't been able to believe her ears. The truth – at long last the truth had come out. *The whole truth*. Bee had lied to her. It was to absolute strangers that Beatrice had decided to unburden herself, to make her confession. In a split second the scales had fallen from Ingrid's eyes and she had seen Bee as she was, with her mask off.

If Ingrid had come back two minutes later, she would have missed the confession. Or two minutes earlier for that matter. Or if the sitting-room door had been closed. Or if Bee had been whispering. Or if they had been playing music, say, one of the interloper's sentimental tunes or his dreary drums. However, Fate – or was it Mighty God Rook? – had decreed differently. That she had been *meant* to learn the truth, Ingrid had no doubt.

She stood watching as a rook descended and perched on a piece of broken statuary. The rook looked at her fearlessly and crowed twice. She stretched her fingers towards it. It was a particularly large specimen. The rook didn't fly away – it seemed to like her! It tilted its head to one side, crowed again and flapped its wings. Ingrid's eyes started swimming with tears. I am starved of love, she thought. Her parents – precious, self-obsessed, narcissistically verbose academics – had barely acknowledged her existence. Her boyfriend had hated her. Her little girl had been snatched away from her. Her best friend had turned out to be a wolf in sheep's clothing–

Ingrid blew her nose. She had a job to do, things to see to. Important things. Matters of life and death.

Bee was going to be punished in a very special kind of way. Bee would be made to suffer for a crime she had not committed. Ingrid nodded to herself and ran her tongue across her lips. Bee was going to be held responsible for the violent murder of Ralph

Renshawe. That, Ingrid reflected, would be so much better than killing Bee – or cutting off Bee's lower lip and thus rendering her pretty mouth unkissable.

Back to Plan A then, as originally conceived. In her bag Ingrid carried Bee's address book. It was covered with Beatrice's fingerprints and of course it had Beatrice's name written on the front page. Ingrid had wrapped the address book up in a clean silk handkerchief and she had been careful not to leave any of her own fingerprints on it. She also carried an exceptionally sharp small knife with a silver handle. Bee had used it to sharpen a pencil. Bee's fingerprints were all over the knife. It was Bee's scent the police would smell in the room. Ce Soir Je T'Aime. Ingrid had dabbed several drops of it behind her ears.

This should provide the police with enough evidence.

She would start with the eyes. She wanted to hear Ralph Renshawe squeal like a hare caught in a trap. She'd leave him one eye so that he could see what was happening to the rest of him. Her only concern was that he might get a heart attack and die after the first cut, but that was something she couldn't do much about.

Despite the increasing heat, Ingrid did not take off her gloves but she saw the birthmark across the palm of her right hand very clearly in her mind. The blood-red naevus. Had she always been meant to be a killer, like Cain?

She must wear her gloves all the time. She mustn't leave any of her own fingerprints. She smiled grimly. She had all the instincts of the successful criminal. She was perfectly capable of committing the perfect murder. She remembered how, in the month Bee got married, she managed to get hold of some cyanide, which she handled very carefully with rubber gloves. Several lumps she used to destroy the wasps' nest in the garden, but the rest of the cyanide she put in a phial and kept at the back of her cupboard. She had toyed with the idea of poisoning the interloper. Well, she'd been unwilling to share Bee with anyone then, least of all with that big lumbering fool.

When Bee was charged with the murder of Ralph Renshawe and put away, the interloper would have a nervous breakdown. The interloper was so besotted with his beloved beautiful Bee, he wouldn't be able to live without her. His existence would become insupportable, so he would probably kill himself.

No loose ends. It would be like one of those meticulously worked-out endings Antonia Darcy specialized in. Ingrid had read Antonia Darcy's first novel, at Bee's recommendation, and had hated it. Ingenious, yes, work of genius, most decidedly no. Ingrid had no doubt that each one of Antonia Darcy's books was a mere commercially motivated replica of its predecessor. Variations on a tried, if tired, lucrative theme. Well-bred characters sitting beside cosy fires, drinking tea, deliberating whodunit ad nauseam.

The rook was still there, perched on the broken statue, looking at her, his head tilted to one side. Mighty God Rook, she whispered and she gave a slight bow. She had no doubt Mighty God Rook knew what was going on in her head. Mighty God Rook approved of what she was about to do.

Ingrid felt filled with superhuman strength and energy, with the kind of 'fuel' that sent rockets blasting across the stratosphere. She started walking fast – broke into a run. She raised her arms a little, like the wings of a bird poised for flight.

Ospreys' steeply pitched roof, the gables and pointed arches danced before her eyes. The sun above seemed to grow larger – an enormous orange of tawny gold. She was heading for the back of the house, for the french windows that led into Ralph's room. She wouldn't have minded entering the normal way, through the front door, but wanted to avoid any possible opposition from the nurse who might say that Ralph was too ill to see her. Well, Ingrid could easily deal with ten nurses if she had to, but she didn't want to waste another minute–

The next moment she stopped short in her tracks.

'Fair is foul and foul is fair,' she heard someone say.

What a relief it was that he didn't have to go to Ospreys after all. Even in normal circumstances Benjamin Saunders was averse to leaving London and his well-established routine. He had never been able to understand his wife's passion for the country, let alone share it. Most of his wife's smart friends seemed to live in the country. All the husbands seemed to play golf. Annabel had been talking admiringly about somebody's husband 'fitting in ten holes between tea and dinner'. Annabel had been trying to persuade *him* to take up golf. How little she knew him! Still, Ralph Renshawe was a highly valued client and it wouldn't have done to displease him – even though he was dying, his word was a command. If the appointment hadn't been cancelled, Saunders would have gone to Ospreys without fail.

He was sitting at his desk, writing with a silver-topped pen. He was a tall distinguished-looking man of sixty-three, with a long straight nose, prim mouth and a lugubrious expression, wearing an immaculate striped suit and silk tie of a restrained pattern. He had loosened his top shirt button, his only concession to the heat wave. On the wall behind him hung framed traditional cartoons by 'Spy' of Victorian legal panjandrums. As one of his clients had observed, Saunders wouldn't have looked out of place in a Spy cartoon himself.

The phone call had been received at eight o'clock that morning, just as he had been making reluctant preparations to leave for Oxford. It had been Nurse Wilkes, Ralph Renshawe's nurse. Ralph wouldn't be able to see him this morning and would Mr Saunders mind *not* coming to Ospreys? She was phoning from a hospital in Oxford. There had been a crisis the night before, but everything was under control now. Ralph had suddenly taken a turn for the worse and she had had to call an ambulance.

She had been sure Ralph wouldn't make it, but it had proved a false alarm, Nurse Wilkes went on cheerfully. Ralph was in his hospital bed, on a drip – but he was making a super recovery. Ralph was in good spirits too, revived by the vitamin injections they had given him. He had been allowed to sit up for a bit and the first thing he insisted on doing was make a phone call to Beatrice, that was Miss Beatrice Ardleigh, Ralph's lady friend – wasn't that nice? Well, the way things were going, she thought they would be back at Ospreys later that afternoon and

140

could Mr Saunders come to Ospreys with the papers *tomorrow morning at eleven?*

Benjamin Saunders frowned. Miss Beatrice Ardleigh – who was she? Someone from Ralph Renshawe's mysterious past? He had the feeling that the reason Ralph Renshawe wanted to see him was something to do with her... Another woman... Would she be as much trouble as Madame Niratpattanasai?

12

The Heiress

'Is – is that Antonia?'

'Oh! Bee! How *are* you? Is – is everything OK?' Antonia felt genuine relief to hear Beatrice Ardleigh's voice.

'Yes, everything is fine. Nothing happened.'

'I am so glad!'

'Well, we didn't sleep awfully well, but that was my fault entirely – my nerves. I am sensitive as an oyster. Poor Len was up and down, all through the night, bringing me pills and drinks and things. No, we haven't seen Ingrid. We heard her crying in her room – it was about two in the morning, I think. Broke my heart! But Len didn't let me speak to her. He can be extremely difficult. I did want to go and give her a hug. I honestly did.'

'Where is she now?'

'She left early this morning. As usual, we heard her but didn't see her. I have no idea where she went. Incidentally, we did barricade our bedroom door last night as Hugh suggested.' Beatrice Ardleigh giggled.

'That made things *so* difficult for poor Len each time he needed to go out. He kept falling over things. Oh dear, I shouldn't be laughing! Sorry. I am hysterical.' She paused. 'How is Hugh?'

Wouldn't you like to know? Antonia thought, pursing her lips slightly. She wasn't going to tell Beatrice Ardleigh that Hugh was in disgrace on account of something *very* silly he did the night before and that she had asked him to sleep on the sitting-room sofa. That was the kind of story Beatrice would relish. Antonia was damned if she was going to make the conversation more personal than it needed to be!

'He is all right. He's in the garden,' she said in neutral tones. 'He's cutting the grass.'

'I adore the smell of freshly mown grass. It's such a lovely morning, isn't it? I adore hot weather.'

Antonia looked out of the open window and saw her husband in his shirtsleeves, leaning against the ancient mower, grimacing piteously at her. Catching her eye, Major Payne brought his palms together as though in prayer. It looked as though he were about to fall to his knees. Earlier on he had scribbled a note, wrapped it around a pebble and thrown it into the room. *Please, darling, forgive, forgive. I love you. I want you so. Do not be cross. H.*

What a clown, Antonia thought, biting her

lower lip in an attempt to remain serious. She had smoothed out the note and placed it carefully inside her diary. For future reference, she had thought. If he does something silly again. She endeavoured to maintain her stern expression.

'Oh Antonia, I must tell you – something *did* happen.' Beatrice had lowered her voice. 'No, nothing bad. *Au contraire*. Nothing to do with Ingrid. Oh, you'd never believe this! It's something – extraordinary – something *stupendous*. The kind of thing that happens in books – in fairy tales!'

'What is it?' Antonia heard Beatrice take a deep breath.

'I received a phone call from Ralph this morning. From *Ralph*, yes. Honestly! I nearly dropped the phone – had to sit down. I mean – Ralph! *After all these years*.'

'Was he – at Ospreys?' Antonia remembered the dark empty-looking house.

'No, no. Ralph was in some hospital in Oxford. He said he felt he simply *had* to speak to me. He nearly died last night, apparently, but he is all right now. He said – you'll never guess what he said – it's quite incredible – staggering – I am still in a state of shock – honestly.'

'Go on. Tell me.'

'He wanted me to know. He wanted to tell me personally and not when the time came, from his solicitor. He also wanted to hear my voice, in case he was going to die before he saw me again. Can you believe it?'

'Sorry – what did he want you to know?'

'That he was leaving me all his money. All his money. I mean – his late wife's fortune. By way of compensation. Horrid word. I don't want compensation. He kept apologizing for the suffering he'd caused me. I was – stunned. Of course I said I couldn't possibly accept, but he said he'd made up his mind and *nothing* could sway him. He's seeing his solicitor tomorrow at eleven.'

'That's wonderful news,' Antonia said.

'You think I should accept? Well, I've already accepted – what else could I do? Poor Ralph! We are talking about an awful lot of money, Antonia. Len did some research – found information about Judith Hartz on the internet. He estimated that it would be nearly – oh, never mind – some fantastic figure. Len is as excited as I am, but he is a bit sceptical. He thinks Ralph might change his mind. Well, both of us are in a state of shock. Ralph said he'd got my phone number from the card I had left – that does mean Ingrid has been going to Ospreys, pretending to be me, doesn't it?'

'It does.'

'But that's incredible! I really don't understand it... Ralph also said he would be very happy if I shared the money with that other unfortunate woman, he clearly meant

Ingrid, and I said I would. He asked if I knew where she lived and so on, and I said I did. I didn't go into details–'

'You didn't tell him it wasn't you who had been visiting him?' Antonia interrupted.

'I am afraid I didn't. I should have, shouldn't I? I couldn't think straight, Antonia. The shock. Honestly. Then – then he rang off. I still wonder whether I might not have dreamt the whole thing!'

'That's very good news indeed... Well, now you know for a fact that Ingrid has been to see him passing herself off as you.'

'*Yes*. But she hasn't killed him, or harmed him in any way. Maybe she too has forgiven him? *But why pretend to be me?* I can't understand it. Len thinks we should call the police and tell them, but I can't possibly *rat* on Ingrid – not after all the years she devoted to me! Not after all she's had to suffer on my account! It would be dreadful – apocalyptic! Can you imagine? Me shopping Ingrid? I already feel so terribly guilty about her. At any rate she's done nothing wrong.'

'Not so far.'

'Why shouldn't she wear a blonde wig and one of my mink coats? It isn't a *crime*.' Beatrice paused. 'If *only* she'd speak to me, I am sure we could work things out. Do you think that's a bit too optimistic? I can't help feeling optimistic on a morning like this – I mean, we are talking about more than

146

twenty million pounds! I still – I still can't believe it. Do you think I'll be spoilt, having so much money?'

Stupid bitch, Father Lillie-Lysander murmured. He panted as he walked round the house. His progress was slow, impeded by his lack of physical fitness and the rough terrain, which comprised a completely overgrown expanse of mature trees and long grass.

He caught sight of ancient statuary, rusting garden chairs, a tumble-down disused fountain and what must have been a conservatory painted shocking pink once, its glazed roof and sides smashed intermittently – he thought he saw a murky concrete pond inside, overshadowed by clumps of bamboo run wild. Eventually he reached the french windows that led to Ralph Renshawe's room. He was holding his mobile phone to his ear and talking into it.

'Yes, Nurse – I have just checked the last one... Sorry, a bit out of breath... Everything's locked. You left in a rush? I don't know if you set the alarm systems – one can't tell, unless one breaks in – you don't want me to do that, do you? Ha-ha. Oh, that's all right, Nurse. Pleasure. Um. I had business in Oxford, but finished early, so I decided to pop in,' he improvised. 'No, it isn't my usual "slot", ha-ha – you are absolutely right... When I didn't find anyone and the front door locked, I got terribly worried, that's why I phoned you. When are you coming back? Later today? I am so glad Ralph is feeling better. That's excellent news. God is merciful. And when is Mr Saunders coming?' Lillie-Lysander asked this casually. 'Tomorrow at eleven...Yes, Ralph did tell me about it... I don't know about "everything". He tells me what his conscience dictates him to... One's conscience operates as a warning bell – if you stop hearing it, there must be something wrong with the mechanism.'

He looked at his watch impatiently. 'We could talk about it some other time perhaps? How it *works*? I am not sure that's the right word when one talks about God – God is not a conjurer, but do let's talk about it later, shall we? Yes, tomorrow. I'll come in the morning, at about ten, if that's all right, since I'll be in Oxford again. It will be more convenient than in the afternoon, yes. I'll see you tomorrow then. Goodbye.'

He wished she didn't keep calling him Father Lillie. Speaking in that arch voice. He hoped she didn't fancy him. The mere idea of it filled him with revulsion.

He was covered in sweat. He wasn't used to physical exertion. Robin had told him he needed exercise. Robin went to a gym regularly, it seemed. Some gyms were notorious pick-up points, or so he had heard. Was that where Robin found – his neophytes? Lillie-

Lysander mopped his brow and neck with his silk handkerchief. His shoes were covered in some ghastly yellow mud. That stupid bitch – well, he needed to be on the right side of Nurse Wilkes, in the light of what he was planning to do.

He dialled Robin's number but found it busy. He looked across the overgrown lawn, shading his eyes with his hand. There was the wishing well, by the beech tree. It dated back to the late 1600s, apparently. He wished this whole business was over. He wished he could give himself another shot of *Papaver somniferum*. He hoped Robin wouldn't think he had got cold feet. So hot. Freak weather–

'Fair is foul and foul is fair,' he said and in a funny way he felt comforted.

He dialled Robin's number again. This time his call was answered at once.

'Oh Robin – it's me. I am at Ospreys, yes. No, I didn't do it. No, I didn't funk it. No, I didn't get cold feet. Your uncle is *not* here–' Lillie-Lysander imagined he heard a noise coming from the rose bushes – the snapping of a twig? Probably a bird or a squirrel. Greedy little beasts, squirrels – should be exterminated. *Who so smites with the sword shall perish by the sword*, he thought inconsequentially.

'What's the matter?' Robin said. Robin sounded exasperated.

'Nothing. Sorry. Thought I heard something. Um. Your uncle was taken to hospital last night – sudden deterioration – apparently he passed out–'

'He didn't die?'

'I am afraid not. It must be terribly frustrating for you. He will be back at Ospreys later today. I don't know when exactly. He is much better, Nurse Wilkes said. It was touch and go, apparently, but he is out of danger now. It'll have to be done tomorrow. Why do I sound squeaky? I don't think I sound squeaky at all. No, I am *not* in a state of blue funkdom–' That was a phrase they had used at school. 'I would do it. I said I would. I'll use the largest pillow, don't you worry. I'll come again tomorrow, at ten... He will be here... You don't believe me? Well, wait until tomorrow and you will see. By ten past ten your uncle will be dead. You have my word, Robin–'

Hidden behind the rose bushes Ingrid crouched and listened. She couldn't believe what she was hearing. At first she scowled ferociously but then her lips curved up slowly into a smile. An interesting complication. A second murderer, eh? It seemed the priest was intent on stealing her thunder.

A challenge. Well, she liked a challenge. Nothing like a challenge to set the adrenalin pumping and catapult her into action.

13

Polaroid

It was the following morning and Antonia was making toast in the Hampstead kitchen. Major Payne said, 'I am truly sorry and I promise never to do it again. *Never.*'

'Why do a silly thing like that?'

'I don't know what possessed me. I really don't. I couldn't resist it.'

'You couldn't resist scaring me?'

'I mean I thought it would be funny.'

'It was extremely thoughtless of you. You did scare me. Is that a smirk, Hugh?'

'No! Of course not,' he cried. 'I am just terribly happy that we are on speakers again. I can't bear you not speaking to me. It's worse than writing five hundred lines of Latin Georgics!'

'I should hope so. I did believe there was blood on the door handle! I did think someone had been killed!'

He kissed her and held her to him and repeated in her ear that he was sorry. He sounded genuinely contrite, so she told him about the phone call she had received from Beatrice Ardleigh. He stared at her. 'Golly.

She went along with the act? I suppose that was the right thing to do in the circumstances. Renshawe is dying – what difference would it make?'

'None whatever,' Antonia agreed. 'It's not as though she's been gaining his favour under false colours.'

'It is funny, when you think about it – dashed ironic – that it should have been Renshawe's deadliest enemy – mad Ingrid – who managed to win him over!'

The clock started chiming nine. They went into the dining room and sat down to breakfast. The warm weather was continuing and the windows were wide open. They could hear birdsong coming from the garden.

'Ingrid needs urgent medical attention, if not the attention of the CID,' said Antonia. 'I do think we should do something about it, Hugh, since Bee doesn't want to get "poor" Ingrid into trouble. Bee would hate to be considered a "snitch". Bee abhors the very idea of "ratting".'

'You don't seem to like Beatrice much,' said Payne mildly. He dug into his bacon and eggs.

Antonia took a sip of tea. 'Not much, no.'

'Well, she's got a husband to advise her. Colville's head seems to be screwed on the right way. Besides, he is no fan of Ingrid's.' Payne glanced at the clock. 'What time was Renshawe's solicitor going to Ospreys?'

'Eleven.'

'If Renshawe does manage to change his will, Beatrice will be one fabulously rich lady,' said Payne thoughtfully. 'However, if he were to die *before* he had seen his solicitor, she would get nothing. This is fascinating, don't you think?'

Antonia agreed it was fascinating.

'A fortune is at stake and it all depends on the purest of chances. Renshawe is a dying man – he can pop off at any moment. Who do you think inherits by his original will?'

Antonia shrugged and said she had no idea. No one had mentioned any children, so she doubted he had any. Illegitimate children? Chaps like Renshawe always had illegitimate sons, Payne said thoughtfully.

'He may have nephews – or a niece or two,' she said after a pause.

'Imagine their shock if Renshawe does manage to change his will.' Payne helped himself to toast and Oxford marmalade. 'Do they know about Uncle Ralph's intentions? Would they approve?'

'I don't see how they could possibly approve.'

Payne looked at her. 'What do you think will happen next?'

Antonia said. 'Nothing, I hope.'

Even at the best of times he was prone to mood swings, to descents into the doldrums, to sudden overpowering 'downers', as Bee put it. Bee had said it was due to the fact he was born under Saturn, the planet of melancholy, that for those born under Saturn there was no lasting escape from the 'black dog'. She had spoken like an expert. *Woof, woof*, she had added. He had managed a laugh – he didn't want her to say again that he was 'deficient in the drollery department' – but the remark had hurt him beyond reason. He had expected greater understanding from her. Well, the truth was Bee had never even tried to enter his feelings.

Leonard Colville sat on the sofa in the sitting room at Millbrook House, leaning against the silk cushions. All the cushions smelled of Bee – of Ce Soir Je T'Aime – her favourite scent. He stroked one particular cushion; there were two golden hairs sticking to it. Then, picking up the cushion, he buried his face in it and inhaled deeply. It didn't help – if anything, his heart grew heavier. A mood of extreme dejection was overtaking him.

She lied to me, Colville whispered, replaying once more the scene at breakfast.

Bee, in her silver-coloured silk peignoir with rabbit fur trimmings, dipping her spoon in her dish of Fortnum and Mason's Soya Porage, bringing it up to her mouth, blowing at it gently, parting her lips. It had been a delight watching her. Bee wrinkled her nose and her green eyes narrowed. Colville caught a glimpse of her even pearly teeth and of her tongue the colour of ripe strawberries. He could have sat and watched her like that for eternity.

Then they started talking about the money – what they would do with it if Ralph Renshawe really did leave his fortune to her. That very morning Renshawe's solicitor was going to Ospreys; a new will was going to be drawn up. Well, darling, Bee said, her voice vibrant with expression, all our financial problems will be resolved once and for all. It was the fairy godfather solution. A cruise – they would go on a cruise, the two of them. A second honeymoon, darling – Bee smiled at him. You would like that, wouldn't you?

He remembered his thoughts. *Never before have I known such bliss – such perfect oceanic peace.*

That was only moments before the telephone rang and Bee rushed to it. Colville chided himself for the unworthy thought, but it was almost as though she had *expected* the phone to ring.

He watched her pick up the receiver. He heard her say hello. He saw her expression change–

Bee listened, then gasped, 'Where *are* you?' The colour in her cheeks heightened and she cast a furtive glance in his direction. (He was sure he hadn't imagined it.) 'Look here – I–' She bit her lip. 'Very well.'

Colville pretended to be absorbed in the *Telegraph* and rustled it ostentatiously.

'Oh, thanks for reminding me, sweetie,' Beatrice said. 'I am such a chump! I forgot. It completely slipped my mind!'

Bee had spoken these last words in an over-loud voice, shouted almost, for his benefit, clearly. She must have a poor opinion of his intelligence, Colville reflected gloomily. Replacing the receiver, she told him it had been Alessandro, her hairdresser. She had completely forgotten that she had made an appointment at the hairdresser's for ten! She stood looking at him, like a bold little girl. There was a curl of hair lying across the side of her forehead and touching her left eyebrow, which the bright sunlight turned to filaments of gold. Colville wanted to run to her, put his arms around her, bury his face in her neck, hold her tight and ask her –no, *beg* her – not to leave him – ever!

Bee had gone up to her room, then re-appeared, wearing a hat made of shiny black straw and dark glasses that instantly transformed the way she looked, imparting to her the mysterious air of the archetypal beautiful spy of fiction. She had put on a mauve shade of lipstick, not her usual dark-rose red, which further altered her appearance. (She didn't want to be recognized, clearly.) She then pecked him perfunctorily on the cheek, turned round and was gone. Her hairdresser was in Oxford and she said she was going to drive; she was taking the Mini. She had looked tense and nervous, but also excited.

Colville buried his face in his hands. He was convinced that Bee was off to a secret rendezvous somewhere. Bee was going to meet a man – her lover – at some roadside motel. Colville's heart stopped at the thought of Bee writhing naked in a strange man's arms, moaning and gasping and laughing. He felt shivers run through his body. Another thought followed. No, not a strange man – *she had gone to meet Payne, Antonia Darcy's husband.*

Colville had noticed that Bee hadn't been the same since the day of the Paynes' visit. Something happened that day.

Bee had laughed even at Payne's silliest remarks. For the life of him, Colville couldn't remember what Payne had actually *said* – some nonsense about the Light Brigade – but he did believe that Payne's remarks had contained hints and innuendo, encoded messages, to which Bee responded. Payne was the kind of man who wooed his women with puns, quotations and oblique compliments. Glances of complicity had passed between them, of that Colville was sure. Although Payne was at pains to conceal the fact, he had been smitten with Bee!

Bee had exercised her compelling power

over him. Like Circe, Bee could unhinge a man with one toss of her tangled blonde curls! Payne had sat pretending indifference, but all along he had watched her covertly, drinking her in, his eyes as busy as coals just thrown on a fire.

The night before, in their bedroom, Bee had initiated an odd kind of conversation. She had started talking about certain African tribesmen who offered their wives to favoured visitors for the night. She knew he was interested in Africa – did he approve or disapprove? Bee had demanded an immediate answer. She had been in a peculiar mood, intense, febrile, peremptory. Well, it was an African custom, Colville said – he neither approved nor disapproved. She had shaken her head and sighed gustily, indicating she found his answer unsatisfactory.

'You disapprove – admit it,' she challenged him.

'I don't disapprove,' he said.

'Then you approve? Say you approve!'

'I neither approve, nor disapprove.'

'You disapprove! I knew it!' Bee had cried triumphantly. It had been the silliest of conversations. When he tried to kiss her, she pushed him away, saying she had a raging headache. She then picked up a book from her bedside table, the biography of the imperial Russian dancer Mathilde Kschessinska. Mathilde, she informed him inconsequentially, had bedded at least five Romanovs and at one stage had lived in a *ménage à trois* with two grand dukes, by one of whom she had a son. Bee's eyes had been very bright and her voice had contained a provocative note.

Was he paranoid to think Bee's choice of conversational topics suggestive?

It was very warm in the sitting room. He couldn't breathe. He was aware he was still hugging the silk cushion. He could hear the loud ticking of the clock and the buzzing of a fly somewhere. He was reminded of his old school – the same mixture of misery and cosiness and numbed longing. He felt his depression deepening.

He reached out and picked up the Polaroid camera that lay on the coffee table, thinking back to the day before yesterday. They had been so happy. Deliriously, insanely happy. *Each one of us should live only for the other.* That was what Bee had said. She had sounded as though she meant it. They had been gazing into each other's eyes. Colville's fingertips caressed the camera. That interval of white thigh between Bee's black stocking and knickers alone was enough to drive him out of his mind...

His love for Bee was no ordinary love. The fire of his passion was a burning forest, spreading fast, leaping rivers, consuming landscapes. Telling her that had been a mistake, he now realized. He shouldn't have put it quite in those terms.

Darling, do you know what? You are becoming too possessive – too Swann-ish. No, not 'swinish', you chump! Swann-ish. Like in Swann and Odette? Remember? Eaten by jealousy. Girls don't really like burning forests. It scares them, so beware.

Bee had uttered these words with one of her light laughs, but it made him wonder. Beware of what? Was she trying to warn him, to prepare him for what she had already made up her mind to do? So that it shouldn't be too great a shock?

Too many heartbreaks and too many betrayals bleed a man dry *and* they lead to the secluded passions of the voyeur. Bee had said that too – apropos of nothing in particular – the silly nonsense she talked sometimes! Colville frowned. She couldn't know, could she, that sometimes, when she was not there, he liked to sneak upstairs and go repeatedly through the soft dresses and perfumed gossamer underclothes in her bedroom drawers and wardrobe. He liked nothing better than to hold them to his face and breathe in their intoxicating aroma...

Colville knew his limitations. He was a dull dog. He wasn't really clever. He wasn't amusing or in any way interesting. He didn't say things that were witty or droll. He didn't read Proust, though he suspected Bee's knowledge of Swann and Odette was derived from the film, that lush costume drama they had watched together last month, rather than from the book... He wasn't much to look at. Well, he was – *middle-aged*. Payne wasn't exactly a youth either, but he seemed to have a certain something he, Colville, clearly lacked. Payne had the slightly pointed ears and the half wistful, half malicious look of a faun.

Colville glanced at the clock. Where was Bee now? Not knowing was worse than knowing the worst! He had thought of following her, of jumping into his car and driving after her at a distance, all the way to her final destination, of lurking outside the motel room door and catching her in the act – but had fought down the impulse. What if she saw him in her rear-view mirror? What if she *was* going to her hairdresser's after all? She would never forgive him. She would be dismayed – furious! If only he had known she was going out in her car, he would have poured sugar in the petrol tank – that would have made driving impossible, though of course it would have destroyed the car engine completely. Too late now!

Swann in Love. Bee had ordered the DVD specially and had watched it a dozen times already. She clearly identified with the courtesan Odette. That poor chap Swann – tormented by unrelenting sexual desire –

crazed by jealousy – constantly pleading – forever declaring his ungovernable love – allowing his craving for Odette to turn his life upside down...Was he really like Swann?

The cuckolded husband, that most pathetic and comical of figures. In farces and low comedies cuckolded husbands did absurd, idiotic things like hiding inside wardrobes, lurking behind screens and curtains, or lying on their stomachs under beds. They groaned and gritted their teeth as they watched their wives strip naked and make love with their secret lovers. Upon being discovered, cuckolded husbands jabbered and croaked and shook their fists in impotent rage, thus making audiences laugh like drains – sometimes they lost their trousers. Why was it that audiences always sided with the lover and never with the husband?

Colville passed his hand across his face. Bee had a tattoo above her instep. Two intertwined snakes – that was what it looked like at first sight, that was what she *said*, but Colville strongly suspected it was the letters B and R intricately interwoven together. *Bee and Ralph*. She had been very much in love with Renshawe. She had admitted as much. Perhaps she was still in love with him? So amusing, she kept saying. He had made her laugh.

Why wouldn't she allow him to take a closer look at her leg? Colville had the idea of drugging Bee and inspecting the tattoo properly... He had acquired a most powerful soporific specially for the purpose... Perhaps he could do it tonight?

Colville hadn't slept at all well the night before, he was feeling like a boiled owl, so now his eyelids drooped and he nodded off. At once he dreamt that Bee had entered the room and sat beside him on the sofa. She looked different somehow. She had a tiara studded with diamonds on her golden head and wore elbow-length gloves. She looked like a royal princess. Her manner was formal and distant to start with but then she gave him a rather suggestive look and put her head downwards towards him, as if expecting him to kiss her on the ear. He could smell her scent. (Ce Soir Je T'Aime.) They hadn't exchanged a word and there was a great tension between them, which he recognized as sexual in nature. Her head went lower. He said, 'I am sorry, ma'am, but I can't hear very well what you are saying.' At this she replied: 'That's because I'm wearing a kilt.' She was in fact wearing a rather glamorous silvery evening dress with a deep décolletage–

Colville woke up with a start. His heart was beating wildly. The sofa beside him was empty. His nerves were pulled taut as marionette strings, his mood one of wretched despair.

He heard the stairs creak.

Was Bee back? No – it was Ingrid, coming down. Ingrid – he'd completely forgotten about Ingrid. As though he hadn't enough worries! What should be done about Ingrid? He had a friend who was a policeman, a Scotland Yard inspector, no less, and Colville had a good mind to contact him and explain the situation. Arthur would listen to him. He looked at the telephone. He sighed. It would cause Bee great distress if he did call Arthur – especially if Arthur decided to take action. (What action? Ingrid hadn't actually committed any criminal act as such. Arthur would probably suggest he contact a psychiatrist.) Bee seemed to think that 'things would be all right', that 'it would blow over' – that Ingrid would 'come to her senses'. Bee could be so naive!

The stairs creaked again. Ingrid was in the hall now.

'*Honestly,*' he heard her murmur to herself, sounding exactly like Beatrice. She'd got her verbal tricks to perfection!

Colville felt nauseous.

He heard the front door open and close. He rose from the sofa. Catching his reflection in the mirror above the fireplace, he winced: his grey hair stood on end, his cheeks were the colour of cranberry sauce, his eyes were round, his expression wild – he had a shell-shocked air about him – as if he had stepped out of an explosion! And he looked ridiculous, hugging that cushion. Why should Bee want to stay with him? He couldn't think of one good reason.

He ran to the window and stood beside it, concealed behind the curtain. My God, he thought, and again– *My God*. If he didn't know Beatrice had already left the house, if he hadn't his own eyes as witnesses, he'd have sworn it was Beatrice he was seeing. It was the same as the other day. No – worse!

Look and be afraid. He stared at Ingrid – the way Rikki-Tikki-Tavi had at the oscillating body of the black cobra with the glinting red eyes and the spread hood.

There she was in all her splendiferous splendour! Wearing one of Beatrice's old suits with padded shoulders and the initials BA embroidered in gold on one of the chest pockets. She had gloves on. Her face glowed – her eyes were dark with mascara – had she used Beatrice's makeup? And what was that she was wearing round her neck? Anger and dismay surged through him. *Not* the Taj Mahal necklace? Bee's Taj Mahal necklace – it had been his engagement present to Bee! How dared this unspeakable creature take it! She'd been in Bee's room, dipping her dirty paws inside Bee's jewel case!

There was a beatific smile on Ingrid's face – she was walking slowly – she appeared to be humming a little tune to herself – and somehow that was much more frightening than an expression of malevolent determination might have been. Ingrid was walking in the direction of the bus stop. There was a spring in her step.

Something had to be done about it. This obscene charade had to stop. (The Taj Mahal necklace – she had no right!) Colville held desperately on to his wits as a man holds on to his hat while crossing a desolate moor in a whirlwind.

He needed to convince Arthur how serious the situation really was.

Ingrid consulted her watch and saw it was 9.10. There was a bus in five minutes. Well, she'd be at Ospreys by 9.35 at the latest. She had thought the whole thing through very carefully. She had managed to pinch Bee's mobile earlier in the morning – it had been lying on the hall table. She was going to phone the nurse and get her out of the way – say that somebody was lying on the ground outside the park gates, bleeding, in need of urgent attention – something on those lines. (When afterwards the police checked the incoming calls on the Ospreys phone, Bee's number would come up.) She'd then walk briskly round the house and enter Ralph's room through the french windows. They were bound to have been left open in this weather but she'd pick up a stone and smash them if they weren't. She'd have finished by 9.45. She wasn't going to stand on ceremony. The priest wasn't coming until ten o'clock, that was what he had said on the phone. She liked the challenge. Who'd get to Ralph first? Nothing like a challenge to set the adrenalin going. Suspense followed by thrills. It was like one of Antonia Darcy's ridiculous plots. Life imitating art? Well, hardly *art*–

Had she got the knife? Now where–?

Ingrid halted and her gloved fingers started rummaging frantically inside her bag.

Colville discovered he was still holding the Polaroid camera. On an impulse he raised it to his eyes and snapped – an instant photograph came out... Ingrid seemed to be looking for something in her bag. He pressed the button again and another photograph started emerging. He rehearsed what he was going to tell Arthur.

This woman has lived with my wife for thirty years... She has started dressing up as my wife... She makes herself look exactly like her... She wears a blonde wig... She puts on my wife's jewels... She's completely off her rocker... She hates me. She hates my wife too... She is jealous. She disapproves of our marriage... She is extremely dangerous–

It sounded feeble and absurd, put like that,

167

the ramblings of an idiot, but how else could he describe the situation? And wouldn't Arthur get the wrong idea about Bee? What sort of person shares a house with a madwoman for thirty years? The question of the exact nature of Bee's relationship with Ingrid was bound to come up... He had wondered himself... Had they been–? Bee had told him not to be silly – but she had also admitted she preferred Ingrid's massage techniques to his!

Well, he would need to explain about the accident and about Ralph Renshawe. He must calm down first – pull himself together – rehearse very carefully what he was going to say – make a few notes perhaps? No, there was no time for notes–

He looked down at the two photos and smiled grimly.

He had proof now. As clear as daylight. The date: *26.11.05* – and the time: *09.12 a.m.* This would show Arthur that he wasn't getting into a flap over nothing! Still, even if Arthur took his story seriously and *did* do something about it, how long would it take before the police got cracking? They were notoriously slack these days, or so he had often heard. Something *had* to be done... There was no time to waste. Ingrid was clearly on her way to Ospreys. That was where she had been going all this time – dressed up as Beatrice. He blinked – had that been the gleam of a blade? He felt the blood draining from his face. Merciful heavens. Did she have a *knife* in her bag? They should be able to arrest her for that, surely?

The next moment Ingrid's intentions became clear to him.

The knife was for Ralph Renshawe...

Something had to be done... White and dazed, his heart thudding, Colville stumbled towards the telephone.

14

Ceaseless Turmoil

In Knightsbridge, in his minimalist flat, Robin Renshawe looked at himself in the mirror and thought: *I wish I felt as cool as I looked.* He was wearing conventional pepper-and-salt tweeds and a black tie, in preparation for the call, which he hoped would come from Ospreys at some point. The phone call would inform him of his uncle's – sad but not unexpected – demise. *In his sleep – it was a peaceful end – it was his heart, Master Robin.* He gave a little smile – that was how Wilkes *would* have addressed him, had they lived in a different age.

Who else would Wilkes notify? If Lily did the job properly, there would be no question of the police being called. That doctor fellow – he was the only one Wilkes would phone – for the death certificate... Saunders of course would already be there... Saunders would have arrived too late...

What if Beatrice ('Bee') Ardleigh turned up? Well, let her. *For him, she was always* the *woman.* Robin sniggered. Bee was bound to be disappointed if she had expected to be left a fortune. By way of compensation Robin would give her a glass of Uncle Ralph's best dry sherry. He already saw himself as taking control of the situation at Ospreys. Well, he *was* his uncle's only surviving relative.

Crossing over to the drinks table, Robin opened a bottle of Chivas Regal whisky and poured some into a glass. Opposite him on the wall hung a Derek Hill portrait of his mother in a lavender dress and a broad-brimmed gardening hat and gloves, contemplating a bed of nasturtiums. He tried to avoid her mournfully reproachful, heart-rendingly patient gaze and quickly glanced at the picture next to it – one of St George Hare's allegorical and suggestively erotic paintings showing a semi-nude captive slave chained to a rock by the wrists with a butterfly hovering over his tousled head. Robin didn't care much for the slave. Too blond – too Teutonic. There had been other, more valuable paintings, including a Poussin and a Freud, but those he had sold.

Lily must be on his way or was already at Ospreys. He had said he would try to get there at five to ten, or earlier. Would he funk it at the last minute and think up some excuse why it couldn't be done? Well, time would show. Robin thought he sounded philosophical when he said the phrase aloud, but he didn't feel philosophical at all.

The truth of the matter was that he felt extremely anxious.

Had it been a mistake to employ Lily as his myrmidon in the first place? No – that had been a happy inspiration on his part. Once more Robin's thoughts turned back to school and the fox... Poor fox... It hadn't stood a chance.

Whack-whack-whack. Robin grimaced squeamishly at the memory. The spectacle had been too gruesome for words. A veritable bloodbath. Lily's intention, it would appear, had been to reduce the fox to a pulp. Robin had turned round only after the whimpering had ceased completely and he had heard Lily say, *Consummatum est.* Lily had been bespattered with blood, a cross between Macbeth *post* Duncan and Hannibal Lecter *post* – well, dinner. Lily had stood there looking at Robin, strutting a little, a jubilant expression on his cherubic face. Had Lily done it to impress him? That he believed to be the main reason – though Lily had also given the distinct impression of having actually *enjoyed* the experience.

Robin took another sip of whisky. Some of the tension started to depart. He smiled. Lily was a natural born killer. The methodical, relentless, rather *rhythmic* way he had bashed away at the beast – as though he had been playing some esoteric musical instrument. He had been totally unmoved by its screams.

The fox had snarled and tried to bite him and that had only speeded up its end.

Still, strange things did happen. Sudden, inexplicable, logic-defying transformations were known to take place in the minds of the most unlikely people. The idea of miracles made Robin nervous, the twinges of anxiety suddenly returned and he drank more whisky. He had a superstitious streak in him, which sometimes manifested itself at times of crisis. I mustn't go down that path, he told himself, but it was already too late. The fear worked like yeast in his thoughts and the fermentation brought to the surface images of likely disasters – the whole catalogue of threats known to the lapsed Catholic rose to haunt him.

What if Lily, having killed his uncle, was suddenly overcome with remorse? What if he had a vision of Our Lady of Sorrows, or saw tears coming out of the eyes of some marble saint, or even heard a voice calling down to him from above? Either of those might send him running to a priest, a *real* priest, one of those pious, interfering bastards. Lily might feel compelled to make a full confession.

Oh father, I have just killed a man–

Miracles did happen from time to time. One never knew. Uncle Ralph had undergone his remarkable conversion the day the doctor had told him that he faced death –

that he had only months to live. Nobody had thought it possible. In his young days his uncle had been a rip, a reprobate and a rapscallion, the black sheep of the tremendously respectable, if not stuffy, Renshawe family. It was death that had changed him – the news that he had only a short time to live.

Would death change Lily? His uncle's death, that was. Robin thought it unlikely, though who could tell? Lily was so fucking unpredictable–

Robin drained his glass and put it down. He looked at the clock. Decorators were coming to his flat sometime after ten. Robin's kitchen didn't really need decorating, but he thought he should have an alibi for the time of his uncle's death. Just in case.

Five minutes to ten. Lily must be at Ospreys. Perhaps he was entering the hall at that very moment, exchanging pleasantries with Wilkes, glancing up at the angels on the ceiling–

Oh father, I have just killed a man. I smothered him with a pillow. It was a friend of mine who put me up to it. It was his uncle, you see – a very rich man.

How reliable an accomplice was Lily? Robin considered the point. Well, Lily seemed to have started cranking himself up – if those pinpoint pupils were anything to go by – and junkies were notoriously erratic in all their dealings. Still, Robin didn't think

Lily was yet at an 'advanced stage', besides Lily was greatly attracted to the idea of easy riches, so chances were that he would pull himself together and do the job properly.

Leaning his elbow against the mantelpiece, Robin pondered the promise he had made. He had told Lily they would go halves... That was an awful lot of money... If he had to be perfectly honest, he didn't feel like parting with half of Uncle Ralph's fortune. In fact he hated the idea of it.

Well, weren't promises made so that they could be broken? It happened all the time. It wasn't as though Robin had put anything in writing or had had his promise recorded on tape. But there was bound to be a reaction, if he failed to abide by his word. Lily could become a nuisance. Lily could turn ... nasty. Lily wouldn't go to the police, for obvious reasons, but he could think of a way of turning the tables on Robin. Lily was clever. He was devilishly devious. Lily could be, well, dangerous. Robin admitted to himself that he was a bit afraid of Lily.

If only – if only Lily, having completed the job, could ... disappear? If Lily could vanish from the face of the earth as utterly and completely as if the devil had snatched him down to hell by the heels...

Kill the killer, eh? That was an idea worth considering, but another body would complicate matters. Dead bodies, no matter how well hidden, tended to turn up sooner or later. Could it be made to look like suicide? Push Lily off a cliff? String him up from a beam? Feed him an overdose of sleeping pills? Feed him to the fish in the river?

No – too complicated – too much bother. How about *scaring* Lily – having him roughed up a bit by way of a warning? More than just a bit. Lily did do crazy things, but he was not really a brave man. Throw a plastic bag over his head – give him a black eye, split his lip, rip off part of his ear, bust his nose, crack a rib perhaps, fracture a finger or two in a lingering kind of way... *Yes*... That would show him what might happen if he tried something. A single phrase whispered in his shell-like ear should do the trick. *Next time it would be much worse, so don't try anything funny.* Something on those lines. It needed to be done soon after Lily had emerged from Ospreys, while the thought of death was still fresh in his mind... That would be the right psychological moment... Yes...

Robin rose slowly and once more he stood before the mirror, empty glass in hand, examining his reflection... He wouldn't do it himself of course... Certainly not. He would be nowhere near the scene of the incident... Perhaps he could have a word with Eric? It was some time since he had seen Eric.

(Why was it that he always thought of Eric when he was drunk?)

176

15

A Splash of Red

The sinner's way, Father Lillie-Lysander murmured, *is tortuous, hazardous, marked by violence, dark, dangerous and insecure.*

He picked up one of the pillows off the bed. Ralph Renshawe went on rambling. Now it was something about Ospreys and Beatrice Ardleigh.

'I have an idea it may be her kind of house. She may decide to keep it and have it renovated. She may enjoy living in it.'

'It's an extremely interesting house,' Lillie-Lysander said.

What was that on the bedside table, on Ralph's right – long and sharp – a *knitting needle?* Yes, it belonged to the damned nurse. He had seen her knitting.

Lillie-Lysander paused, the pillow poised in his hands. For some reason he found the sight of the needle unsettling; it made him feel a trifle queasy. It also had a somewhat mesmeric effect on him. A knitting needle would make a messy murder weapon – it would be madness to use anything like that.

He thought he heard a noise from the

177

direction of the garden and looked towards the open french windows. He imagined he caught a movement. No, nothing. Rooks. Circling over the garden, screeching their heads off in their unfathomable way. Ugly creatures–

Why were they so agitated? Had something alarmed them?

The grandfather clock in the hall chimed the half-hour. Half past ten.

Time for Father Lillie's tea. It was always at half past ten that Nurse Wilkes made it. She had been sitting in the kitchen, her headphones on, listening to Madonna sing 'Material Girl', leafing through the latest issue of *Hello!* and daydreaming what she would do if she had big money. Nathan, her boyfriend, did the lottery every week, so far without success. Well, if she ever got a lot of dosh, she'd buy Nathan a Porsche, that was what he talked about all the time, and then they would get married and go on a cruise around the world, with her mum and dad and his mum and dad, only Nathan would probably be bored because he didn't like foreign countries much. But he'd like the Porsche. Oh yes, she'd also buy one of those super-large plasma TVs, so that Nathan could watch his football big. He would like that very much, but then she wouldn't be able to get him off the couch!

Nurse Wilkes filled the electric kettle with water, then turned it on.

She had tried to knit earlier on only to discover one of her knitting needles was missing. Could she have dropped it in Ralph's room? She'd been sitting beside his bed when it had looked as if there might be another attack coming, but that proved to be a false alarm. She didn't want to disturb Father Lillie, so she hadn't gone back to look for her needle. She liked knitting. Nathan laughed at her and said it made her look like an old woman. She didn't mind. She was an old-fashioned girl at heart. The jumper was going to be for Robin Renshawe. She had promised him. Even if he didn't like it, it'd amuse him. She hadn't said anything about it to Nathan. Nathan might be jealous.

China tea. Leaves, not teabags. No milk. Father Lillie was most particular about things. He always had Lotus tea. *Bone* china, he had specified, since it released the fragrance in a way no ordinary china could, apparently. He had taken a fancy to one of Ralph's Spode cups, so that was the one she was using. The cup was the colour of ivory, extremely pretty.

Did Ralph really have so much to confess that he needed a priest so often? Nurse Wilkes had read somewhere that some people made things up to keep the priest busy, or because they felt guilty if they had nothing to confess, or because they liked the attention. Once she'd squatted by the door with her ear to the keyhole but she had heard nothing. Not a word. Well, Ralph's voice was like the whispering of dry leaves.

The tea, once brewed, looked weak and bilious and smelled faintly fishy, like something that had started rotting, or like somebody's unwashed socks, but every man to his poison. This reminded Nurse Wilkes of the morphine that had disappeared so mysteriously. Where could the ampoule have gone? She had looked everywhere... It couldn't have been Father Lillie, could it? Well, who else was there? Linda was the only one of the two cleaners who was allowed to go into Ralph's room, but it couldn't be her. Out of the question. That left Father Lillie. What would Father Lillie want with an ampoule? Well, he *was* an odd one. Nathan had decided he was a poof when she told him about him.

No sugar. No biscuits. No cake. No bread and butter even – Father Lillie never had anything to eat. Why was he so fat then? There was *something* about Father Lillie that actually gave her the creeps, she couldn't quite say what.

She wished there was a proper staff, but it was only her and the two women who came to clean three times a week. When Ralph had first bought Ospreys, there had been at least six servants and a gardener, she had been told. But once he got cancer and became a Catholic, he'd dismissed everybody. Stupid thing to do – a house of that size! Most of the rooms were shuttered – well, hardly anyone ever visited. Ralph had pots of money in the bank, real big money, but he clearly regarded it as sinful, keeping a large staff. Something he didn't deserve. That kind of malarkey. Robin thought the dismissal of the staff an unwise thing to do, but then Robin's opinions didn't cut any ice with his uncle.

Ralph disapproved of Robin on 'moral grounds'. She had heard him use the phrase. That was interesting, given that when he first moved into the house, Ralph had had a live-in mistress, apparently – a big Thai woman with glittering black eyes and a name no one could pronounce. Madame something-or-other, that lawyer, Mr Saunders, had called her. Ralph sent Madame away when he became ill and got religion, but she had become so attached to him that she didn't want to go, or so the story went. Apparently she made a terrible scene. She got really violent, screaming and smashing things, so they had to call the police! Some of the woman's stuff was still in the house. There were several boxes. Nurse Wilkes had taken a peep.

Some extremely colourful outfits, of the kind people wore at carnivals. Joss sticks. A fan made of peacock feathers. Plastic flowers. A rook rifle. (Apparently Madame had liked taking pot shots at the rooks!) A feather boa. Several Barbara Cartland paperbacks, the more difficult words under-lined in purple ink and the Thai translation penned in the margin. A love-making manual that looked really dirty. (Nathan said he wanted to see it.) A bronze statuette of Buddha. Ten pairs of silk stockings. Handcuffs. Three old-fashioned garters. A stuffed monkey and a bottle of Grecian Ivory Number 2 make-up.

Nurse Wilkes had never met the woman, but she felt sorry for her. Such a heartless thing to do, kicking out someone who loved you! Not Christian. Well, converts were much worse than cradle Catholics, it was always said. Much more fanatical. Much more – extreme.

There had been another nurse when Nurse Wilkes first started; a male nurse, Eric, but he too had had to leave. Ralph had sacked him. She had liked Eric. He was a former prison warder. Not particularly bright but exceptionally strong. Eric had a zip of black beard in the cleft of his chin, like one of those musketeers, and a golden earring. A body-builder, but very quiet, very softly spoken. Eric could crack a walnut between his thumb and index finger! So useful to have around the house. She had felt safer with Eric round. She hadn't thought him threatening in any way. Eric liked to paint his nails very pale green, which was a very nice colour...

The house could be quite scary at night. Sometimes Nurse Wilkes found it difficult to sleep. All those empty rooms... On several occasions she imagined she could hear someone walking about, laughing and talking gibberish, and had got it into her head it might be Madame, the Thai woman, come back, mad with grief, the way it happened in books – or that she might have topped herself and was haunting the house! Eastern women were very loyal, to the death, she had heard.

Nurse Wilkes took her headphones off and picked up the small tray. Linda had told her she had seen Eric in Coulston. He seemed to have got a local job of some kind. Linda was coming at eleven, same as Mr Saunders. Nurse Wilkes had phoned her at Ralph's request. She and Linda were going to be witnesses to the new will Ralph was making... Was Ralph going to disinherit his nephew? It certainly looked that way. And the new beneficiary? Wilkes had no doubt it would be Beatrice. Who else? The way Ralph's face lit up each time she entered the room! He had been very much in love with her once upon a time, she had gathered, then they had been separated or something. It was a very romantic story.

Nurse Wilkes believed Ralph's brain wasn't functioning properly. The cancer must be killing his brain cells. He had odd fancies. After Beatrice's last visit, Ralph said, 'I'd rather be struck down by the Angel of Death than die of cancer.' He had spoken in a funny kind of voice, as though he had seen the Angel of Death. What did he mean exactly? To Nurse Wilkes' way of thinking, the Angel of Death and cancer were very much the same thing. Death was death. Ralph also seemed to suspect his nephew Robin and Eric of having had an affair. That was why he had turned against them. Well, even if that was true, it was none of her business. Live and let live, that was her motto. She liked Robin; he was a charmer. His mother had been a Lady – Lady Violet Trelawney.

What was that noise? Nurse Wilkes stood and listened. Sounded like all the rooks outside were having a riot! As though something had scared them. When Mr Saunders came later on, she'd ask him about getting another nurse. She could do with some company. She must be careful though – she didn't really want to give the impression she was complaining in any way. They paid her a good salary – an *extremely* good salary, in fact. Better than anywhere else she'd been before. Besides, Ralph told her he had remembered her in his will.

She walked across the hall and paused outside the door. She didn't want to interrupt a confession. No, nothing. Silence. Absolute silence. Maybe Ralph had fallen asleep and Father Lillie was praying for the salvation of his soul. She wanted to talk to Father Lillie about how exactly this thing worked. As she pushed the door to Ralph's room open, she heard a buzzing noise – *flies?*

Instinctively she looked at the french windows first. When Father Lillie had come, they had been left ajar – now they were gaping open. There was something on the floor that hadn't been there before. She drew in her breath.

A red trail–

She traced it back, from the windows to the bed – that was where the trail was coming from.

Nurse Wilkes didn't drop the tray, the way they did in films, didn't scream either, but stood very still in the doorway, staring at the glistening wet redness at the head of the bed. Ralph lay slumped against his pillow. There was blood on his face. On the pillows and the sheet as well. Ralph's head was at an awkward angle.

She had no doubt that he was dead. From where she stood she couldn't see the wound, but she imagined his throat had been slit, or his jugular pierced. There were flies buzzing in the room, attracted by the blood. It must be all this hot weather. A hornet too, by the sound of it.

Nurse Wilkes was used to the sight of blood, but she started shaking now. Who did this to him? Where was Father Lillie?

One of the wardrobe doors was ajar. A crazy thought popped into her head: what if moon-faced Father Lillie was lurking inside, clutching a knife, waiting for her?

16

Lazarus

Antonia took her coffee and the vanilla-cream macaroons she had bought at the local Chez Paul to her study, sat down at her desk and opened her diary. Hugh had asked her what she imagined would happen next. She had said, *nothing* – but she could do better than that, surely?

She picked up her pen and started writing.

A double bluff. What no one realizes is that there is another plot at work. It has never occurred to Ingrid that she is being duped. Ralph is not Ralph. The dying man by whose bed Ingrid has been sitting is not dying at all. He is an actor hired – and handsomely remunerated – by Ralph to impersonate him. The dreadful appearance is nothing but clever make-up and prosthetics. For some reason Ralph is keen on keeping up the pretence that he is mortally ill, that indeed he is dying. What reason though?

'Well, he has enemies. Ingrid Delmar is not the only one who is after him.' Hugh had come into the room unnoticed, and was standing behind her, looking down at what she had written. He stroked her hair, then put his hand on her shoulder. 'We may start with the strong presumption that Ralph Renshawe had a serious reason to leave America. Gentlemen at his time of life do not change all their habits and exchange willingly the delightful climate of Florida for the solitary life of an English squire in a bleak Gothic mansion on the border between Oxfordshire and Berkshire.'

'How did he make his enemies?' Antonia tapped the pen against her teeth.

'When he lived in Calgary and later in America he managed to get involved in various dubious deals. He cheated and double-crossed a great number of people.'

'Perhaps he even ventured into the territory of organized crime? Yes. It was fear that drove him away.'

'He had been getting death threats—'

'Ralph Renshawe chose Ospreys very carefully,' said Antonia. 'Ospreys' main attraction lay in the fact that it was isolated and hard to find. Remember how long it took us to get there?'

'Indeed I do. That was a matter of desperate necessity. Renshawe settled down at Ospreys — but the fear didn't leave him. Night after night he lay in bed, thinking about his enemies. He then hit on an ingenious plan—'

'By pretending to be mortally ill, indeed, dying,' Antonia said slowly, 'Ralph Renshawe hopes to discourage his enemies from bumping him off... But if the cancer is fictitious, the resident nurse would know it, surely?'

Payne waved his hand. 'Squared. Part of the set-up.'

'The doctor–'

'Ditto.'

'Ralph Renshawe – the real Ralph Renshawe – is also at Ospreys. He occupies a secret attic room. He has been monitoring the situation from above. He's had CCTV cameras installed and everything. What he doesn't realize–' Antonia broke off. 'Can you think of a final twist?'

'I think I can. What Renshawe doesn't realize is that the nurse and the actor have fallen in love,' suggested Payne. 'They have guessed about Ingrid and her murderous intentions. The murder takes place quite late in the story. When a body does turn up, it is the *real* Ralph Renshawe and it looks as though Ingrid has killed him – she seems to have discovered the truth – but as a matter of fact it is the nurse and the actor who are the killers. The actor is in fact Renshawe's illegitimate son–'

Colville was on the phone, talking to his friend Arthur Manning.

'Yes, both Bee and I are absolutely sure and we are extremely concerned... For

Ralph Renshawe's safety – as well as for our own… For Ingrid too – well, yes. She has tried to commit suicide in the past. No, she hasn't come back yet. I do believe she went to Ralph Renshawe's place… Ospreys, yes. That's the name of the house. It's outside a village called Coulston. Not far from us… I tried to phone them, warn them, tell them who she is and that they should be careful, but there was no answer… Ingrid's visited Ralph Renshawe several times already, we know that for a fact… I took a photo of her earlier on – through the window – two photos, actually. I happened to have my Polaroid at hand – she was walking towards the bus stop – there's a bus that goes to Coulston… No evidence? What are you talking about? Why else dress up like Beatrice, for heaven's sake?'

Colville listened with pursed lips. 'Isn't there a chance of you taking a look at Ingrid? Make up your mind about her? You do have a degree in criminal psychology after all… The doctor who treated her when she had her breakdown? I have no idea who he is, but I can ask Bee when she comes back.'

He looked at the clock. Twenty-five past eleven. Where *was* Bee? 'Yes. Yes. He might be able to help, you are right. I know you are busy, Arthur, but– Yes, I know. All right. Thank you.'

Colville put down the receiver. His hand

was shaking. Well, it was as he had suspected it would be. Arthur did think he was making a mountain out of a molehill. Arthur was too busy tracking down criminals, *real* criminals.

Colville pressed his fingertips against his temples. He had so much on his mind, so much. He couldn't think straight. The day so far had had a nightmarish quality about it. For the life of him he couldn't separate what had happened from what hadn't. Outside the heat shimmered and the sun, bright as fire, glared on. He mopped his brow with his handkerchief. Suddenly he started up. As in a dream, or as if he was looking at something in a play, he became aware that Ingrid was standing outside in the garden, her face pressed against the window pane, looking in. Ingrid's eyes were yellow-red and luminous, like a wolf's, and she was acting like a thing possessed – grimacing horribly, baring her teeth, mocking him, taunting him. Then she pulled back a little and he distinctly heard her say, *'Le comte est mort.'* He saw her draw the side of her hand slowly across her throat, then let her tongue hang out obscenely, as though imagining his French might not be good enough – but of course the second he blinked, she was gone.

Ingrid had been nothing but a mirage. Colville's neck prickled. Their back garden was empty of any human presence; it was smooth as velvet, its herbaceous borders tidied up for winter. There had never been anybody there.

He was covered in sweat. 'I am not well,' Colville said aloud.

Twenty-seven minutes past eleven. Twenty-eight. Why wasn't Bee back? Where *was* she? Then a thought struck him.

Could she have gone to Ospreys?

'So, apart from various minor provisions, you want Miss Beatrice Ardleigh to be your sole beneficiary. Your decision is final and irreversible?' Benjamin Saunders said expressionlessly, looking down at the old man who sat propped up between four pillows. He was impressed by their gleaming whiteness, by the fresh smell they exuded.

'Yes, yes,' Ralph Renshawe said. 'Final and irreversible. Good way of putting it.'

Saunders cleared his throat. 'This is a lot of money—'

'It's *my* money. I am of sound mind. I know perfectly well what I am doing. Get on with it, Saunders.'

He didn't look too bad – for a dying man. In fact he looked better than the last time Saunders had seen him. He had some colour in his cheeks – his eyes were brighter – and he was in a belligerent mood.

'According to your current will, it is your nephew, Robin Renshawe, who–'

'No longer. All that's changed.' Ralph

Renshawe sounded impatient. 'Robin gets nothing. All for Bee.'

'Very well. Miss Wilkes. Mrs Brown. Would you come over?' Saunders made a courtly gesture. 'Sign here, please... On the dotted line, yes... It doesn't matter who goes first.'

As Nurse Wilkes signed her name, the solicitor noticed that her hand shook so much that she had to stop and start again. What was wrong with her? He had been wondering. She had said she wanted to talk to him about something... When she opened the front door for him, he was struck by her extreme pallor. As white as one of Ralph Renshawe's sheets. She hadn't been her usual chatty self, which was another peculiar thing. She was unaccustomedly subdued. The other woman had noticed it too – Mrs Brown. He saw her shooting puzzled glances at Wilkes. Was Wilkes ill? Had something happened? She looked as though she had received a shock of some kind... Or it could be the heat... He dabbed at his face with his handkerchief... So terribly hot... He didn't feel too good himself... It seemed incredible that it was the end of November!

Was the job getting to be too demanding for poor Wilkes? Ralph's room was spotlessly clean, the floor was still slightly damp and it smelled of some superior disinfectant, which suggested that Wilkes had finished cleaning it only moments earlier. Mrs Brown – Linda – was one of the two women who came to clean three times a week, but today wasn't one of her days, she had said. Which meant that it was Wilkes who, on top of all her other duties, had been scrubbing away in Ralph's room. She had also changed his sheets – all the linen was crisp and spotless... Had Ralph made a mess earlier on? Saunders had heard such horror stories about cancer patients. His long sensitive nose quivered squeamishly but no, there was nothing – he had to admit that there wasn't the slightest whiff of any offensive effluvium.

When the new will had been signed, all formalities completed and he was back in the hall, about to take his leave, he asked Nurse Wilkes whether everything was all right.

'Yes. I am just tired, I suppose.' She tried to smile. 'Actually I am getting married.'

'Getting married? Congratulations. Well done.' He patted her arm, though he had an immediate sense of foreboding. 'I suppose you'd like – um – some time off?'

'Yes. As from tomorrow, if possible... That's what I wanted to talk to you about.'

'Of course. As from tomorrow... We'll need another nurse urgently.' Saunders pulled at his lower lip. 'Very well. How many days?'

'I want to take two – no, three months.'

'Three months? That long?' Saunders was

taken aback. Three months! Ralph would have gone by then. That meant adieu to Wilkes, rather than au revoir. From tomorrow too. She *was* in a hurry. 'Very well. I'll see to it... We'll need to settle your salary first–'

'No need. Ralph's already paid me.'

'He has? Are you sure?'

'Yes, I am sure. It's all settled.'

Saunders' eyebrows went up a little. That was unusual. Had something – happened? Wilkes' manner struck him as odd – strained, furtive – she gave the impression of having been upset by something – she wasn't meeting his eye.

Had Ralph perhaps made a pass at her? Saunders remembered the luscious Madame Niratpattanasai and the trouble they had had ejecting her from the house. It had taken four uniformed policemen. How she had screamed! Wilkes was a completely different physical type, still Ralph's Catholicism might extend to his tastes in women... He mustn't be flippant... No, no – out of the question – a man in his condition! So long as Wilkes was happy, he didn't need to worry his head about what might have happened.

'We need to have that doorbell repaired,' he murmured and soon after he left.

'What's the matter with you today?' Linda nudged her.

'I don't know what you mean,' Nurse

195

Wilkes said.

'Don't give me that. You look like something horrible has happened. As though – I don't know. You are not yourself. What's up? Has Ralph been giving you aggro?'

'No. No. I'm knackered. The heat, I suppose...'

17

The Mortification of Moriarty

At four in the afternoon Robin Renshawe drove to Athlone Place. He rang the bell twice and waited several moments before pushing his hand into his pocket. He didn't really expect Lily to be lurking inside.

The lock was a rather ordinary one and it took him exactly thirty-five seconds to pick it with the special piece of wire he had brought with him. He let himself into the flat. He shut the door behind him and stood beside an ornate hall lamp, which dangled from the arm of a marble caryatid. Nobody had seen him, not even the concierge. He had managed to slip by his desk in the hall. The concierge was some ancient duffer, a hearing aid sticking out of his left ear, *and* he had been engrossed in a book. If all crimes were to be made that easy!

Robin hadn't taken off his gloves. They were tan-coloured and made of the finest thin leather and fitted his hands like another skin. He pulled all the curtains across the windows and turned on a table lamp. He stood looking round Lily's sitting room.

Everything in pristine order, rather like in a museum. What an absurd setting Lily had created for himself. A cross between the Brompton Oratory, the Savoy and the Athenaeum – with more than a hint of a *fin de siècle* bordello! An Aubusson carpet. A Turkish cabinet. Two palms in Japanese-style porcelain pots. Intricately carved bookshelves. Two marble busts of unidentifiable ancient sages – or were they Roman emperors? A divan upholstered in red velvet – candelabras – two gruesome religious paintings on the walls, also some framed Max Beerbohm caricatures, authentic, he bet – silk and satin cushions – a polished Sheraton bureau–

Robin looked at the books that lay on the bureau. *Hadrian the Seventh* by Frederick Rolfe. De Quincey's *Opium Eater* and *Murder as a Fine Art*. No surprises there. *The Leopold and Loeb Case Revisited*. How curious. Robin opened the book – turned a page. Had Lily seen a parallel between himself and Robin and those two? They were nothing like them. Leopold and Loeb had killed one of their fellow students solely for aesthetic kicks. Besides, they had had an affair – and Robin couldn't imagine anything more ghastly than having an affair with Lily, not even for a bet.

He opened a drawer, then another, examining their contents. A photo of a very old woman, strabismic, wearing small round glasses. *Gwen Ffrangcon-Davies' last appearance in 'The Master Blackmailer'*. What freakish tastes Lily had, Robin had forgotten.

More photos. A portly man with a bald head and the lips of a highly disciplined voluptuary. Lily's papa, the prosperous banker – there was a resemblance. Another photo, of a rather forbidding woman with a Roman nose. Mrs Lillie-Lysander, née Lushington. Lily's mamma. She was wearing an elaborate hat, which suggested a wedding or a garden party. Robin remembered meeting them once – they had come to Antlers in a Daimler. They had been extremely formal with Lily – a handshake and a pat on the shoulder – no kisses – Lily's mother hadn't even taken off her gloves. She had known exactly how many sons of Catholic dukes there were at the school at the moment.

Papers. Bills... Bills... *Bills*... Lily must have been desperate... Loans from three banks. Catalogues from sales – Christie's – Sotheby's. A gilt-edged card with the Midas club address and phone number. He had several of those himself. A book: *Unbreakable Systems*. Lily seemed to have taken roulette rather seriously. Another book: *Satan's Seraglio*. Had Lily been planning to sell his soul to Satan or had he already done so? A mahogany humidor filled with cigars.

Expensive tastes. A Masonic tie-pin. Nothing of a remotely personal nature. No suspicious-looking brown envelopes.

Robin found himself thinking back to the scandal of Father Canteloupe – everybody had been talking about it – it had happened in their second year at school – there had been rumours that the school might be closed down. Father Canteloupe had committed suicide the same day the police had raided his study and discovered hundreds of what the press called 'disturbing images'. Father Canteloupe had been found hanging in the cricket pavilion – as though the cricket pavilion hadn't seen enough horrors already.

No, no dirty pictures of any kind. Robin had been hoping for something esoteric – something *recherché*. How terribly disappointing. *I don't believe that he ever experienced what one might call a stirring in the undergrowth for anyone – man, woman or child.* That was what Nico, the least screwed-up of the five doomed Llewellyn Davies brothers and the last to die, had said about his 'Uncle Jim' Barrie. Lily, Robin imagined, was very much in the same category. Yes, Lily seemed to be one of those astonishing asexuals who went through life without any of the destructive passions known to man. Apart from gambling, that was.

It was for anything that could connect him, Robin, with Lily that he was looking.

Well, there was a school group photo. There he was – had his hair really been that long? Well, that had been in 1979. Apart from the hair, he had changed little, he thought. He had the same dashingly chiselled cheekbones. Where was Lily? The overfed cherub on his right? Good lord. Yes. They weren't standing side by side, Lily and he – there were no names written on the photograph. Still, Robin put it into his pocket – better play it safe...

He picked up a booklet bound in maroon leather. It looked familiar somehow. *The Mortification of Moriarty.* As he read the title, his heart missed a beat. Of course. It was the one-act play he and Lily had written together, though they had never got to perform it. Robin was going to play Moriarty – Sherlock Holmes's nemesis. What was it all about? Robin leafed through it. He had forgotten. Something about Moriarty falling victim to one of his own cunning schemes? Pulling strings – getting people to commit all sorts of crimes for him, but not realizing – what? For the life of him Robin couldn't recall the twist. Holmes didn't appear at all, but it was all rather clever and had this terribly ironic denouement–

Putting the play into his pocket, Robin opened the last drawer.

No, nothing. Nothing at all.

Had he given Lily any of his joke cards?

Robin Renshawe, Gentleman of Leisure. Robin's address and phone number were printed on it. Where was the card? Lily had placed it inside his wallet – it all came back to Robin now... Well, Robin had instructed Eric not only to rough Lily up but to remove every scrap of paper from his pockets as well. He had also asked him to dispose of Lily's mobile, which would have a record of all the calls Robin had made to him. The idea was that there should be nothing to connect Lily with Robin. Then, even if Lily became difficult and unpleasant and, say, attempted to blackmail him in some way, he would not be able to prove that he had been acting under Robin's edict...

Lily had promised to send him a message as soon as he had accomplished his assignment, but he hadn't. Robin didn't want to ring Ospreys and draw attention to himself. He had rehearsed what he was going to say – the casual tone of voice in which he would ask Wilkes some totally silly question – had she knitted his pullover? And of course, if his uncle *was* dead, Wilkes would tell him at once. But wouldn't they have called him anyway if his uncle had died? No one had called him so far, which suggested that all was in order at Ospreys.

Where *was* Lily? It was half past four now. Six hours! What if Eric had executed the 'roughing' task without the finesse it required – a little bit too roughly, perhaps? So far Eric hadn't contacted him, which suggested that Eric might have killed Lily and was too scared to admit it.

Robin knew in his bones that at some point of the operation something had gone spectacularly wrong. He sat on one of Lily's heraldic chairs and reflected that the worst scenario would be if his uncle was still alive and it was Lily who had ended up dead.

Robin had phoned Eric at five minutes to ten in the morning. By then he had drunk two thirds of the whisky. Eric of course had been delighted to hear his voice. Eric was like a puppy. *Oh Robin, so nice to hear from you. How have you been?* Eric was in Coulston, taking care of a Mr Stanley who was an invalid. It was Robin who had got him the job after his uncle had sacked Eric. Robin knew Mr Stanley from the Midas. Mr Stanley had been a regular at the roulette table until he had had his stroke. He could hardly move now. Eric was deeply grateful to Robin for getting him the job.

Yes, Robin. Anything. Anything... I see... You don't want me to get anywhere near the house? Wait further down the road and watch the gates? A Catholic priest – I'll recognize him by the collar? Stop his car and tell him I have a message from you? Ask him to follow my car? Take him to the disused quarry? I know the quarry very well, yes. Then you want me to–?

(Robin had wished the slow-witted fool hadn't repeated everything he said.)

If Eric *had* killed Lily, what had he done with the body? What had he done with his car?

Then another thought struck Robin. When asked, old Saunders would certainly say that it had been Robin Renshawe who had recommended Father Lillie-Lysander. Well, what if he had? That proved nothing. All he needed to say then was that they had been to school together, that was how he knew Lily. Still–

The irony would be if they arrested him, Robin, for Lily's death. Lily then would have the last laugh from beyond the grave. Robin smiled grimly. Something like that had happened in the play they had written together, *The Mortification of Moriarty*, hadn't it?

How prophetic that would be – and how pathetic.

18

The Hound of Death

Nurse Wilkes sat in the kitchen at Ospreys, lost in a daze, thinking back to what had happened, trying to make sense of things.

The moment she had started walking towards Ralph's bed, she heard a voice.

His voice. 'Wilkes–'

She had stopped short and stared. Ralph had stirred – raised his hand – so he wasn't dead after all!

'Don't stand and stare. *Clean.* Quick.' Ralph had spoken sparingly, using single words, as though saving his energy. He had stirred and pointed. 'Blood. Half an hour. Saunders. Get on with it. Clean.'

'Aren't you – hurt?' she had heard herself say.

'No.'

'But – the blood? Whose–?'

'No idea.'

'I don't understand.'

'I don't either.'

'Where's Father Lillie?'

'Don't know. Asleep. When I woke up, he'd gone. Blood all over me. *Clean.*'

Likely story, she thought. When she didn't move, he said, 'Twenty-five minutes. One thousand pounds for each minute. Twenty-five thousand. All yours. Clean. Everything spotless. Get pillow off.' There had been a pillow lying across his stomach. 'Pyjamas. Change. Sheets – *everything*.'

She had done as he had asked her. She would always remember those crazy twenty-five minutes – as long as she lived. She had hurried back to the kitchen, placed the tea tray on the table, opened the pantry door and pulled out the box with the bottles of various cleaning liquids in it. Then she had got hold of the mop and several cloths – filled the bucket with water – put on rubber gloves–

She had run back to his room. She had had to clean him first – get rid of his bloody clothes. She had wiped his face clean with wet tissues, then with a sponge – his throat, his neck, his chest – ran out again – brought back fresh underwear and another pair of pyjamas – as well as a basket for the bloodied things–

He hadn't said another word, neither had she. He had felt dry and scaly – nothing but skin and bone – disgusting to the touch – but alive. There hadn't been a scratch on him.

As the clock had ticked away the seconds and the minutes, she had mopped and washed and scrubbed the floor. She had found a bloody hand print on the little white wardrobe where Ralph's clothes were kept. She couldn't swear to it but she believed that one of Ralph's shirts as well as a pullover were missing. She had wiped clean the print. She hadn't asked Ralph about the missing clothes since she didn't think he would give her an answer.

She had then wiped clean the bloody trail that led from the bed to the french windows – it looked like some ferocious beast had dragged its prey out. At one point she had felt sick. She had been about to throw up but managed to hold it in. A nightmare, that was what the whole thing felt like. A proper nightmare. *No idea*, he had said. *No idea*. He had no idea whose blood it was! She was sure he was lying.

Surely the blood was Father Lillie's? Couldn't be anybody else's, could it?

She'd felt goose-bumps go up and down her spine. Her stomach too had continued to feel funny. There had been drops of blood outside on the steps leading down to the garden and she had wiped those away too, to the best of her ability. She'd expected to hear a growl – she really had – the monstrous beast, having devoured Father Lillie, coming back for more fresh meat – the *hound* – slobbering jaws – foul breath – fangs like knives–

That had reminded her. Now where was

her knitting needle? There had been nothing under the bed. She had started looking round the room, but hadn't been able to find her knitting needle anywhere. She had found a keyring with keys on it, though. Car keys. The keyring bore a monogram: *L-L*.

She had got rid of the flies and bluebottles and shut the french windows. She had even drawn the curtains across them.

'*Good*. Not a word about this. To anyone,' he had said. 'What's the time?'

'Five to eleven.'

'And no sign of Saunders yet? Excellent. Well done, Wilkes. My cheque book – the desk.'

He had then proceeded to write her a cheque not for twenty-five thousand but for *thirty-five* thousand pounds. 'No questions. Not a word to anyone,' he had repeated.

She said, 'Father Lillie's car is still there, I think.' And she had shown Ralph the keys. 'Lillie-Lysander.'

'His keys, yes. Good thinking, Wilkes. Go and get his car into the garage. Plenty of space. You can drive, can't you? Be quick about it. Saunders mustn't see it. Don't want distractions. The new will. Mustn't die before I've signed the new will. How much did I give you?' He looked down at the cheque. 'You deserve better than this.' He picked up his pen once more.

The killer must have got some blood on

him. Was that why he had taken clothes from the wardrobe, to change? Ralph *must* know who it was. She was sure Father Lillie had been murdered. Ralph must have seen the killer. Or could he have passed out? Who'd want to kill Father Lillie beside Ralph's bed? *Why?*

She had found some blonde hairs on the back of the chair by the bed. Beatrice hadn't come today. She had said she would but she hadn't. A good thing too. Nurse Wilkes gave a little smile. All she'd needed was Beatrice appearing in the middle of it all, as she'd been mopping up the bloody mess!

19

The Vanishing

'Your hair's not done. What happened to your hairdresser's appointment?' Colville asked, trying to sound as casual as possible.

'Oh, don't ask!' Beatrice flapped her hands. 'The most awful calamity. Honestly! You won't believe this, darling, but they suddenly found themselves without any electricity!'

'Without electricity?'

'Yes! There was a loud crack as I was entering. Some kind of short-circuit or power cut or something. Can you *imagine?* Alessandro didn't know where to look – so terribly embarrassed, poor boy. Then I ran into Cressie. D'you remember Cressie de Villeneuve? Oh no, you wouldn't. She and I used to be great chums but had rather lost touch. She's come back from Brazil – where her husband's our man – brown as a nut! We were at finishing school together, in Switzerland. The last time she saw me, I was in my wheelchair, so she didn't recognize me at first. There was a lot of catching-up to do. She wanted to hear all about you.'

210

'She did?'

'Yes! Her people apparently knew your people. We went to have lunch at a place called Tiddly Dolls – such fun – the most divine Spanish omelette I've ever had – I completely lost track of the time! Then we went shopping – Cressie needed to buy a handbag and she wanted my opinion.'

She prattled on. It was half past four now. It turned out she had lost her mobile phone too; she had absolutely no idea where her mobile had disappeared, that was why she hadn't been able to ring him. (A likely story! How could she have lost her mobile?) She had *meant* to ring, honestly. (A contradiction, surely? A moment earlier she had said she had lost track of time. He kept catching her out. She wasn't really taking care, was she? She must have a very poor opinion of his intelligence. Didn't she realize that all he needed to do was phone Alessandro's and check whether there really had been a power cut?)

'You haven't been *worried*, have you? My poor darling, you do look terrible! Has anything happened?'

'Nothing's happened.'

'You look different somehow. You look tired. *Years* older.'

'Rubbish,' he bristled. She had been with some young man, that was why he appeared older to her now. She was seeing him with 'new eyes'. Or she had lain in the arms of somebody who looked younger and was more vigorous than his years – was it Payne?

'Is it the heat? You aren't awfully good in the heat, are you?' She reached out and touched his forehead. Her fingertips felt cool. He shivered. Her power over him continued undiminished.

'It must be the heat,' he said.

'Is Ingrid back?' Beatrice heaved a deep sigh and shook her head when he said no.

Something rustled in his pocket. His fingers closed on the folded sheet of paper he had found in the pocket of the mink coat Ingrid had abandoned on the landing upstairs. The coat belonged to Bee. Ingrid had worn it until the weather had turned, as part of the Beatrice disguise. Ingrid had drawn a plan of Ospreys on it – it showed Ralph Renshawe's french windows, the terrace and the wishing well in the garden. The police would certainly be interested in it. He wondered whether to show the drawing to Bee.

He saw her pull something out of her bag. It was an oblong in scarlet, black and gold: a Tiddly Dolls menu. Making a silly face, what she called her 'duck face', Beatrice waved the menu under his nose. 'In case you don't believe I had lunch there.'

Why had she brought the menu with her? She had *stolen* it from the restaurant. She had panicked. She felt he needed convincing – she had been worried he might not believe her. She wouldn't have done it if she had been innocent. No. She didn't realize that the menu was proof of her guilt. 'Cressie de Villeneuve' was an invention. Well, Bee might well have had lunch at Tiddly Dolls – in the company of her lover.

Was it Major Payne?

Two days later, at one o'clock in the afternoon of November 28th, Major Payne sat at the kitchen table, a whisky and soda in his hand, his unlit pipe lying on the table before him, his attention divided between watching his wife make salad, playing Patience Solitaire with a pack of cards and leafing absently through an early edition of London's *Evening Standard*. It was another very warm day and the kitchen window was wide open.

'So, plenty of olive oil but no garlic? You sure about the garlic?' Antonia said.

'Absolutely. No garlic,' Major Payne said firmly. 'You don't have to follow Miss Elizabeth David so slavishly. We don't want to feel more Mediterranean than we already do, do we?'

'I wouldn't mind. I'd rather be hot than cold.'

'So would I.' He squinted at the row of Antonia's cookery books. 'I bet you don't know what Mrs Beeton's first name was.'

'I don't.'

'Isabella.'

'I would never have thought it possible. She doesn't sound like an Isabella at all, if her recipes are anything to go by. Do you remember the pink blancmange?'

'Vividly. The pink blancmange should never have been attempted. The whole Victorian dinner idea was a mistake from start to finish. I nearly died of indigestion that night.'

'The oyster soup wasn't too bad. Do you find Beatrice Ardleigh attractive?'

'There we go again. *Not in the least.*'

'That's what Colonel Christie must have said when Agatha asked him the very same question about Nancy Neale,' Antonia said with a smile. She then went on to say that perhaps detective story writers should not marry military men. It didn't seem to work.

'What absolute rot,' Major Payne said.

'If I were to disappear for twenty-six days, you would know why.'

'I'll lead the search party straight to the Harrogate Hydro.'

'Do they say when this "front" is going to leave these shores?' Antonia asked after a pause.

Payne looked down at the paper. 'No... People have been splashing about in the fountains in Trafalgar Square and members of the Queen's mounted guard have been seen hosing down their horses in an attempt to cool them. *Good lord,'* he exclaimed as he reached page four.

'What is it?'

There was a pause. The newspaper rustled in his hands. 'I am *not* making this up, Antonia. *Mysterious disappearance of a Catholic priest. The alarm was raised after Father Lillie-Lysander, 40, failed to keep an appointment with his bishop and there was no response to any of the calls made to his landline or his mobile phone. Father Lillie-Lysander was last seen on the morning of November 26th at Ospreys, a country house in Oxfordshire, the property of Mr Ralph Renshawe.'*

'Are you trying to say Ralph's father confessor has disappeared?' Antonia stood very still, a lettuce leaf in her hand.

'That's what it says here, it must be him. A second priest on the scene would be *de trop.'*

Antonia put her head to one side. 'You are making this up.'

'I am not. Golly. *Wait.* There's been a *second* disappearance!' Payne cried. 'It's reported on the very same page! They always report disappearances on the same page... Only a short paragraph... No, this is too much. You won't believe this,' he said. 'Listen... *The police are very concerned about the whereabouts of Ingrid Delmar, 50, who has been missing from her home since the morning of November 26th.'*

'You are making this up. We did talk about it, Hugh.'

'I am not making anything up! *Miss Delmar, who has had a history of depressive illness, lives in Wallingford, Oxfordshire. She shares a house with friends of hers, Mr and Mrs Colville. It was Mrs Colville who contacted the police. A search is under way.*'

Antonia continued staring at him. 'This is another of your jokes.'

'I can understand why you should think that, but it isn't another of my jokes. Well, read it for yourself.' He tossed the paper across the table.

Wiping her hands on a tea towel, she picked up the paper.

He was gratified to see her expression change. She turned the paper over and scrutinized the front page as though to convince herself this was indeed today's paper, an authentic paper, and that he wasn't playing some trick on her. One *could* produce a fake newspaper, as part of some elaborate hoax, he supposed. There was a place somewhere in London, where they did that sort of thing, he was sure. Somewhere near Covent Garden?

'Incredible,' he heard Antonia say. 'Sorry, Hugh. I can't believe this...'

'What was the technical term for the doctrine of chance?' Major Payne picked up his pipe.

'What doctrine?' She lowered the paper.

'We were talking about it last night.'

'The Calculus of Probabilities?'

'That's it. Well, according to the Calculus of Probabilities,' Payne said slowly, 'coincidence in these particular circumstances is *not* very likely. You agree?'

'I don't see how it could be coincidence.' Antonia frowned. 'Two disappearances – on the very same day – both missing persons with links to Ospreys and Ralph Renshawe. Something – something must have happened to them. People don't just – disappear.'

'*Omnia exeunt in mysterium,*' Major Payne said. 'Everything dissolves in mystery... Perhaps there is some human Bermuda triangle encompassing Ospreys?' He put his pipe in his mouth and produced a match.

'No, not in the kitchen, Hugh, I've told you.'

'I need to smoke,' he said. 'Helps me to think.'

'Oh very well, but only this once.' She sat down slowly. 'Where *have* they gone? Something must have happened.'

'Maybe the padre and Ingrid decided to elope and set up house together? Emotionally labile people attract one another. Plenty of examples. Bonnie and Clyde. Elizabeth Taylor and Richard Burton – they got married, then got divorced, then remarried,

217

then got divorced again. Hinge and Brackett – young men masquerading as old women. The Papen sisters–'

'The Papen sisters were *sisters*, Hugh. They couldn't have attracted one another.'

'Wasn't there a touch of incestuous lesbianism about them? Garbo and Gilbert.'

'Gilbert and George?' Antonia said despite herself.

'Absolutely. See? The list is endless.'

'Why would Father Lillie-Lysander and Ingrid want to elope?'

'Because of the padre's vows... Um... They need time to think ahead – plan the future – think of the best way to break it to the cardinals–'

'For a man whose intelligence has been described as "subtle", Hugh, you do talk a lot of nonsense.' Antonia frowned. 'Are you sure Gilbert was emotionally labile? I mean Garbo's Gilbert?'

'He thought he was the greatest actor who ever lived. He drank himself to death.'

'We don't know if Father Lillie-Lysander was emotionally labile.'

'Well, he's been listening to strangers describing their unspeakable fantasies for heaven knows how long. *Through a grille.* Try to imagine what that could do to a chap. Don't you think the grille is a form of peephole to one's most private peep show?'

'No, I don't. Really, Hugh–'

The next moment the telephone started ringing. Payne felt delighted at the interruption – he didn't at all like the expression on Antonia's face. 'I'll get it.' Jumping up from his seat, he picked up the kitchen extension.

'Oh, hello, Beatrice.' He grimaced at Antonia. 'Actually, we just read it and were talking about it. Yes, terrible thing to happen... I can imagine... What? *Now?* I see. I don't know – um– Oh, I am sorry. Just a moment. Let me ask Antonia.' Putting his hand over the receiver, he whispered, 'She wants us to go to her place. *Now.* She is in a state. She's had a row with Colville and he's dashed out of the house. *She's been abandoned by everybody.* She is in floods of tears ... *hysterical.*'

'Oh dear.' Antonia glanced down at the salad bowl. 'I suppose we'd better go.'

She was not sure whether she said yes out of concern for Beatrice Ardleigh, or because she was curious about the amazing turn of events. The latter, she admitted to herself. A double vanishing was most certainly worth investigating. Beatrice, on the other hand, was perfectly capable of coping on her own. Beneath that vulnerable fluttery exterior Beatrice was actually quite tough, Antonia felt sure. Why indulge her unduly? And it wasn't as though they were her oldest – or her best – friends... Beatrice was after

Hugh... Beatrice had probably been hoping she would be able to get Hugh on his own...

'Doesn't Poe refer to the Calculus of Probabilities in *The Mystery of Marie Celeste?*' Payne said as they were getting into the car.

'You mean *The Mystery of Marie Roget.*'

'Do I? Oh, of course. Association of ideas. *Marie Celeste* was the ship from which everybody disappeared mysteriously and without a trace...'

20

The Scapegoat

Once again they were at Millbrook House.

They heard the eerie sound of drumbeats, which should have been incongruous in Oxfordshire but somehow felt appropriate under the blazing sun. The front door opened even before they had rung the bell and Beatrice flung herself on Antonia's neck. Between sobs and gasps, she managed to say that she had never felt so frightened in her life. *Everything* had gone wrong. Ingrid had vanished into thin air. The police had been noxious and officious. The police had acted as though she had something to do with Ingrid's disappearance. Worst of all, Len had left her!

'I am sure you are wrong,' Payne murmured. 'Colville worships the ground you walk on.'

'No more,' Beatrice whispered. '*No more.*'

'What happened?' Antonia asked.

Len had been extremely cross with her – Len was a prince among men, but she'd never seen him so furious – he had gone off – she seriously feared he'd never come back.

Or that he might do something silly. It would serve her right if he did – she'd been telling fibs – she had been deceiving Len. She didn't deserve Len. She was responsible for the whole catalogue of misfortunes. She was the architect of the disaster. She had brought all these troubles on her own head. She was terrified. She had always known she'd die alone. And it was less than a month to Christmas!

What had that got to do with anything? Payne thought. The bloody woman was hysterical. And those drums – enough to drive anybody mad! They were still standing in the hall. Payne strode into the sitting room and turned off the CD player. As he did so, he inadvertently pushed some CDs off a shelf and they spilled on the floor. Damn, he said, but didn't pick them up. He could hear Beatrice sobbing uncontrollably in the hall. He went over to the drinks table, poured some brandy into a glass and brought it back to her.

'Thank you, thank you, dear friend.' Beatrice clutched at his hand. 'You and Antonia are the only friends I have. My only true friends.' After this extravagant statement Beatrice gulped down the brandy. It made her splutter and cough, but she clearly felt better for she started examining her face critically in the mirror. She said she looked a 'fright'. She asked Antonia whether she could borrow her lipstick. 'I can't find mine. We use the same colour. I noticed the first time I saw you,' Beatrice breathed.

Antonia opened her bag and took out her lipstick, but in the process her diary fell out. She picked it up, not noticing the slip of paper that dislodged itself from between the book's pages and fluttered down to the floor.

Having painted her lips, Beatrice led the way into the sitting room. Her arm was linked through Antonia's. 'What's your favourite scent?' she asked.

Antonia said she didn't have a favourite scent. It struck her that she probably gave the impression of being rather puritanical. She needed to loosen up. Hugh was bound to start thinking her a nuisance sooner or later.

'Mine is Ce Soir Je T'Aime. My life is incomplete without it,' Beatrice said. She then promised to send Antonia a bottle of Ce Soir Je T'Aime for Christmas.

Beatrice's hair had the sheen of Mycenaean gold; she wore preposterously high heels, a rather chic black cocktail dress and a heavy ornate necklace that didn't really seem to go with the rest of her. (Had she dressed like that to impress Hugh?) On close inspection the necklace turned out to be made of miniature Taj Mahals. Payne had also taken note of the Taj Mahal necklace – he thought it an impossibly kitsch-y artifact

– an affront to good taste.

'Len had it specially made for me when we got engaged. He drew the design himself. They'd never had to make anything like it before,' Beatrice explained. 'The Taj Mahal was built by some Indian emperor for his beloved wife, wasn't it? Len's such a silly romantic. He paid a fortune for it. I don't wear it often. To tell you the truth,' Beatrice lowered her voice, 'I don't care much for it, but I put it on for Len's sake. So that when he comes back, he will see that I am wearing his necklace and then he will forgive me. I am an idiot, I know!'

A novel by Françoise Sagan, *A Certain Smile*, lay on the coffee table beside an open, rather depleted, box of marrons glacés and a half-full glass of Tia Maria. Beatrice explained she had been trying to comfort herself and urged them to help themselves to marrons – or would they prefer drinks? 'Do sit down, please!' She then went into the kitchen and came back several moments later holding before her a tray loaded with cheese straws, smoked almonds and black Kalamata olives.

Only Beatrice and Major Payne had drinks. She stuck to brandy, which she drank out of an enormous globular glass, he had a whisky and soda. She saw him hold his pipe and insisted that he smoke it. She *adored* the smell of pipe tobacco. Payne told her, in serio-comical tones, how Antonia had banned him from smoking in their kitchen and Beatrice gasped in mock-horror– 'No.'

Something like an easy intimacy was developing between them. Antonia didn't like it at all. Beatrice leant towards Payne. 'I don't suppose you liked the drumbeats? It isn't everybody's cup of tea, I know. As a matter of fact that's the authentic sound of a North African courtship ceremony. Honestly. It was Len's idea.' Beatrice's nerves gave every appearance of having steadied themselves. 'You'd never believe this, *but Len serenaded me with it.*'

Payne was surprised. He'd have thought that something on the lines of 'Song at Twilight' would be more Colville's style. Or 'Fools Rush In', he thought unkindly as he watched Beatrice totter across the room on her high heels. Mistaking his look for one of sensual admiration, Antonia said in a voice that sounded over-loud, 'No news of Ingrid's whereabouts then? Since you reported her disappearance to the police?'

'No. No. Nothing... It was Len who reported it, actually. He has a friend at Scotland Yard. Arthur – Something-or-other?' Beatrice looked at Payne as though she expected him to know the man's surname. 'Len's already told Arthur about Ingrid, you see,' she went on. 'Oh, the police were awful! I was right not to want them told about Ingrid. That was the reason why Len got so very angry with me. The idiotic questions they asked! Was I sure it wasn't me who'd suggested it to Ingrid to dress up as me, as a sort of lark? Hadn't it really been *my* idea that she visit Ralph pretending to be me?'

'It wasn't your idea, was it?' Antonia said with a smile.

Beatrice stared at her. 'Shall I tell you something, but you *must* promise not to breathe a word?'

'Cross my heart and hope to die,' Payne said in solemn tones and he gave the Boy Scout salute.

'Well, you see, I *did* suggest that Ingrid dress up as me once, but that was aeons ago,' Beatrice said. 'I thought it might cheer her up. It did make her smile! I helped her with the make-up and everything. I did think it funny. Of course I never thought she'd want to do it again, if you know what I mean?'

'Did she look like you?' Payne asked.

'She did! It was uncanny. Oh, the police were ghastly. They gave me the third degree. All those questions! Hadn't I had concerns about Ingrid's state of mind before? Why had I failed to seek medical assistance? What medication had Ingrid been on? I was terribly vague about it and it made them suspicious. It doesn't take much to make

226

the police suspicious! I couldn't find any of Ingrid's prescriptions – all her pills seemed to have vanished from her room. She's probably thrown them away, wretched thing – she never liked the idea of being considered "loopy". Oh my God.' She clapped her hand over her mouth. 'Did you notice? I'm already talking about her *in the past tense!* I don't really believe that she is dead. I honestly don't, but somewhere, at the back of my mind I *must* be thinking it. Isn't that awful of me?'

'Did you see her on the morning she disappeared? Two days ago, was it? That was what the paper said.' Payne relit his pipe. '26th November?'

'Yes. No, I didn't see her, but she–' Beatrice broke off. 'All right, I'll tell you. I didn't tell Len. I lied to Len, and I lied to the police, but I will tell *you*. You see, she phoned me – it was the morning of 26th November, that's correct. Sometime after nine. Len and I were having brekkers.'

'Ingrid phoned you? Where from? Where was she?' Antonia asked.

'She said she was in Oxford – but she was in her room upstairs, so she must have rung me on her mobile! I didn't know at the time she was in her room. How do I know she was in her room? Well, apparently, she came down just a few minutes after I'd left. Len told me – he saw her! It never occurred to

227

me to doubt her when she said she was in Oxford – why should I? I suppose I am terribly naive. I told you she went out an awful lot. I was so happy when she said she wanted to see me.'

'Is that what she told you? That she wanted to see you?'

'Yes, she said she wanted to talk to me. *Urgently*. I was *so* glad. You see, I'd been trying to talk to her for the last month or so, ever since she stopped talking to me – but she wouldn't. And there she was now, asking me to meet her at a café in Oxford – a place called the Way to Heaven, not far from the Ashmolean Museum. She explained how to find it.'

'You went?'

'I did.'

'Why didn't you tell Colville?' Payne asked.

'Because, Hugh, I knew he'd fuss. He is a terrible fusspot. He'd have been scared Ingrid might do something to me. Len's too protective. Could be tedious about it. Don't you see? *He'd have tried to stop me.* So I lied to him. I told him I was going to the hairdresser's. That's why we had the row today, you see. He is convinced I'd gone to meet a man.' Beatrice looked at Payne fixedly, then rolled up her eyes. 'It's perfectly awful. You would never believe it, but Len is jealous.'

'Really?' Antonia said. Surprise, surprise,

she thought.

'*Yes*. I had no idea. Frightfully jealous.' Beatrice seemed pleased with her discovery. 'I was already cross with him, you see – *really* cross, for spilling the beans about Ingrid. I mean he told the police everything – the whole horror story, about Ralph and the accident and the dead baby and Ingrid coming to the hospital – I mean, *everything* – from start to finish. Oh, he looked terrible – bug-eyed and red and glistening. I thought he'd have a heart attack. I had no idea he hated her so much. He waved his arms in the air and raved and ranted like – like–'

'Like Lear of the heath?' Major Payne suggested. At once he put down his glass and cleared his throat. 'Sorry. Shouldn't be saying things like that.'

Beatrice giggled. 'Oh dear, yes. *Yes*. So apt. Quite impossible!' Then she became serious. 'Len let them see all those little girls – he had no right to! I mean the photos in Ingrid's room. He also showed them that poem Ingrid wrote ages ago – to prove how mad she was. He wasn't himself. He's been in a ghastly state these last couple of days. His battery has been discharging faster than it could charge. The police took copious notes. Len exaggerated terribly – that's what made me angry, you see. He made Ingrid sound like some dangerous lunatic – some homicidal maniac. Well, I was really nasty to

229

him afterwards. I mean – really nasty. I shouted at him and said some very unkind things. I should have been more under-standing but I lost my temper. Poor Len's got an awful lot on his mind. He is terribly worried about his letting business, poor pet.'

'What letting business?' Antonia asked.

'Len owns property. Several houses in London and in Oxford, which he rents out to people. He's got tenants,' Beatrice explained. 'Sounds a marvellous thing, doesn't it, being the wife of a *rentier*. Everybody immediately thinks of the Duke of Westminster. Oh, you've got houses – you must be rolling, everybody tells me, but the truth is the poor darling is not terribly good at it. He has had horrendous problems with some of his tenants. He's been losing pots of money – he's had three lawsuits in the last two months! I think *he's on the brink of bankruptcy*.'

'Surely not?' Major Payne said.

'I am afraid so. Yes. He doesn't want me to know, he doesn't want to upset me, but I've looked through his papers. Oh, he is too good, too decent, too unassuming, too *gentlemanly*.' Beatrice looked at Payne and lowered her eyes, as though to suggest that she considered him to be of that vanishing breed too.

'What exactly is the problem?' Antonia asked.

'Well, unscrupulous common people think of Len as a soft touch and they take advantage of him. *Everybody* has been taking advantage of him – his solicitors, his accountant, the estate agents – the exorbitant bills they send him! I couldn't believe my eyes. Quite ridiculous, really. Inflating the already bursting coffers of the legal profession! All right. Len is *not* terribly enterprising – it's simply not in his blood. The Colvilles are of the untitled aristocracy, you see. I know one shouldn't say things like that but on the other hand, why not?'

'They are all in the Landed Gentry,' murmured Payne.

'They are. A fine old yeoman stock. Once the backbone of the empire. The Colvilles go back to the sixteenth century – Henry VIII employed a Colville as his Esquire of the Body. Once upon a time they were frightfully rich and influential, but they have fallen on bad times – one of Len's cousins is being investigated for tax evasion – an aunt of his is in rehab – she is eighty-seven. Terribly depressing.'

'*Tempora mutantur.* Or should one say – *Sic transit gloria mundi?*' Payne said, putting his forefinger to his cheek – like Rodin's *Le Penseur*, Antonia thought. Or rather *Le Poseur* – if ever there was a statue of Major Hugh Payne, that was the inscription it should bear.

She said, 'So Ralph Renshawe's money will come in quite handy, I suppose?'

'Oh yes, Antonia. Dear me – yes! It will be the kiss of life Len needs – *we* need. The fairy godfather solution. I will let the poor darling have every penny he needs... Would you like another drink, Hugh?'

'No, thank you. Back to your secret assignation,' Payne went on. 'I assume Ingrid didn't turn up?'

'She didn't. I sat at a table and waited and drank I don't know how many cups of coffee, but she didn't come... What time did I get to Oxford? Well, at about ten to ten. I drove there in my car. We have two – Len drives a Peugeot. I found the café easily enough and I sat there until twenty past eleven. There was some perfectly dreadful man who sat at a nearby table. He made advances – offered to buy me a drink. He was quite insistent.'

'Did you accept?' Payne asked.

'Of course not. Hugh!' Beatrice giggled. 'Oh, the whole thing was so dreary! I don't really blame that man. I mean I was suspect – woman on her own, all made up and wearing a hat – he must have taken me for a tart, but then thank God Cressie de Villeneuve turned up – a dear, dear old chum of mine I hadn't seen for ages, so we went and had lunch together–' Beatrice broke off. 'What was the meaning of that phone call? Have you any ideas? I mean – *where is Ingrid?*'

There was a pause. Payne asked, 'Is Colville sure he saw her?'

'Positive. Ingrid was dressed up as me, wig and all. He saw her as she left the house and started walking in the direction of the bus stop – it's further down the road. The number 19 takes you to Coulston and it stops practically outside Ospreys... Len was standing by the window– Oh I'll show you!' Beatrice rose to her feet. 'He snapped her.'

'Snapped her?' Antonia echoed.

'I mean, took a photo of her – with the Polaroid.' Beatrice pointed to the camera lying on the small desk beside the window. 'He thought of it on the spur of the moment. He had a brainwave. He decided it would be a good idea to show Arthur – his Scotland Yard friend – what Ingrid got up to, in case Arthur didn't believe him.'

'Did he show the photo to the police?' Payne asked.

'He certainly did. They took it away with them, but there's a second photograph. Len took *two* photos.' Beatrice opened the top desk drawer and took out a photograph. 'It's got the date – and the exact time. 26th November, 9.12 a.m.... Look... Frightful, isn't it?' For a moment it looked as though Beatrice was going to sit on the arm of Payne's chair. 'Poor Ingrid. She does look like me on a bad day. She's put on weight.'

'She's wearing a jacket with your mono-gram on the breast pocket,' Antonia observed.

'Oh, *that* suit,' Beatrice said dismissively. '*So* '80s. Look at the horrible padded shoulders. To think that was all the rage, remember, Antonia? Power dressing! Always made me look *enormous*. I've only worn it once or twice. She's welcome to it.'

Payne said thoughtfully, 'So that was the last time she was ever seen... She asked you to go to Oxford while she – she went to Ospreys... We are assuming she went to Ospreys...'

'Why ask me to go to Oxford when she had no intention of going there herself?' Beatrice leant forward. 'Why send me on a wild-goose chase? Why ask me to wear dark glasses and a hat *and* insist I continue wearing them in the café? Why ask me to put on different lipstick? I did everything – to humour her. It made me look a bit like Joan Collins, but I followed her instructions to the letter. In case she came along, saw I didn't look the way she expected and left. Ingrid can be wildly temperamental.'

'She asked you to wear a hat and dark glasses at the café – and different lipstick?' Antonia was frowning. 'While she herself was dressed up as you... Ostentatiously so – with your initials emblazoned in gold on her chest, for the whole world to see...'

'I still don't understand–' Suddenly Beatrice gasped. 'No – I do. I do under-stand. Oh my God. *Oh my God.* I see it now. Antonia, you don't think she went to Ospreys to kill Ralph – and she wanted to make it look as though I had done it?'

'That's the likeliest explanation.'

'She must really hate me. Oh, how she must hate me,' Beatrice whispered. 'Well of course, it all makes perfect sense now. The ingenuity of it! *She didn't want me to have an alibi for the time she was at Ospreys.* She didn't want me to be recognized by anyone who saw me at the café. *I was to be her scapegoat.* Oh my God. And she warned me *not* to tell Len where I was going! It all fits in. Oh, why does she hate me so much? Why?'

'Your marriage,' Antonia said. 'Your part in her daughter's death. What *she* sees as your part in her daughter's death.'

'So you do believe she heard me – the other night? As I was telling you about it? When she came in?'

'Yes.'

'All right. *All right.* Let's be rational about it,' Beatrice said. 'Ingrid was last seen going to Ospreys. Let's assume she was going to Ospreys. Did she disappear *before* she got to the house – or could it have been *after?*'

'That,' Major Payne said, 'is the million dollar question. Before – or after?'

'Well, she didn't kill Ralph, that's for

certain. We'd have known by now if she had. The police phoned Ospreys from here, as it happened – a nurse answered – a male nurse, apparently – everything seemed to be fine. I mean Ralph is alive.'

Payne cleared his throat. 'Renshawe was going to change his will in your favour on the morning of the 26th – correct?'

Beatrice stared at him out of guileless doll-like eyes and spoke breathlessly. 'Yes. Yes. He said he'd instructed his solicitor to go to Ospreys at eleven in the morning, but I have absolutely no idea whether their meeting took place or not.'

She spoke as though she had forgotten all about it – or as though it couldn't matter less. Antonia felt sure her indifference was feigned.

'Len was dismissive about the whole thing. He thinks it was just the ramblings of a mortally ill man,' Beatrice went on. 'But Ingrid *couldn't* have known about the will, could she? I am dreadfully befuddled now. If Ingrid did go to Ospreys, it was to kill Ralph as an act of revenge and make me take the rap for it... It couldn't possibly have had anything to do with the will, could it?'

'No. Though I have a feeling the changing of the will may be important in some way,' Major Payne said. 'If Renshawe had died *before* eleven o'clock in the morning, you wouldn't have become his sole beneficiary.

Only he didn't. Who was the beneficiary from the previous will, do you know?'

'Ralph's nephew Robin,' Beatrice answered promptly. 'Ralph told me when he phoned, you see. Said Robin had been a great disappointment. He said Robin was forty, but hadn't done an honest day's work in his life.'

'Renshawe has an idler of a nephew, eh? Is he a Catholic too? Forty – same age as Father Lillie-Lysander,' Payne said in a thoughtful voice. 'Do you know anything about Father Lillie-Lysander? That's the priest who visited Renshawe.'

'No, I don't.' Beatrice shook her head. 'Oh my God. The Catholic priest! He too has disappeared, hasn't he?'

'He has.'

'I read about it in the paper. Do you think there is a *connection* between him and Ingrid?'

'Both of them knew Ralph Renshawe,' Antonia said. 'They visited him at Ospreys. Father Lillie-Lysander was Ralph's father confessor. It is not inconceivable that they did bump into one another at some point. They disappeared on the same day. I believe that is a line of inquiry the police will want to follow – are probably following at this very moment.'

'*Assassins at Ospreys*. I don't know why I said that. Sorry.' Payne waved his hand. 'It just struck me as a damned good title for a detective novel.'

'It's fantastically clever,' Beatrice breathed. 'Alliterative – or do I mean onomatopoeic?'

Antonia said nothing. Her face remained blank. She would never use a title like that, *never*, she determined.

There was a pause. 'I think it's time we went to Ospreys again and took a look round,' Payne said, glancing at his watch. 'It's half past three. What do you say, my love?'

'Excellent idea,' Beatrice said. The next moment she giggled and her hand went up to her lips. 'Sorry!'

'All right,' Antonia said. I can't believe she did that, Antonia thought.

'Did you say "again"? Have you already been to Ospreys?' Beatrice frowned.

'Yes. We did go to Ospreys the day we came here, or rather the night,' Payne explained. 'We wanted to make sure Renshawe was all right. But we found no one at the house.'

'That must have been when Ralph was rushed to hospital. As a matter of fact, I too want to go to Ospreys,' Beatrice declared. 'I'd like to come with you, if I may... *Please.*'

'Well, you are perfectly entitled to a visit. After all, he did ask you to visit him,' Major Payne said. 'I think it's time Ralph Renshawe saw the person to whom he left his fortune. The real Beatrice Ardleigh.'

21

Without a Clue

'...but the priest, as you say, got in her way – perhaps he tried to defend Ralph Renshawe, so she killed him. Then she panicked and fled. It *could* have happened that way, but then if it did, where is Father Lillie-Lysander's body? You couldn't get any sense out of Ralph Renshawe, could you?'

'No. We did try. I don't think he was aware who we were. He kept talking gibberish. Said that when one's mind was fixed on death, everything started to spiral and to magnify. He asked if I knew how many spirals there were. Then he told me: double helixes, spiral galaxies and corkscrews.' Inspector Hopper tapped his forehead with a forefinger.

'Ralph Renshawe is gravely ill, isn't he?'

'Yes. Dying, apparently. Cancer. There was a nurse there – a man – not the original nurse – he was new. South African. Came last night. There's no other staff, which is odd enough for a big house like that. We are trying to track down Nurse Wilkes. She left yesterday. Seems to have gone off. Somewhere abroad, I gathered. She's been with Ralph for a couple of months at least. She might be able to tell us something. Did she let Ingrid Delmar into the house? Was the priest already there? Did she see the priest go? It's odd, her leaving so suddenly...'

'It is odd, yes... You found nothing of interest at Ospreys?'

'No. It all seemed in perfect order. Nothing suspicious. We saw no need for a proper search at this stage.'

'Perhaps the murder took place outside. Perhaps Ingrid ran into the priest as he was leaving. He might have become suspicious – realized that she wasn't Beatrice Ardleigh – and challenged her? That was when she killed him – she might have had a knife – or cracked his skull with something heavy – picked up a stone. Then she put him into the boot of her car – no, she hadn't a car. But if she did kill the priest, what did she do with the body?'

'Hid it somewhere on the grounds... Or inside the house?'

'Could she have done that – dragged the body into the house?'

'No. I don't see how – not without the nurse becoming aware of it. It was broad daylight – morning.'

'Nurse Wilkes would have heard the noise... There'd have been blood... Perhaps Nurse Wilkes was in on it too. Wilkes might have helped Ingrid dispose of the body?'

'She might have... Well, we should get a warrant, go back to Ospreys and do a proper search. Yes. It's imperative that we speak to Nurse Wilkes... Where *is* Ingrid Delmar? Where's she vanished to?'

'On the run. Hiding somewhere. At some hotel. Some B and B. Skulking under a bridge. She's a nutcase. Keen on revenge. Pretending to be the other one. All those photos of little girls in her room. She claimed they were her daughter. And she wrote a poem – "Madrigals for Mad Girls". Serious hair-raising stuff. She should never have been allowed to walk free. We'll get her sooner or later. She's conspicuous enough, with her black gloves and blood-red hand.'

'If she keeps her gloves on, her blood-red hand won't be noticed... She might be dead.'

'You mean it's the other way round? The priest killed Ingrid?'

'I meant she might have committed suicide. She's harmed herself in the past, hasn't she?'

'She has. Apparently she talked about suicide – discussed ways of doing it. Been violent too.'

'Couldn't get over the loss of her unborn child. Leonard Colville said so and Beatrice Ardleigh confirmed it. She confirmed it rather reluctantly. Great tension between those two. Haven't been married long. He was keen to tell us all about Ingrid's madness and masquerades, and she wasn't too pleased... Sensible chap. I found Beatrice Ardleigh's attitude rather puzzling.'

'What is she like?'

'Beatrice Ardleigh?' Inspector Hopper frowned. 'Speaking unprofessionally, I'd say kittenish, stupid-clever and, in normal circumstances, I imagine, an amusing talker – but circumstances were far from normal.'

'Attractive?'

'Attractive... She bit her lip when I suggested she might have had a hand in this dressing-up business – avoided my eye... Denied it of course, but I think she's in it, somehow... Looked guilty as hell... Strange business.'

'You don't think Beatrice knows where Ingrid is – that she might be helping her hide somewhere? Or could Ingrid be lurking somewhere inside Ospreys? Whacking pile of a place, you said – most of the rooms not in use?'

'Yes. Furniture shrouded in sheets, from what I could see. You mean she might be lying doggo, hiding under one of those? Well, she might – she's a nutcase. What was that?'

'*Monster in the Closet*... There was a film of that name – saw it as a teenager twenty years or so ago. Scared the hell out of me.'

'Don't get too fanciful, Bancroft,' Inspector Hopper said. 'Let's see about that search warrant, shall we?'

22

The Monster in the Closet

Antonia had the feeling that in the course of the conversation something very important had been said – or was it something she had seen? Some object in the sitting room at Millbrook? Yes. She believed it was something visual rather than verbal...

Something that belonged to Beatrice... Yes... What *was* it? Antonia shut her eyes and thought back. High heels? Necklace? Scent? It would come to her. It always did. Soon, she hoped. Cocktail dress? Cigarette? Golden hair? (Beatrice didn't wear a wig, did she? No. Beatrice's hair was her own. It was Ingrid who wore a wig, to make herself look like Beatrice.)

No, that was all wrong – it was something that *shouldn't* have been there.

What an odd thought. Antonia opened her eyes. What exactly did she mean by that?

They were in the car bound for Ospreys. Major Payne was driving and he expressed the hope that they would not clash with the police. If the house was under some sort of guardianship, they would certainly not be

243

allowed in. The police didn't like amateur investigators meddling in their business.

'Why are amateur detectives always cleverer than the police?' Beatrice looked at Antonia over her shoulder. Beatrice's spirits appeared to have revived completely. She sat next to Payne in front while Antonia sat in the back of the car. Antonia didn't quite know how that had happened.

'It's a convention in detective fiction,' she said.

'Don't you think you should break it? Isn't that what conventions are for?' Beatrice laughed. 'I mean, write a novel in which things happen *the other way round?* Have the amateur detective lose the battle of wits to the professional policeman?'

'A jolly good idea,' Payne agreed heartily. 'Don't you think?' He addressed Antonia, but she remained silent. She was annoyed because he was right. It *was* a good idea.

'Just imagine we are characters in a detective novel,' Beatrice went on after a pause. 'We are hurrying towards the scene of a crime, but it is only the author who decides what is going to happen next... Perhaps the author doesn't even know at this point who the victim is – he may not even know who the killer is going to be. That's quite scary, don't you think? I mean it could be *anyone*. It could be the padre – it could be Ingrid – it could be Ralph – it could even be me!'

'Yes, it could even be you,' Antonia agreed. 'What was that called? *Meta*fiction?'

Showing off, Antonia thought – trying to impress Hugh.

Beatrice had spent half an hour in her room, getting ready. Her make-up, when she appeared, was revealed as flawless. She had changed into a wasp-waisted tweed suit and more conventional but still smart shoes. She had replaced the rather embarrassing Taj Mahal necklace with a string of pearls. She wore a scarf of unusual yellow-green colour – *yerba de mate*, she told Antonia – intricately wound round her head and had elegant dark glasses on. She looked as though she might have stepped down from some 1950s advertisement... Advertising what? The best way to steal a husband, that's what, Antonia thought. There'd be a bubble coming out of her mouth, saying, *Husband-snatching is such fun.*

Beatrice kept leaning towards Hugh, laying her hand on his arm. She was doing it again now, at this very moment. She was laughing. He had said something, which had amused her. Antonia pursed her lips. She regretted not having got in front first. Was she being unreasonable?

'That's not how it happens in real life, is it?' Beatrice went on. 'How many private investigators do you know who tumble to the truth while the police fail lamentably?

Are there private investigators any more?'

'They are in the Yellow Pages, apparently. I have never checked, so don't quote me,' Payne said.

Beatrice looked over her shoulder once more. 'Do you know any private detectives, Antonia?'

Antonia said she didn't.

Beatrice then asked whether they went to the theatre and the opera often. Living in London they probably went every week? No, not every week, Antonia said. Beatrice missed London terribly. Wallingford was utter ghastly drears – a cultural desert, really. Not a single person to have a decent conversation with. Nothing but tiresome county types. Philistines and oh so smug with it! A woman called Pamela Montdore had referred to Beatrice as the 'soul of pampered self-absorption', which Beatrice had found extremely hurtful. Len seemed keen on cultivating the friendship of a husband-and-wife duo called Sutcliffe, but she couldn't stand them, Beatrice said.

She went on speaking in a wistful voice. Even when they did go to London, things happened to prevent her from enjoying herself. Len grumbled about parking and he hated the sight of too many people. Len wasn't terribly keen on theatre, and he was even less enthusiastic about opera. He fell asleep during a performance of *Othello* and afterwards it had taken Beatrice *ages* to explain about the significance of the handkerchief.

Beatrice looked over her shoulder. *Othello* was one of the first psychological thrillers, wasn't it? *And* it contained elements of the classical detective story – that handkerchief – so clever! Well, yes, Antonia agreed. There was a pause, then for no apparent reason Antonia's husband started telling Beatrice how to make an Opera cocktail. He listed the ingredients: gin, red Dubonnet and maraschino liqueur.

'Sounds awful,' Antonia said.

'Not so if you shake it properly with ice and strain it into an appropriate chilled glass!'

'Delicious. I would love to try it,' said Beatrice. 'Hugh, may I have a light?' She had produced a cigarette from a silver case, which she was holding in an inexperienced, almost gauche, manner, as though she had no idea what to do with it. The femme fatale had been replaced by an ingénue. Beatrice suddenly seemed utterly helpless. For a moment it looked as though Hugh was going to abandon the wheel and strike a match for her – she seemed to expect it. Antonia gasped in horror – they were just about to negotiate a roundabout!

'I smoke nothing but Turkish. One can only get them at a little place in New Bond

Street,' Beatrice said. 'They are a treat, really – I smoke only rarely and I *don't* inhale.'

Antonia was seething. What was Beatrice giving herself a treat for? For succeeding in vamping Hugh? Why had she dolled herself up, if not for Hugh's delectation? What a bitch, she thought. She didn't trust her one little bit. She wouldn't be surprised if Beatrice turned out to have killed both Ingrid *and* the priest. Well, a fabulous fortune was at stake – and Beatrice had admitted to an agonized craving for the *luxe*.

Who will rid me of this turbulent priest? Antonia didn't think Father Lillie-Lysander was anything like Thomas à Becket. Now, why would Beatrice want to kill the priest? She might want to kill Ingrid to prevent her from killing Ralph and thus make it possible for him to sign his new will – but why kill the priest? Unless the priest was another assassin? Assassins at Ospreys. How ridiculous.

Antonia knew she was being irrational. Well, she was jealous. Extremely jealous. Terrible thing, jealousy. It made her feel insecure. Hugh had denied being attracted to Beatrice – did he tell the truth? That was how things had started with her first husband – it had been the beginning of the end–

Soon after, they reached Ospreys.

Ingrid came to, slowly. She tried to rise and a sharp pain pierced her head – she had banged it against some hard surface. The left side of her face was numb. She felt confused and disoriented. She could smell petrol and oil. She wondered if she had been in an accident. Or was it a dream? Was she dreaming about *the* accident? She sometimes did, though not recently... Where *was* she?

Her hands – something had happened to her hands. She couldn't feel her hands! Had they *gone?* No – her hands were behind her back – tied – they had gone numb, that's why she didn't feel them.

How dark it was. She seemed to be in a box of some kind. For some reason she thought of a closet or a small wardrobe. No, she was horizontal, not vertical. A coffin, she thought. I am in a coffin. Not only bound but gagged. She could hardly breathe because there was a rag of some sort in her mouth and some kind of sticky tape across the lower part of her face. The rag – was it a handkerchief? – reeked of something, a smell she knew well. She could only breathe through her nose, just about.

Her head hurt badly, where the blow had fallen. She believed she had bled from the side of her head. She could smell blood. She could taste it too. Her lip had burst. Well, she was no stranger to blood. Years ago she had used to cut her arms and thighs. The sight of blood had excited her. She hadn't minded the pain one little bit. Each time she made a cut, she wanted to see how deep she could go...

Ingrid's legs were numb too. She tried stretching them and failed. She tried wriggling her toes but couldn't do that either. She had lost all feeling. Pinpricks sparkled faintly through her calves... She was bound and gagged. She was incarcerated. She was at her enemy's mercy–

Her enemy. Who was her enemy? If only she could think more clearly...

Minutes went by... Hours... Ingrid had no idea how many. She must have passed out and then come to. She made an effort to remember what exactly had happened. She tried to trace the exact sequence of events that led to her being placed inside this ... coffin? Was she *really* in a coffin? Had she been buried alive? A premature burial, like in Poe... Well, she remembered being dragged across the garden – someone pulling her by the shoulders... She also remembered the knife glistening in the sun... That had been earlier on.

Ingrid had got on a bus – then – then she had arrived at Ospreys. She had walked up the drive. There had been rooks again, circling above her head, shrieking. Yes. She remembered the rooks. She had known at once there was something wrong. The rooks were her friends and they had been trying to warn her. She had started running...

She had arrived late, not at the time she intended. And the reason? Something had distracted her. She had seen a little girl on the bus – for a moment she had thought this was her daughter, her little Claire, but of course that was impossible. If her daughter had lived, Ingrid reasoned, she would have been thirty now. Ingrid had stood gazing at the girl, listening to her prattle to her little brother. She had wanted to reach out and stroke her fair curls – pinch her cheek. She wanted to pick her up and give her a kiss–

She had missed her stop, that was it! She'd had to walk back. That was why she had had to run... Yes... Across the garden... How the rooks had screeched and flapped their wings! Catching sight of the well, she made a wish. *Please, Mighty God Rook, let me be the first to get to Ralph.*

She had opened her bag and taken out the knife. She had wondered whether the priest would be there already. Her thoughts came back to her. *I'll be damned if I let him kill Ralph. With a soft pillow? An easy death? Oh no. That is not the death Ralph deserves.* She had heard the priest talk about using a pillow into his mobile the day before – she had been concealed among the rose bushes in that overgrown garden.

The priest had been talking to Ralph's nephew. What was the nephew's name? Robin? Yes. Ralph didn't trust Robin – well, with good reason! How funny that there should have been a *second* plot to kill Ralph – the kind of thing Antonia Darcy might have dreamt up. *Assassins at Ospreys* – some such ridiculous title.

So she had been right about the priest. She knew that he was a dodgy one the moment she laid eyes on him, though a less likely hired killer one could not possibly imagine. Who would get to Ralph first? She had liked the challenge. She'd relished the adrenalin rush. She had been convinced she'd beat the podgy padre to it, oh yes, she had no doubt.

As Ingrid came round the corner of the terrace, however, she heard the priest's voice coming from inside Ralph's room. Father Lillie-Lysander was speaking in conversational tones. *Did you say your solicitor was coming at eleven? You are definitely leaving all your money to Miss Ardleigh? No change of heart?* She realized at once the french windows of Ralph's room were open. Exactly as she'd anticipated them to be on a warm day like that. The priest had beaten her to it! Well, no – not quite. Not yet. *Ralph was still alive.* There was time. She had halted and now she looked down at the knife in her hand. The blade caught the sun and for a moment she had been dazzled. She remembered her thoughts: *Now I will have to kill the priest as well.*

She had started walking across the terrace but the next moment had stopped short.

She had stood and stared.

She hadn't been able to believe her eyes—

23

Lord of the Flies

'Good afternoon,' Beatrice said with her most winning smile, removing her dark glasses and revealing her bright green eyes. 'I'd like to see Ralph – Mr Renshawe, that is. I've been to see him several times before. Would you tell him that it is Beatrice? My name is Beatrice Ardleigh. He knows me very well, yes.'

She was a born liar. Despite herself, Antonia found herself admiring Beatrice's chutzpah. What poise – what sangfroid – what confidence! Bee hadn't batted an eyelid. Or was that unfair? Well, she *was* Beatrice Ardleigh – but she had never been to Ospreys before.

They had had to knock hard – the doorbell still didn't work. The young man who had opened the door wore spotless white overalls. He was fair-haired and had a pleasant face. He was the gentle giant type and spoke with a South African accent. He had *I Love Cape* tattooed on his muscular right forearm. Antonia saw Beatrice shoot him an appreciative look. He was smiling broadly. A male nurse? Antonia had expected a woman. Ralph had mentioned a woman called Wilkes, Beatrice told them.

'Sure, madam. Come in... Your friends too. That's fine. I am new here, but I'm sure it's all right for friends of Mr Renshawe to visit him. My name is Greg. Mr Renshawe hasn't been too bad, to tell you the truth. His appetite seems to be returning. He actually asked me to make him crème caramel!' Greg held open the door for Payne and Antonia. 'That was what he used to love eating best when he was a boy... He also asked me to bring him a feather fan that had belonged to a lady friend of his!'

They walked into a gloomy hall where it felt distinctly cooler than outside. Major Payne looked round. Empty, but for two Pugin chairs and a rusty suit of armour that seemed to have been made to accommodate a colossus. William and Adelaide gothick wallpaper. Was it *faux?* No – it looked authentic. He ran his hand across the wall – felt authentic too. The great staircase was made of black wrought iron and had red mahogany balustrades. Glancing up he saw angel faces with sly heavy-lidded eyes and outspread wings that seemed to have sprouted from the back of their heads hanging suspended from the hammer-beam vault above. They brought to mind monstrous bats poised for flight – or attack more likely, by the look of it, which was not what one would have expected from angels – something jolly unsettling about them – he felt they couldn't be trusted. Surely that was not the way angels were supposed to affect one?

'I will try to get as much out of him as possible,' Payne heard Beatrice whisper.

'This way, madam.' Greg pointed to a door. 'Oh, you know it – you've been here before.'

They watched Beatrice trip across the hall – as though she had done it hundreds of times – as though the place belonged to her! As she opened the door, they heard a thin voice pipe up, 'Bee, my dear – is that you? How lovely to see you!'

The situation was curious, to say the least – well, surreal. Would Ralph see it was not the same one? Antonia wondered. And would it make any difference to his decision to leave his money to her if he did?

'Would you like a drink? There's orange juice and iced tea.'

'Good idea. Thank you,' Payne said and they followed Greg down a long corridor into the kitchen.

The kitchen was a large cavernous room with a round oak table in the middle. All the windows were open. 'You wouldn't think it was November, would you? All these flies and bluebottles! They keep coming in.' Greg waved his hand.

'It's hot. They've crept out of their hibernation pad.' Major Payne produced his pipe. He started patting his pockets.

'If you smoke, they'll probably go,' Greg said. He went up to the fridge and took out a jug full of orange juice. It was very fresh. He had squeezed it himself some quarter of an hour earlier. The old man – he meant Mr Renshawe – loved orange juice. Mr Renshawe ate next to nothing, but he loved his orange juice.

'You said there's been an improvement?'

'Well, yes, ma'am. I was told Mr Renshawe had been pretty bad, expected to die any minute, but he didn't strike me as a dying man when I saw him. And he's been even better today.'

'You made him a crème caramel,' Payne murmured.

'That's excellent news,' Antonia said.

'It is, ma'am. I don't like it when my patients die.' Greg poured juice into two tall glasses. He looked across at Payne. 'Aren't you going to light your pipe, sir? The nasty creatures are sure to fly out, if you do, I reckon.'

'Sorry. Can't find my tobacco pouch. Bloody nuisance. Don't know what's become of it. So you are new?'

'Yes, sir. I arrived last night. Here you are, ma'am. Sir.' Greg handed them the glasses.

257

'The agency supplied me with instructions. I met Mr Saunders. He was here, waiting for me. Mr Saunders is Mr Renshawe's solicitor.'

Antonia asked what happened to the woman who used to work for Ralph. Did Greg know where she went?

'Nurse Wilkes? Oh, she left, ma'am. It was very sudden. She got a lot of money, Mr Saunders let drop. I think she won the lottery or Premium Bonds or something. Going to get married on one of those ocean liners, apparently. Lucky girl!'

'Lucky in love as well as at cards or indeed the lottery. Doesn't happen often.' Payne shot a glance at Antonia and saw her give a meaningful nod. Jolly timely, he thought. A double disappearance and the nurse suddenly exits the stage. Unusual coincidences were always interesting. Still, one mustn't jump to conclusions. 'I suppose that's her knitting over there?' He pointed to a side table with the stem of his pipe.

'I don't know, sir, but it must be hers, yes. It was there when I arrived.' Greg laughed. 'Seems she no longer wants to knit!'

'She can't anyhow – not with one needle.' Payne had strolled over to the side table and picked up the knitting. He stroked his jaw with a thoughtful forefinger. 'Where's the other needle, do you know?'

Greg shrugged his massive shoulders.

'Haven't seen it anywhere. Lost, I guess.'

'Did Nurse Wilkes leave other things unfinished or undone? Tasks for you to complete?' Payne went on in casual tones.

'Well, not that much – the place was spick-and-span.' Greg stood with his arms folded before him. 'I am talking about the ground floor. I don't know what the situation is upstairs. It's a big house. So I haven't had to do much. Apart from those bloody sheets.'

'I'd have hated to arrive at a place and start cleaning. This is delicious.' Antonia took another sip of orange juice.

Greg frowned. 'I did try to wash them but they were completely ruined, so in the end I threw them away.'

Payne cocked an eyebrow. 'When you said "bloody", did you mean it as an impolite term of exasperation – or did you mean the sheets were covered in blood?'

'Covered in blood, sir. There seems to have been some sort of an accident. With Nurse Wilkes or the old man. There were bed sheets and three pillowcases and a pair of pyjamas – Mr Renshawe's pyjamas, they had his monogram on the breast pocket – all bloodstained. Actually I don't think Mr Renshawe cut himself or anything like that. I'd have noticed but there wasn't a scratch on him, so it must have been Nurse Wilkes.'

'Could she have bled over Renshawe and his bed?' Payne murmured.

'That's what I wondered, sir. Nurse Wilkes had put the bloodied things into the washing machine and seemed to have forgotten about them. It was useless trying to wash them. So, as I said, I put them in a bin-liner and threw them away.'

'Did you ask Mr Renshawe what happened?'

'I did, sir. He said he had no idea what I was talking about. He seemed annoyed. He told me to dispose of the sheets at once. He seemed pleased when I told him I'd already done so.'

'How very interesting,' Payne said thoughtfully. 'Um. Changing the subject, do you know whether Nurse Wilkes used to do any knitting in Renshawe's room?'

Patterns, Antonia thought. He is as bad as me – trying to fit seemingly random details into a recognizable logical pattern.

'It's funny you should ask that, sir.' Greg smiled. 'The first time Mr Renshawe saw me, he asked whether I could knit. Said he'd got used to needles clicking in the background. He found the sound soothing. I said I couldn't. He said that perhaps I should take up knitting. I don't know whether he was joking or not. He seemed serious, but then I don't know Mr Renshawe well. He does say funny things – fancy him asking me to bring him that feather fan!'

'Very funny, yes,' Payne said.

Some men knitted as therapy, Antonia said. Knitting was proven to have a calming effect on people recovering from nervous breakdowns. Hadn't the Duke of Windsor been fond of knitting? Or did she mean embroidery?

'So Nurse Wilkes *did* knit in Renshawe's room.' Major Payne felt the point of the knitting needle with a forefinger. 'Ouch! This *is* sharp. It isn't the smell of blood that's attracting the bluebottles, is it?'

'Oh. You are probably right, sir. The bin-liners are still outside. There is a collection tomorrow. There were a lot of bluebottles in the garden this morning. They seem to be coming from the direction of–'

'Did you mention the bloodied sheets to the police, Greg?' Antonia asked.

He blinked. 'Sorry, ma'am?'

'The police were here, weren't they? Earlier today?'

The young man gaped slightly, revealing perfect teeth. 'How ... how did you know? Two policemen did come earlier on. Yes. About an hour ago. Very polite gentlemen. Nothing like South African police. They wanted to know if I knew anything about the Catholic priest who used to visit Mr Renshawe. The priest seems to have disappeared. I told them I didn't know anything. I told them I was new.'

'Did they want to know anything else?'

261

'They asked whether Miss Beatrice Ardleigh had been to see Mr Renshawe. I said no one has been to the house, not while I've been here... Oh, was that the lady who came with you? Your friend?' Greg looked towards the door.

'Yes. The very same.' Payne nodded. Only it wasn't. How terribly confusing. One kept forgetting. The police had meant Ingrid Delmar, dressed up as Beatrice Ardleigh. The police knew the whole story now.

'The police also asked for Nurse Wilkes' address, but I said I didn't know it,' Greg went on. 'I am afraid they didn't find me very helpful. Then they wanted to speak to Mr Renshawe and they let me stay in the room, but they didn't get anything out of him either. Mr Renshawe wasn't himself. Mr Renshawe kept talking about angels and demons and that there was a constant battle in the heavens. Then he started talking about spirals.' Greg laughed. 'I saw them exchange looks and shake their heads. They couldn't get any sense out of him, which was funny because Mr Renshawe recovered the moment they left!'

'Did he now?' Payne murmured. He had started walking slowly towards one of the open windows.

'Yes! That's when he asked me to make him the crème caramel, sir.'

'How terribly interesting. Did the police

262

search the premises?' Payne could hear a buzzing sound – bluebottles?

'Search the premises?' Greg looked startled. 'Oh no, sir. They were very polite, very pleasant. Real gentlemen. They only asked if anyone else lived at Ospreys and I said, no one. Apart from Mr Renshawe and me, that is. I did tell them that Mr Renshawe was a very sick gentleman, but they could see that for themselves. Then they left.'

'So you didn't mention the bloodied sheets to them?' Antonia said.

'Well, no, I didn't think it was important. Do you think it is, madam?'

It was Payne who answered – he was now standing by the window, looking out. 'I think so. Yes... Extremely important.' He spoke absently. 'Lots of bluebottles outside, you are perfectly right. Where are Ralph Renshawe's windows? I can't work it out... That monstrosity over there must be Moira Montano's pink conservatory?' He pointed.

'Whose conservatory, sir?'

'Moira Montano. She was a B-movie actress. Well before your time. I imagine she made films with titles like *Stains of Scarlet* and *The Reek of Dread*... Are the bin-liners somewhere on this side?'

'Oh no, sir. On the other side.' Greg waved his hand towards the door that led to the garden.

'That's odd then because the buzzing's

definitely coming from somewhere this side... Are those Renshawe's french windows?' Payne pointed again.

'Yes, sir. Those are Mr Renshawe's windows.' Greg had joined Payne beside the kitchen window.

'And what's that thing over there in the garden?' Payne shaded his eyes. 'Not a well, surely?'

'It is a well, sir. An ancient wishing well, Mr Renshawe said. That's where the buzzing is coming from, I guess, sir. I meant to go and investigate.'

'Let's go and do it now, shall we?' Payne turned towards Antonia. 'The well is in a direct line from Renshawe's windows.' Something in his voice made Antonia look sharply at him.

'Shall I lead the way, sir?'

'By all means, old boy. Am I right in thinking you've been in the army?'

'Yes, sir. For two years.'

'What I thought. Good man.'

Antonia and Major Payne followed Greg out of the kitchen door and into the garden. They turned left, then left again...

The garden resembled a jungle, Antonia thought. She was conscious of a rising sense of uneasiness inside her. Yews and birches and, startlingly, tall bedraggled Chinese palms – as well as rose bushes that were as tall as the trees – all interwoven with ivy and various other creepers. And weeds, weeds everywhere. They passed a dilapidated grotto bench with fantastic undersea carvings and a pagoda-like structure, shrouded in ivy. It was the kind of landscape one associated with the Sleeping Beauty's castle...

Greg had stopped and he raised his hand. 'Those are Mr Renshawe's windows.'

Like a bloodhound on the scent, Payne advanced to the steps leading up to the dilapidated terrace. The stone surface was invisible under a carpet of dead leaves. The french windows were ajar and Payne caught sight of Beatrice sitting on a straight-backed Empire chair beside the bed in which Ralph Renshawe sat propped up among several pillows.

A toad-like, even Gila-monsterish, face the colour of mouldy old bone, but the eyes struck Payne as bright and animated. Not the eyes of a dying man. Renshawe was wearing an outlandish garb – what appeared to be a Japanese kimono in apricot and black, and across his lap lay a large white feather fan. Major Payne was put in mind of Graham Sutherland's controversial portrait of the octogenarian Somerset Maugham that had made the grand old man of letters look like the dissolute madam of a Shanghai brothel.

Stationing himself between an empty plant tub made of black marble and an ornate, rusting wire garden chair, Payne took in more details. There was a crucifix on the wall above Renshawe's head. Renshawe was holding Beatrice's left hand between the skeletal fingers of both his. He has no idea it's a different one, Payne thought – or has he? Renshawe was saying something. Beatrice was leaning towards him, nodding her blonde head as though in agreement. She had a very serious expression on her face. They looked like fellow conspirators. Not a word could be heard. Payne wondered what he was saying to her.

A moment later Payne walked back and rejoined Greg and Antonia. Suddenly he didn't seem to be in a hurry at all. He stood looking at the well. It appeared he was trying to estimate the distance between the well and Ralph Renshawe's windows. 'You don't think–?' Antonia began.

'I don't know, my love, but it strikes me as a definite possibility. See these rusty stains?' Payne had kicked at a heap of dead leaves on the ground. Antonia frowned, then nodded. 'You'd better tighten your tummy. It may not be a pleasant sight.'

Greg was the first to notice the little cloud that hovered above the well. 'Bluebottles! I thought so! Sir, shall I–?'

'Go on, old boy. Lead the way.'

Spotting an oblong piece of cardboard in a clump of yellow grass, Payne stooped over and picked it up. No, not an ordinary piece of cardboard. He turned it over. Gilt edges. Somebody's visiting card. *Robin Renshawe, Gentleman of Leisure.* The nefarious nephew, eh? He whom Uncle Ralph had disinherited. Had the rogue Robin been here then?

'Would be remarkable if he really did drop his card, just like that,' Antonia pointed out. 'That was blood, wasn't it?'

'I think so. Let's follow the buzzing trail.'

Above them the rooks screamed and flapped their wings. The silly things appeared to be in quite a state. Antonia stopped for a moment and gazed up. As the three of them drew nearer to the well, the ferocious buzzing increased... The cloud moved slightly to one side but didn't disperse entirely – not even when Greg waved his arms at it.

Antonia gasped as a fresh swarm of flies burst out of the well the moment they stood beside it. Furious at the disruption of their unspeakable feast, she thought. For a moment she feared she might disgrace herself and be sick.

'This wouldn't have happened if the weather had been cooler,' said Payne.

'Some animal must have fallen into the well, I guess.'

'Animal... I imagine you've seen a great

many terrible things in the veldt?'

Greg looked at him with a frown. 'You don't think it's something else, do you, sir?'

'As a matter of fact, old boy, I do think it's something else.'

Greg leant over the edge of the well and looked inside. He kept brushing away at the flies with his right hand. 'There's something inside. I can see it–'

'What is it?'

'Something black, ma'am. No, *white* – round – covered in flies!' The next moment Greg swore. 'What the devil's that?'

He had drawn back as though he'd been stung by something. 'It's – it's a face, sir! A human face! I swear. There's a face down there – somebody inside – looking up! I saw the eyes – the mouth too, gaping open. I can't tell if it's a man or a woman but they are dead – covered in flies – must be dead!'

24

Unholy Dying

She had been deceiving him. She had been carrying on outrageously behind his back. She'd been having an affair. She had set all discretion at defiance and thrown every caution to the winds–

She had had her lover in the house.

Dazed and dismayed, Colville stood in the middle of the sitting room, staring down at the tobacco pouch in his hand. He was overcome with violent giddiness and feared he might collapse. Earlier on he had managed to persuade himself that he was wrong, that he had been imagining it all, that there was an innocent explanation for things. He was a fool! Well, here was the proof now – the absolute, irrefutable proof of Bee's perfidy.

An arch betrayer of true love. That had been said about Marie Antoinette but the description fitted Bee perfectly. Bee was like one of those shiny apples which you bite into, only to spit out the brown rotten flesh. A Jezebel of a woman. Nothing but a two-faced whore.

He had already phoned Alessandro's, Bee's hairdresser's in Oxford. No, they hadn't had a power cut. They never had power cuts. The woman who answered Colville's call had sounded extremely surprised. Was the gentleman by any chance from the Health and Safety department? Colville put down the receiver. No. Of course there had been no power cut. He had always known that was a lie. He had then rung Tiddly Dolls, the absurdly named restaurant, and asked the manageress – a Mrs Derwent-Delahaye – if a golden-haired woman with green eyes had had lunch there two days before in the company of a military-looking man. He would have liked to say that Mrs Derwent-Delahaye sounded like a tiddly doll herself, but she had spoken with the intimidating gravitas of some superior schoolmarm.

What an extraordinary query, Mrs Derwent-Delahaye had said repressively; she feared that it would be difficult and time-wasting to ascertain whether a couple of that description had had lunch at her establishment – besides, it wasn't within their practice to divulge information regarding their patrons – unless there was a serious reason for it? 'She stole your menu!' Colville shouted into the phone before slamming it down. He had been shaking. Knowing full well that he had made a fool of himself, he sat with his face buried in his hands.

The pouch was made of fine black leather, was zip-operated and had the initials *H.P.* on it. Hugh Payne. Major Payne. Antonia Darcy's husband. Colville had found it on the small table beside one of the armchairs. He had been right. He had suspected Payne from the very start. *He had been right.*

The sitting room reeked of Payne's tobacco. Payne had been smoking his pipe. Payne had made himself at home, clearly. Payne had had drinks with Bee. His glass was on the little table beside his pouch. Colville picked it up and sniffed at it. Whisky. Bee had drunk brandy; her glass was smeared with her dark-rose lipstick. No third glass – there had been only the two of them. Antonia Darcy, he was sure, had no idea. Of course not. So much for the famous intuition of women. So much for crime writers' much vaunted powers of observation! He gave a mirthless laugh, but tears were already rolling down his face. Bee must have called Payne as soon as he, Colville, had left the house. Perhaps Bee had initiated the row with that aim in view? It was Payne she had been to see the other day when she said she'd been to the hairdresser's!

There were CDs strewn around on the floor. 'The Way You Look Tonight'. 'Moonlight Becomes You'. 'Unforgettable'. 'Fools Rush In'. These, as it happened, were some of his favourite songs. He picked them up and replaced them automatically on the shelf. Things seemed to have got ... passionate ... rough... Perhaps that was how Bee liked things. He swallowed. Yes. Payne had pushed Bee against the shelves and started kissing her throat–

Falling down on all fours, Colville started examining the carpet. Crumpled – closer to the door than it had been before – the fringe disarranged. One didn't need to be Sherlock Holmes to deduce that Bee and Payne had been dancing. Yes. Smooching. Pressed together, shamelessly close. Colville saw them very clearly in his mind's eye. Payne's arms around Bee's body, Bee's golden head on Payne's shoulder, her fingers linked behind his neck...

Whispering in each other's ears – laughing... People often danced as a prelude to greater intimacies.

Colville swallowed. He was remembering how Bee managed to get rid of her clothes – it was a trick she had – she did a sort of *shrug* and everything slithered to the ground – it was as though skirt, blouse and pants were all a bit of a piece. What a revelation that had been. It had left him breathless. It had happened on the first day of their honeymoon in Java. He recalled the double bed with the silk sheets – the green window shutters – the hot tropical afternoon pulsing outside... It all felt like a dream now...

Colville felt sure Payne was a marvellous dancer. Payne had carried Bee along with sinuous and effortless grace. Colville could hear Bee's laughter, her exclamations of delight, her gasps as she clung to her lover. She might even have wept, the way women did when they were in the throes of ecstasy.

He gripped the back of a chair. Everything was crumbling round him. His mind felt as though it was going to explode. His greatest fear was that he might be going mad. Become like Ingrid–

An hour earlier he had given himself a fatuous injunction: *Nil desperandum*. Well, he had convinced himself that all would be well after he had discussed matters with Bee. He had returned intent on reconciliation. He had been going to say sorry. He had meant to ask for forgiveness. Fall to his knees, if necessary. He'd have done anything for her smile – for her touch – for the lightest of her kisses – anything!

He was a fool. No fool like an old fool. So Ingrid had been right when she said all those ghastly, those truly shocking things about Bee when he had first moved into the house. Ingrid had regaled him with lurid tales of Bee seducing strangers, of trying to persuade Ingrid to procure for her – even while she had still been wheelchair-bound and then after her recovery – and of how, on two occasions, Ingrid had succumbed. Ingrid called Bee a 'voracious bird'. She claimed that Bee had even had an affair with

273

her doctor, Dr Aylard, who must be at least sixty... Colville had been convinced Ingrid was trying to poison his mind against Bee.

Well, Ingrid was jealous of him – resentful of his proximity to Bee, of his very presence in the house – she had a name for him – 'the interloper'! He had absolutely refused to believe that Bee had taken lovers, but now he wondered. Yes, he wondered very much... *Could the devil speak true?*

Suddenly he was eager to *know* and he felt at once impatient and terrified – rather like Bluebeard's young bride nerving herself to enter the forbidden chamber. He wanted to go and ransack those old velvet and satin hatboxes Bee kept in her wardrobe – tear them apart. The boxes had belonged to Bee's mother and seemed to be full of papers. He might find something – love letters – suggestive notes – mementoes – photos–

Photos other men had taken of Bee? Bee wearing outrageous outfits – naked – in suggestive poses – performing unspeakable lewd acts–

He passed his hand across his face. He started walking towards the door – halted. *No.* He needed to attend to other, more important, things first. There was the letter from his solicitor about that damned court case – he needed to write back as soon as possible. A bonfire. He needed to make a bonfire as a matter of some urgency, though he couldn't remember the exact reason for it. Burn dead leaves? Burn all of Bee's dresses, as an act of revenge? All those damned expensive Chanels and Balenciagas and Valentinos... No, it was something else he needed to burn – what *was* it? I am going mad, he whispered.

Had Payne and Bee gone to a hotel? Or were they perhaps at that very moment in the back of Payne's car? It must be Payne's car, since her Mini was in the garage. Were they lying on a blanket in the grass in some secluded spot – the obvious thing to do on a warm day like that. He could just see them. Smoking Bee's Turkish cigarettes – Bee's golden head on Payne's chest – discussing their future together – making plans – laughing – wondering about the most tactful and painless way of breaking the news to him.

Colville walked slowly into the hall, he didn't quite know why, and stood examining his reflection in the mirror. He looked distraught – wild-eyed – pouchy. He had aged over the last couple of hours. No woman would want to go with him – unless he paid her. Well, he had employed the services of tarts once or twice – years ago, when his first marriage had started going wrong – he deemed it a most unsatisfactory experience. He didn't want a tart. He wanted Bee. *He wanted Bee.*

But perhaps – perhaps everything was not

yet lost? Suddenly he felt a surge of optimism, heady and intoxicating – the kind of euphoria he had experienced when Bee said yes to his marriage proposal. Perhaps Bee was merely infatuated with Payne. It might be nothing but a crush. She might already have recovered from it, the way people recovered from bouts of illness. Yes. She might have resisted Payne's advances. The ultimate might not have taken place yet. Perhaps at that very moment she was saying, 'I am sorry, Hugh, but this is totally wrong. Please, take your hands off me. I don't know what possessed me. I must go back to my husband at once.'

Yes... He saw his reflection in the mirror smile back at him. I must go and make that bonfire, he thought. My future happiness depends on it. The next moment he noticed a small folded sheet of paper lying on the floor underneath the mirror. He stooped over and picked it up.

Please, darling, forgive, forgive. I love you. I want you so. Do not be cross. H.

H. for Hugh. Hugh Payne. Major Hugh Payne. Payne had written to her. She had dropped Payne's note. Not very careful, was she? Or maybe she no longer saw any point in concealing the affair. 'Forgive' and 'Do not be cross' suggested of course a previous secret meeting. They appeared to have had a tiff. *A lovers' tiff.* Well, Bee had clearly forgiven Payne. She had engineered the row with Colville, so that she could get Colville out of the house. She had then phoned Payne and asked him to come over–

It was all over. He had been a fool to imagine otherwise.

I must see to that bonfire, he thought.

Back at Ospreys Major Payne was taking command. 'I would like you to call the police,' he told Greg. 'Say we've found the body of Father Lillie-Lysander.'

'Is that him? The priest who disappeared?'

'Yes. The blood on the sheets and on Renshawe's pyjamas is his.'

'The priest's blood!'

'Yes. Nurse Wilkes will have to answer some awkward questions.'

'Oh, that's too bad!' cried the good-natured Greg. 'Just when she won the lottery–'

'She didn't win the lottery. What I think she got was part hush money, part reward. I think Nurse Wilkes was generously re-munerated for her cooperation. Where's that bin-liner exactly? The one with the bloody things?'

'In the big container.'

'Better get it back into the house – make sure it is the right one. The police would be jolly interested in the bloody things.' Payne paused. 'Lord of the flies.'

'What's that?' Antonia said.

'Beelzebub... Remember Beelzebub, my love? The priest's face was covered in flies. An association of ideas,' Major Payne explained. 'The Pharisees accused Jesus of performing miracles in the name of Beelzebub, who was a demon – some say Satan himself... I don't know. Not fair, perhaps, at this early stage. I shouldn't make precipitate judgements. I may be doing the priest a terrible injustice, but then the cloth does attract some strange individuals. I mean I am assuming he was a bad hat. I'll tell you what. Let's have a word with the Master of Ospreys. I want to see him before the police arrive. Come along. It should be jolly interesting. Though I doubt if he'll tell us the truth. Why should he?'

They saw Greg pick up the phone. When they were in the hall, Antonia asked, 'What do you think happened?'

'Well, I may be entirely wrong, but I have an idea that it was Ralph Renshawe's hand that held the fatal knitting needle that unleashed the gore – which doesn't necessarily make him into a killer, if you know what I mean.'

Antonia said, 'He wouldn't have had the strength for a powerful lethal upward thrust, would he?'

'No. He wouldn't have been able to get the body out of the room and drop it in the well either. Someone helped him.'

25

Le Malade Imaginaire

Ralph Renshawe squeezed her hand. *'Listen.* I've worked it all out. It is my nephew who was behind it. Father Lillie-Lysander was Robin's agent. He was a friend of his, apparently. They were at school together. Saunders told me about it. It slipped out – he didn't intend to tell me, but he got muddled. The old fool.'

'You didn't know they were friends?'

'I had no idea. Of course not. I am very cross with Saunders for not finding a priest himself. I commissioned him – and he left it all to Robin. To Robin! I am sure the priest was acting on orders from Robin. They were planning to share my fortune. I am sure it was all Robin's idea. Money, my dear, is the root of all evil.'

'Money's horrid. I entirely agree,' Beatrice breathed. *'Yes.'*

'I'd have shown Father Lillie-Lysander the door right away,' Ralph Renshawe went on. 'I'd have banned this perfidious priest from coming anywhere near the house. To think that I'd been confessing to the Devil! Oh

Bee, I will never forget those eyes above me – getting closer – cold, inhuman, the eyes of a beast! There was a smile on his lips – *he looked as though he was enjoying himself.*'

'You must tell the police about it, Ralph. Honestly. You must tell them about the connection between your nephew and the priest.'

'No – for my late sister-in-law's sake, I won't. My sister-in-law was a saint.' Ralph Renshawe picked up the fan. 'But Saunders will probably tell them. Saunders is scared, shaking in his boots. Well, I intend to sack Saunders. I feel hot, Bee. This seems to be a good sign. I was always cold before.' He had started fanning himself. 'Do I look terribly eccentric?'

Bee giggled. 'You do, rather.'

He pressed her hand again. 'I hope to see more of you in future, my dear. You will come again, won't you?'

'Of course I will.'

'Won't your husband mind?'

'He doesn't need to know.'

'Wicked girl,' he said. 'Would you give me a kiss, or am I too repugnant?'

'No, of course not, my sweet. Here.' She bent over and kissed his forehead. 'When you do feel better, Ralph, we can go to Baudolino's, for a symbolic drink – to exorcize the past,' she whispered. 'Or would that be in poor taste?'

The door opened and Antonia and Major Payne appeared.

'Who are these people?' Ralph Renshawe asked.

'Dear friends of mine. Hugh and Antonia Payne. They brought me here.'

'Sorry for barging in like that. I was wondering whether I might have a word with Mr Renshawe.' Major Payne was at his most clipped.

Ralph Renshawe had dropped the fan and slumped down between the pillows. 'With me? What about?'

Antonia stared at the lipstick mark on his forehead. Can't be dying, she thought.

Payne cleared his throat. 'The police will be here any moment—'

'They've already been here,' Ralph Renshawe said. 'The police don't scare me. They are looking for Father Lillie-Lysander. Well, I can't help them. I know nothing about his whereabouts. Nothing at all.'

'He's turned up, actually.' Major Payne paused. 'In a short while Father Lillie-Lysander will be in the capable hands of the scene-of-crime fellows.'

Beatrice gave a little gasp. 'What do you mean, Hugh?'

'I should have said his body. He is dead. He's been murdered.'

Ralph Renshawe's pale tongue flicked across the lips. 'You found his body? Where?'

'In the garden.' Payne waved towards the windows. 'The priest's in the hole. I mean the well.'

'In the wishing well!' Beatrice clutched at her throat.

'That is where the body was dropped. Somebody clearly wished him dead.' Payne paused but Ralph Renshawe said nothing. 'Father Lillie-Lysander was stabbed with one of Nurse Wilkes' knitting needles. It was on your bedside table, wasn't it, Renshawe?'

'I don't know what you are talking about.'

'I think you do. The needle pierced the priest's jugular. There was blood. Father Lillie-Lysander bled over your bed. You made Nurse Wilkes clean it up. You paid her handsomely to keep her mouth shut. It happened on the morning of the 26th. Two days ago. Your solicitor was coming at eleven o'clock. Father Lillie-Lysander died at least half an hour before that – the question is why? Why did he have to die?'

Ralph Renshawe looked at him. *Who are you?*

'I have a theory. The padre was about to bump you off – no, not with the knitting needle – by some other ingenious means.' Payne frowned thoughtfully at the pillows at the foot of the bed. 'However, the murderous attempt was foiled.' Payne raised his eyebrows at Beatrice who had stifled a cry. 'I do believe someone popped in through the french windows and rescued you.'

'You sound like one of those vacuous army majors.'

'I am a major, but I am far from vacuous.'

'Bee, my dear, would you tell your friends to go away? I am afraid I am awfully tired.' Ralph Renshawe shut his eyes.

'It had something to do with your will, hadn't it?'

'I know nothing about it, Hugh,' Beatrice whispered. 'Nothing at all.'

'I didn't mean you–'

Ralph Renshawe murmured, 'Why should I tell you anything?'

The sound of a siren came from outside.

'The police,' said Antonia.

Beatrice had kept her hand at her throat. She was tugging at her pearls as though they were choking her. And then it suddenly came to Antonia, what it was she had seen at Millbrook that was of importance.

Of course. It was the Polaroid photograph of Ingrid dressed up as Beatrice. The photograph held the clue.

That ridiculous necklace with the Taj Mahals – Ingrid was wearing it in the photo – the photo had been taken on the morning of the 26th – two days ago. That was when Ingrid had disappeared. Well, Ingrid hadn't been found yet – but when Antonia and Hugh arrived at Millbrook House earlier in the afternoon, the necklace – the unique Taj

Mahal necklace – had been adorning Bee's neck…

That, Antonia reflected, could mean only one thing.

'I haven't the foggiest what happened. I must have fallen asleep. I could hear the clacking of his rosary beads. It was a hypnotic kind of sound. Then – nothing. Total oblivion,' Ralph Renshawe told Inspector Hopper. His head lay on the pillow and he spoke in a halting, breathless voice, quite different from the voice in which he had spoken to Beatrice Ardleigh earlier on.

'Please try to remember. It is extremely important.'

'I had a rather frightening sort of dream. A nightmare, you may say. I often have nightmares. Only moments ago I imagined I heard the Grim Reaper sharpening his scythe. I am a very ill man.' Renshawe's eyes were half-closed, but he was watching his interlocutor covertly. 'When I woke up, I saw I was covered in blood. I *smelled* it first. A metallic kind of smell, slightly fishy. At first I thought I was still dreaming – that it was part of the nightmare, but then I touched it and realized the blood was real.'

'And Father Lillie-Lysander?'

'Gone. Vanished. He wasn't in the room any longer. His rosary was on my bedside table.'

Inspector Hopper leant forward. 'Father Lillie-Lysander's car was found in your garage, Mr Renshawe. We believe he died in this room. Your sheets were covered in his blood. We found bloodstains on the terrace outside and on the garden path. Father Lillie-Lysander's body was dragged out of here through the french windows, down the terrace steps, across the garden and pushed into the well.'

The old man cackled. 'You don't think it was me who did the dragging? I mean – look at me.'

'I never for a moment thought it was you. Somebody else dragged him out.' Inspector Hopper took out the card Major Payne had given him. 'Robin Renshawe. That's your nephew, isn't it? Was it your nephew who helped you?'

'Robin wouldn't try to help me. *Quite* the reverse.' Ralph Renshawe shut his eyes. 'You keep getting things wrong. Please, go away.'

'Was it your nurse? The woman who left your employ so hurriedly – Nurse Wilkes?' No answer came. 'Who helped you?' Hopper persisted. 'Whoever it was, you must have seen him.'

There was a pause. Ralph Renshawe's eyes remained shut but he started speaking deliriously. 'Who helped me? You want to know who helped me? I do know who helped me. Oh yes. It's all coming back to me. I'd never seen my saviour before, but you see, I recognized my saviour at once.'

The inspector leant forward, pen poised over notebook. 'Who was it? Would you describe him, sir?'

'*Him?* Oh no, it wasn't a man.'

'A woman? Who was she?'

'What a literal mind you have.' Ralph Renshawe sighed. 'They have no gender.'

Hopper blinked. 'No–?'

'I thought you knew. Don't you read your Bible?'

'What's the Bible got to do with it?' Hopper frowned. Was Ralph Renshawe really off his rocker or was he playing games with him?

'It's all in the Bible,' Ralph Renshawe said. 'You want to know who my saviour was? It was an angel, inspector–'

'An angel!'

Ralph Renshawe drew back a little, a pained expression on his face. 'Be kind enough to moderate your voice, inspector. Yes, an angel – but not a common or garden one. Oh no. It was *my guardian angel*. My guardian angel came to me in my hour of need.'

'What need?'

'Sorry – didn't I say? Do forgive me. I keep falling prey to fugues and fancies. The monstrous monsignor attempted to murder me.'

'Father Lillie-Lysander tried to kill you?'

'Is that a better way of saying it?' Ralph Renshawe frowned in a puzzled manner. 'Well, I prayed for help and my prayer was answered. I was helped in my hour of need, inspector, *exactly* as the Bible promises. You want me to describe my guardian angel? Smooth-faced, seemingly delicate but in fact exceptionally strong, with golden hair and golden crown and golden wings, brandishing a sword, exuding goodness and mercy, but also breathing fire—'

26

Strong Poison

The discovery of Father Lillie-Lysander's body in the grounds of Ospreys was announced later that evening on the ten o'clock news. He had been murdered – stabbed to death. The camera lingered on the theatrically Gothic pile with its absurd gables and turrets, then swept across the wildly overgrown garden, parts of which looked distinctly un-English due to the late Moira Montano's now dilapidated pink conservatory, ragged palms, fantastical grotto benches and clumps of bamboo; it all brought to mind a decayed Mediterranean film set.

The camera came to rest on a rook perched on the edge of the seventeenth-century wishing well. The rook – rather a large specimen – gazed straight at the camera, flapped its wings and crowed. There was no perceptible change in the newscaster's voice when he said that the priest's body had been at the bottom of the well. It had been a particularly brutal attack. At the time of discovery, the body had been in the

early stages of decomposition. The perpe-
trator was unknown and the motive for the
crime remained unclear. The police were
conducting an investigation and they were
anxious to speak to Miss Ingrid Delmar.

'Good lord, that's not Ospreys, is it?' Sir
Marcus Laud said, peering at the TV screen.
'It is Ospreys,' Lady Laud said.

She was thirty years younger than her
husband and his fourth wife. She had
reappeared soon after he had got rid of
Ospreys and since then they had been
leading a life of unadulterated bliss in South
Kensington. Sitting on the floor beside his
chair, resting her auburn head against his
knee, the fourth Lady Laud – who had read
English at Oxford and was something of an
expert on Kipling – sighed and once more
she told the story of what had made her run
away that day.

She had been aware of a little grey shadow,
as it might have been a snowflake against the
light, floating at an immense distance in the
background of her brain. She had then been
plunged into overwhelming gloom. Her
amazed soul, she said, dropped gulf by gulf
into that horror of great darkness which is
spoken of in the Bible, and which, as
auctioneers say, must be experienced to be
appreciated. Despair upon despair, misery
upon misery, fear after fear, until she found

herself in a state of absolute panic. She hadn't seen any ghosts or heard any voices – nothing like that, but, nevertheless, she had felt the overpowering urge to be as far away from Ospreys as possible. And again Sir Marcus – who had never read Kipling's story 'The House Surgeon' – said comfortably that he wasn't the least bit surprised. It was that sort of place.

(The truth was of course quite different and much more prosaic, and it had something to do with an unexpected phone call from a past lover who had suggested that they have one last month of passion in the Caribbean.)

The conversation then turned to Moira Montano.

'In one of her films she comes out of a lake on a freezing cold night and hovers above the surface,' Sir Marcus said. 'There's a chap in a boat and for some reason he's got stuck in the middle of the lake. She is beautiful as a dream. Golden hair, enormous green eyes, a wide red mouth, but when she smiles at the chap, her teeth show white and pointed, sharp as needles – as many teeth as a strange fish.'

In Knightsbridge, reclining so far back in his chair that he was horizontal in front of his TV set, his arms crossed behind his head, Robin Renshawe too watched the broadcast. A glass and a whisky bottle stood on the table before him. He had started by mixing himself whisky sours with grenadine, fresh lime and crushed ice, but had ended up drinking it neat. The ice cubes in the bucket had all melted. He was rather drunk; he was on the point of reaching that highly desirable state in which relaxation and irresponsibility mingle.

'Who the fuck is Ingrid Delmar?' Robin asked aloud. There hadn't been much regret in his reaction to Lily's demise. He had always regarded Lily as expendable. As disposable as a cocktail stick. *Requiescat in pace*, he had murmured and he had raised his glass. He had then wondered if it would be worth the trouble of sneaking into Lily's flat and collecting the marble bust of Cicero or whoever that was. It seemed to have caught his fancy, oddly enough. *No.* That wishing well might have been swarming with flies, but Lily's flat would be much worse – it would be swarming with *les flics*. Robin laughed at his joke, but his heart was far from light.

Another of his lieutenants gone. A couple of minutes earlier he had received a call from Eric at long last. Eric had told him he *hadn't* been able to do what Robin had asked him. *I am very sorry, Robin.* The silly ass had given the most *pathetic* reason imaginable for failing to go to Ospreys on the morning of the 26th. Eric had been most apologetic in that absurd lisping voice of his. That famous saying, *Looks like Tarzan, speaks like Jane*, might have been invented with Eric in mind. Robin should have known better.

'Why do I always associate with people like that?' Robin murmured. 'Why? *Why?*' He shut his eyes.

Golden ... golden ... hair and eyes ... and paradise. The words of a song floated through the open window in the warm night. Some people, it seemed, were managing to have a good time.

Everything had gone wrong. Lily was dead while his uncle was alive. Robin had been on the phone to Saunders, trying to pump him for information about the will. He had wanted confirmation – *was* there a new will? Saunders, however, had been terribly tight-lipped about it. Saunders had given him the cold shoulder. Saunders had been much nicer to him in the past, but then of course Robin had been his uncle's main legatee. Now Saunders treated him like a leper. All solicitors were bastards. Profiteering hypo-critical bastards. Robin had then called Wilkes. It was she who had told him about the new will, which she had witnessed – together with one of the cleaners. Well, she had confirmed what he had known all along. Everything to Beatrice fucking Ardleigh!

Christ. The whole Judith Hartz fortune. Wilkes had commiserated with him. She had been on her way to the airport, apparently, off to get married or something.

'Why Ingrid Delmar? Who is this Ingrid Delmar?' Robin cried. 'It is to Beatrice Ardleigh you should be speaking! You fucking ineffectual *flics*. It was Beatrice who killed Lily – must have done! Who else?'

His front doorbell rang. He remained seated. He yawned. He stretched his arms. He was not at home. The doorbell rang again. A manservant would have been able to deal with the matter in a smoothish kind of way. *Mr Renshawe is not at home. May I take a message?* Well, he couldn't afford a manservant, unless he asked Eric to do it for free? Eric would look jolly presentable in a black alpaca coat and striped trousers. No, not Eric – he was finished with Eric – not even if Eric, like his famous namesake in the book, learnt to do things properly, *little by little*.

What the fuck was that? Robin couldn't believe his ears. Someone was forgetting this was Knightsbridge and not fucking Redbridge. Manners, *please*. Fists had started banging on his front door. A voice shouted: 'Mr Renshawe? We know you are there! Open up. Police!'

Robin remembered how as a boy he used to read the Norse myths and how he cheered on Loki, the trickster malcontent and shape-shifter, who was doomed to agonized failure in his persistent battles with the Asgard gods... They must have found something... Saunders must have talked, blast him... His uncle must have been saying things... Had Eric too talked? Eric tended to want to 'share' things with people in the girlie way he had... Would the Asgard gods batter down the door if he didn't open it?

They couldn't put him in jail – there wouldn't be enough evidence – but they were capable of making his life distinctly unpleasant for a while. *The Mortification of Moriarty*. How ironic, Robin Renshawe thought. It was almost as though Lily had known some such thing would happen all those years ago when he had devised the twist at the end of their play.

At her enemy's mercy...

Who *was* her enemy? Ingrid was sure she knew. If only her head didn't hurt so badly, if only so many thoughts didn't insist on crowding round her brain, it would come to her... The name or the face... So hard to think of one particular enemy, when one had so many! Ralph. The interloper. Bee. Father Lillie-Lysander – no – Father Lillie-Lysander was dead – killed like a pig.

How he had bled!

What was it the handkerchief in her

mouth reeked of? It was *such* a familiar smell. A mixture of tobacco and scent. A smell she associated with someone she had once loved dearly. No, not Claire... Claire didn't smoke. Claire was too young, completely unspoilt... Her little girl... Lovely lips like a rosebud, clear blue eyes, hair like lint, so fair it hardly made any shadow on her pale forehead. Where *was* Claire?

Ce Soir Je T'Aime and stale Turkish cigarettes. That was it – the malodorous *mélange*. To think that there had been a time when she hadn't minded the smell of either, that she had actually *liked* it since they were both part of Bee... She had been dabbing drops of Ce Soir Je T'Aime behind her ears as part of her impersonation – but it was not something she wanted in her mouth.

For no apparent reason a memory floated into Ingrid's head. A balmy day in early August. The sun shimmering off the river in bright waves. Bee and she sitting contentedly within a nest of large brocade cushions. A starched tablecloth on the grass. A picnic lunch. Pimms, grilled salmon-trout, sautéed potatoes, green salad, a bottle of white wine, followed by lemon sorbet and, finally, thick black coffee out of exquisite Meissen porcelain cups, which Ingrid had brought over from the house carefully wrapped up in two silk shawls. The summery buzzing of bees in the air. Bluish smoke rising from

Bee's Turkish cigarette. Bee reminiscing once more about the grand hotels in the South of France where she had stayed with her father – vanilla and strawberry palaces in their *vastes parcs fleuris*, sheltered by parasol pines and fountaining palm trees – sleek-headed bellboys in duck-egg grey uniforms – taps that filled the bath in thirty seconds and caused it to overflow in thirty-five... Then the wild beating of wings – two ducks fighting on the river. How they had laughed! *Quack, quack*, Bee had said in her droll way. *Quack, quack, quack*. Ingrid remembered her thoughts. *This is too perfect.*

Ingrid had reached out for Bee's left hand, held it palm upwards and compared it with her own. *Look, our hands are practically identical.* Bee had hastily withdrawn her hand – didn't Ingrid know it was unlucky to compare hands? Ingrid had told her not to be silly. Ingrid hadn't really expected anything bad to happen, but had felt a little disconcerted when the following morning at ten a man introducing himself as 'Leonard Colville' phoned and asked to speak to Bee. Ingrid had put her hand over the receiver and whispered – *Sounds like some pompous fool – hope you won't be too bored.*

Ingrid realized that she was dead already. Her parents had killed her, her boyfriend had killed her, Ralph had killed her, Bee had killed her, the interloper had killed her, the wasted years had killed her. When the heart was dead, all was dead, though the victim might not fully be aware of it for a long time–

She tried to scream but all that came from her mouth was a faint moaning sound. What kind of a box was this? As a child she used to be punished by her father by being shut up in a wardrobe or small cupboard, where she had imagined that a small creature was trying to bite off her toes. *Had* her toes been bitten off–

She was delirious again.

Was the mixture of Parisian scent and Turkish tobacco in her mouth going to make her throw up? If that happened, she would choke on her own vomit and die a slow horrible death. Maybe that was the intention?

No, that was *not* the intention. Ingrid knew she was going to die a violent death, but she believed there was a purpose as to why she had been kept alive so far. There was a good reason why she hadn't been killed outright in the garden at Ospreys, the way the priest had been, why the first blow hadn't been followed by a second, lethal one.

The priest had struggled – that had been his undoing. There had been a spurt of blood – then another. The priest had thrashed about and then had lain on the floor twitching. Yes, she had seen the priest perish. She had stood outside the french windows and watched, fascinated, hypnotized by the sight of the blood...

It was only moments later that she had made her presence known. *Hello.* The shocked look on his face – those foolish bulging eyes, that gaping mouth, those cheeks the colour of ripe tomatoes! It had made her laugh. He had been dragging the priest like a sack of potatoes across the terrace towards the stone steps that led to the garden.

She had started speaking. The things she had said! She had let all her frustration, all her resentment, all her bitterness, all her hatred spill out, but she had also, in a strange kind of way, enjoyed herself. Oh yes. She smiled at the memory. She had felt extremely powerful and in complete control. The torrent of words unleashed from between her lips had been frightening.

She had let rip.

Do you think you will be allowed to get away with this? Your interloping days are over. You are finished. You'll spend the rest of your days in jail. You will end up as some big boy's bitch. I will see to it. They may even kill you. You'll never be allowed to touch your beloved again. I'll see to it. But it was when she had started with the more specific taunts – *Bee's got a rating system, you know – she rates all her lovers – if you only knew what she said about you, how she laughed when she said you lacked that significant It in the boudoir department, you wouldn't want to live!* – that the blow had fallen.

Suddenly the lid opened and Ingrid was blinded by light–

An electric torch had been flashed into her face. She moaned – it burnt her eyes. She felt the tape being removed from her mouth, roughly and painfully peeled off, the handkerchief pulled out. Air! She coughed and gasped. Bright spots swam before her eyes. Then, in negative black and white, she saw something familiar. Wasn't that the holly tree in front of Millbrook, the house she and Beatrice had shared for thirty years? Of course it was. The holly reached up to her bedroom window – why, she had trimmed it only last week!

Then she saw where she was. In the boot of a car – not in a coffin. She opened her mouth wide – not to scream but to breathe. She filled her lungs with air. Had help come? Earlier on she had been praying to Mighty God Rook–

No. Ingrid couldn't make out the features of the face looking down at her, but she knew very well who it was. It was – *him*. I will have you for assault and illegal constraint, she wanted to shout but the next moment she smelled bitter almonds. She tried to bite the hateful fingers that were pushing the lump of cyanide into her mouth – how she would have liked to crunch them off! – but failed. She snarled – she felt her chin being pushed upwards. She heard her teeth click. She felt the cyanide gliding down her tongue, like a boat down a sluggish river, sinking deep into her throat. She gasped again – choked – gurgled–

Then, in the couple of seconds she had to live, Ingrid saw why she had been kept alive so far and brought to Millbrook House. It was one of those instant flashes of intuition.

The plan was that her death be made to look like suicide. It was *her* cyanide, she knew. The cyanide she kept in a phial in her room. Her cupboard had been raided. Suicide – wasn't that what loopy people like her did when they reached the end of the line? The police were meant to assume that it was *she* who had killed the priest – that he had tried to protect Ralph, that they had had a fight – and she had stabbed him. No doubt they would discover the fruit knife in her pocket – it would be suitably smeared in the priest's blood. They would assume she had panicked and bolted – that she had been hiding. She would be found stretched out on her bed beside her daughter's photos–

One last gasp – one last convulsion – and she was still.

27

Esquire of the Body

Ingrid's face was fiercely distorted. One eye, large and staring, moved slightly to the left as if it had become unmoored. The other remained fixed on her killer.

Ingrid's body was dragged through the front door of the house and up the stairs, to the room which she had once occupied. There were a lot of photographs in silver frames on the bedside table. Several showed the two dogs Ingrid had once loved but had eventually had put down – these had black ribbons across the left corner. The majority of the photos were of similar-looking little girls. About six or seven years old – smiling faces – dimpled chins – blonde curls. That was what her daughter *would* have been like, Ingrid had felt certain. Six photographs showed the same girl in a playground; that had been her *best* Claire; Ingrid had found her after hours of searching, and taken photos of her without the mother noticing. She had seriously considered abducting the girl and bringing her up as her own – but there had been too many people around.

The body was laid on the bed. The hands and the feet were unbound. An open phial which contained traces of cyanide was placed between the fingers of her right hand. For a moment the killer hesitated – she *was* right-handed, wasn't she? The blonde wig was still on Ingrid's head but it was a rag now, covered in congealed mud; blades of grass and dead leaves stuck out of it. Ingrid's face was badly bruised – it was black and blue and no longer looked anything like Beatrice's, he was pleased to note. The nose seemed broken, one of the eyes terribly swollen. The lips too. Well, the police would assume that Ingrid Delmar had sustained her injuries in her fight with the priest. The fruit knife, covered in the priest's blood, would be discovered in her pocket.

He stood looking round the room. Sea-green walls, very faded, bordered with a pattern of roses on a black background. On the dressing table, beside a bowl of dead flowers, so black it was impossible to say what they had been when fresh, lay a book. He picked it up and held it in his gloved hand. George Trevelyan. *On Reincarnation and Other Psychic Matters*. He leafed through it. A sort of erudite madness, from what he could see. The book was covered in dust, like the rest of the dressing table. What was it Ingrid had wanted to believe? That her unborn daughter might have come back as some other little girl? He wiped his gloves with his handkerchief.

A musty smell hung on the air. Heaven knew when the room had been cleaned and aired last... Was there anything else he needed to do? He had already disposed of the knitting needle. The police would never find it... Earlier on he had managed to burn his bloodied clothes as well as the shirt and jumper he had taken from Ralph Renshawe's wardrobe. He had done it in the back yard. He had made sure the clothes had been reduced to ashes, then scattered the ashes over the river... He remembered Ralph's eyes following him as he had walked across the room. Ralph – his former rival in love! Of course Ralph had had no idea as to who he was. Ralph had nodded and mouthed his thanks. Not a word had passed between them. At one point both of them had looked at the clock. They had had the same thought in mind, the same purpose – that nothing should interfere with the signing of the will.

He had dropped Robin Renshawe's card in the garden; he had found it in the priest's wallet. The more false leads the police had to follow, the more hares to chase after, the better. Though of course, inevitably, it was all going to culminate here, in this room. That was how it had to be. He didn't turn off the light. Casting one final glance at Ingrid's body, he left the room.

He descended the stairs and went out of the house without locking the front door.

He got back into his car.

He sat trying to collect his thoughts. Suddenly he felt empty – anticlimactic.

It would be up to Beatrice to discover the body and inform the police. Whenever she and Payne came back. *If* they came back... They were bound to notice the light in Ingrid's room... It might be quite late – midnight or even in the small hours of the morning... *Would* they come back? They might decide to spend the night at an hotel – or at Payne's pied-à-terre. Fellows like Payne always kept a pied-à-terre... Payne's wife clearly had no idea of what was going on, preoccupied as she was with her writing, inventing murders and victims and alibis. Shouldn't he write to Antonia Darcy and apprise her of her husband's infidelity? Anonymously – signed 'Well-wisher'? No – what would be the point? It wouldn't change a thing – too late.

He stared in front of him into the gathering darkness. He had prepared an alibi for himself. Now what *was* it? He frowned. He needed to concentrate. He gripped the wheel between his gloved hands and shut his eyes. No, he didn't need an alibi. No one would ever suspect him. Why should they? He would need to clean the boot though – dispose of the handkerchief and the paper with the house plan–

Colville groaned. He had felt the beginnings of a depression, the powerful daemon he had never been able to understand, counter or control. It started as usual with the familiar sinking sensation – thoughts of futility and pointlessness – a nameless dread nagging at his mind, like some ancient curse. What had Bee said the last time he had complained? *By no means let the black dog pounce! It's all a question of silly biochemistry, darling – one of those rogue enzymes.* Bee hadn't been exactly helpful. The truth was she had never understood him – she hadn't even tried.

What good would all this money be to him without Bee's love? Even if she stayed with him, for appearances' sake, she'd continue to sneak out to meet Payne. Of course she would. Colville clearly lacked that significant It in the boudoir department... Love trysts... Secret and not-so-secret assignations... Bee would expect him to condone her ways – she regarded him as a mere blind, doting dullard... He took Payne's pouch out of his pocket and stared down at it.

Then another thought struck him. If Bee did leave him for Payne, which she probably would do in the end, he'd get nothing ... not a penny. He could never tell Bee what he had done... All his efforts – to keep Bee and Payne in state! He examined his bruised knuckles. The risks he had taken – the danger he had put himself in – so that those two could enjoy a life of plutocratic leisure–

He started the car. He had no idea where he was going.

'Oh, but you *must* come in and have a bite to eat,' Beatrice said when they delivered her at Millbrook House shortly after ten that evening. '*Please*... I feel a wreck. I look a wreck, don't I?' Opening her eyes wide, she turned to Antonia. 'Don't I?'

'Not really,' Antonia said.

'Oh, I can't get Len on his mobile... I could do with some company.' Beatrice shot Payne a sidelong glance, but Antonia no longer minded. Earlier on Beatrice had been saying how absolutely thrilling she found that young man's South African accent. She meant Greg. It wasn't at all 'common', nothing like the way Australians, say, spoke – it sounded warm and unusual and well, *sexy*. She had given a laugh and made a funny face – her 'duck face', she informed them.

At one point she and Greg had started talking about tattoos and she had confided in him that *she too had one*. She would have shown it to him, she said coyly, if *only* she didn't have to remove her stocking. They had stood in the kitchen at Ospreys, drinking brandy. Greg had opened one of Ralph Renshawe's bottles of Armagnac. They had all needed a drink. Father Lillie-Lysander's body had been taken away. The police had gone.

Well, Beatrice couldn't help herself. She was that sort of woman. Still, they needed to talk to her seriously before long. What would be the best way to break the news to her? Beatrice wouldn't have hysterics, would she? Antonia couldn't bear the thought of a scene. They would probably end up staying the night at Millbrook House. (Where *was* Ingrid's body? What had he done with the body?)

'Heaven knows where Len has gone... He seems to have had a bonfire earlier on, can you smell it?' Beatrice had opened her door but seemed reluctant to leave the car. 'Such a pleasant, *Christmassy* kind of smell... I am sure that's our back garden... Why are you so quiet? You look as though you know something I don't. Don't tell me I am imagining things. I saw you whispering, just before we left Ospreys... What is it? Why are you looking at me like that? You are frightening me!'

Antonia pretended she hadn't heard. Keeping Beatrice in the dark afforded her an unworthy frisson of sadistic pleasure. 'It's getting colder,' she said. 'The weather's turning, have you noticed?'

'All right.' Major Payne cleared his throat. 'Beatrice, there's something you should know–'

Beatrice interrupted. 'Oh my God, look – *look*. The light's on in Ingrid's room!' She pointed. 'Ingrid seems to be back... Now you simply *must* come in... You can't possibly leave me alone with her. We may have to call the police and you can do that so much better than me.'

28

The Taj Mahal Necklace

Four weeks later it was Christmas and they had Major Payne's aunt staying with them. Lady Grylls had recovered from her cataract operation, but she still wore a piratical patch across her right eye – because she fancied herself in it rather than out of any real necessity, Antonia suspected – and was eager for entertainment. Lady Grylls loved stories of mystery, mayhem and murder, so, with the Christmas pudding and the black coffee, they told her this one. The whole lamentable affair in which greed, revenge, despair and madness all played a part.

'Colville gave every appearance of a man who stands on his feet, representing solidity and permanence, but he became a double murderer,' Major Payne said. 'Well, he wasn't a particularly effectual landlord. His business had been going to the dogs. He needed money badly and, having this magnificent windfall come to his wife, he wasn't going to allow it to be snatched away, just like that. What was hers was going to be his. They had a joint bank account. We are

309

talking about a fabulous fortune here. Big money.'

'How big?' Lady Grylls asked. She liked details in a story.

'Very big. Thirty-five million pounds. Well, money is a great catalyst. He decided to follow Ingrid moments after he'd seen her through the window and snapped her with his Polaroid. It was a spur-of-the-moment decision. He saw her make for the bus stop. He had no doubt she'd get on the number 19 bus, which would take her to Ospreys. Maybe he saw her get on the bus. His one and only concern was that Ralph Renshawe should be alive at eleven o'clock and sign the will which made Beatrice his sole beneficiary.'

'I love reconstructions like that.' Lady Grylls helped herself to more cream. 'It's almost as though you were there. You are terribly clever.'

'Not at all. Much of this is pure speculation, darling, so we may be well off the mark about an awful lot of things... I wouldn't presume to know exactly what went on in Colville's mind, but it is doubtful whether he had a plan as such, not when he set out. His idea was to stop Ingrid inflicting any harm on Ralph Renshawe. Intervene, if necessary. So he ran out of the house, got into his car and drove to Ospreys.'

Lady Grylls frowned. 'Why didn't he alert the nurse over the blower if he was so concerned? He could have phoned Ospreys and saved himself the trouble. Or rung the front doorbell when he got there – and explained to her what was happening?'

'He could have, but he didn't. Good point, darling,' said Major Payne. 'My only explanation is that Colville was in some peculiar mental state that day, that he wasn't thinking straight – worried silly about money, his tenants, the forthcoming court case and heaven knows what else. He had been under a lot of pressure.'

'The front doorbell was out of order – Colville might have tried ringing it,' Antonia put in.

Payne stroked his jaw. 'He might have feared it would delay things if he started explaining the situation to the nurse. On the other hand, he might have been looking for an excuse to deal with Ingrid in his own terms – he seemed to have hated her as much as she hated him. Too fanciful? He phoned a policeman friend of his and told him how concerned he was about Ingrid, but that was *after* he had put her in his car boot. Anyhow, he got to the house and walked round to the back. He knew Renshawe occupied a room on the ground floor that looked out on the back garden and the wishing well–'

'How did he know that? And why didn't the nurse hear his car?'

'The nurse was in the kitchen, which is in

a different part of the house. I don't imagine you can hear much from there. Colville had a rough drawing of Renshawe's part of the house in his pocket. The police believe it was done by Ingrid – they found her finger-prints on it – and Colville chanced upon it somehow.' Major Payne took a sip of coffee. 'Colville saw the french windows were open. It was a very warm day, remember. He went closer and looked in. Well, it was Ingrid he had come to protect Ralph against, but what he saw was Ralph's father confessor holding a pillow over Ralph's face, pressing it down, clearly smothering him–'

'I can't quite imagine a C. of E. clergyman doing that kind of thing, can you?' Lady Grylls said.

Antonia took up the tale. 'Colville ran into the room and pulled Father Lillie-Lysander away. He probably resisted and Colville wrestled him down – against the knitting needle, as it happened. Colville was much bigger and stronger. The knitting needle had been on Ralph's bedside table and Ralph had managed to reach out for it and was holding it aloft, but of course he was too feeble to put it to any effective use.'

'So the padre got skewered?'

'So the padre, as you so picturesquely put it, darling, got skewered,' Major Payne said. 'I don't believe Colville *intended* it to happen that way, but there it was. Colville started

312

dragging the priest's body through the french windows, across the terrace in the direction of the well. It was at that point Ingrid appeared on the scene.'

'It is almost as though you were there,' Lady Grylls said again. 'I imagine she taunted him – threatened to tell the police...'

'Ingrid's face was badly bruised, so were Colville's knuckles,' Antonia said thoughtfully. 'Which suggests that Colville dealt her several blows with his fist. She fell to the ground, hit her head – passed out. Which allowed him to drag the priest's body to the well. He also managed to cover the blood trail with dead leaves... Then he got Ingrid round the house to his car. He bound and gagged her–'

'He gagged her with Beatrice's handkerchief. He had kept it next to his heart,' said Payne. 'The handkerchief was later found in the boot of Colville's car. It bore an imprint of Ingrid's teeth. They also found hairs from her blonde wig. And bloodstains. It was Ingrid's blood.'

'At some point Colville forced Ingrid to swallow a lump of cyanide, arranged her body in her room and made it look like suicide. That's where we found her,' Antonia said, giving a slight shudder at the memory.

There was a pause.

'We used to know some people called Colville,' Lady Grylls said. 'I am sure they

313

were called Colville. We met them in the South of France. Stayed at the same hotel – the good old Palais Maeterlinck. D'you remember it, Hughie?'

'Of course I do. The good old Palais Maeterlinck.'

'They kept having spats – all on account of Mrs Colville spending too much time in the arms of some gigolo or other. She insisted he was teaching her the cha-cha-cha. Must have been 1956 or '57.'

'One doesn't dance the cha-cha-cha in anybody's arms. You do it in line,' Antonia pointed out.

'*Precisely*, my dear. That was the bone of contention. *Forward, back, cha-cha-cha, back, forward, cha-cha-cha. Two, three, cha-cha-cha. Hey, hey, I can do this, cha-cha-cha, it's easy, cha-cha-cha!*' Lady Grylls sang out and wiggled her shoulders. 'Ah, those were the days.' She helped herself to another slice of Christmas pudding. 'Now then, at which point did you puzzle out it was Colville?'

'I remembered the Taj Mahal necklace,' Antonia explained. 'Beatrice had it on that day, when we went to Millbrook House. It had been a present from Colville. He had had it specially made for her when they got engaged. On the morning she disappeared, Ingrid had put on the necklace as part of the Beatrice get-up. It could be seen in the Polaroid photo Colville took of her. There was only *one* Taj Mahal necklace. Yet, Beatrice was wearing it two days later at the height of the search for Ingrid! How *did* the Taj Mahal necklace find its way to Bee's neck? Bee couldn't have had anything to do with it – on the fatal morning she was in Oxford.'

'You think it was Colville who brought it back to the house?'

'*Only* Colville could have brought it back to the house. He couldn't allow Ingrid to wear what was clearly an object of supreme sentimental value to him. So sometime after he knocked her out and put her in the boot of his car, he took the necklace off. He brought it back to the house and replaced it inside his wife's jewel case. It never occurred to him to consider the implications. Beatrice of course had no idea about any of this, so she took the necklace out and put it on. She and Colville had had a row and she wanted him to see her wearing the Taj Mahal necklace when he came back.'

'What a silly woman. *Is* she a silly woman?'

'Not quite. She is a strange mixture–' Major Payne broke off. He had seen the expression on Antonia's face.

'What happened to her?' Lady Grylls asked.

'She is seeing Ralph Renshawe's nurse. A young South African called Greg,' Antonia said. 'In fact she has moved in with him at

Ospreys. He is twenty years younger than her, but they seem very happy together. We went to see them the other day.'

'I know her type.' Lady Grylls nodded. 'Oh yes. For some reason women like that are always all right in the end. One always thinks – *hopes* – they'd end up disastrously but they don't, not always, isn't that extraordinary? Does she wear palazzo pants? Women like that always wear palazzo pants.'

'As a matter of fact she does,' Antonia said. 'She did wear palazzo pants the other day!'

'Is Ralph Renshawe still alive then?'

'Yes. He has had a miraculous recovery. The doctors couldn't believe it, but it's not such a completely unknown thing to have happened, not even among seemingly hopeless cases. Beatrice and Greg are looking after him and he seems delighted with the arrangement. Not quite a *ménage à trois*. When he dies, Beatrice will inherit his fortune, but that may not be for a while. He's left his bed and propels his way round in a rather superior motorized wheelchair. He's talked to us and told us more things than he told the police, mainly thanks to Beatrice,' Antonia conceded. 'Last time we went they were watching a Moira Montano film – they found a trunkful of old reels in the attic and Greg had them transferred on to video.'

'Ah, Moira Montano. I remember Moira Montano. Hughie's uncle was mad about

Moira Montano,' Lady Grylls said. 'She died some bizarre death, I think.'

'Renshawe's Christmas present for Beatrice is a fine Rolls, its silver snout professionally inscribed on what might be the left nostril, BEE... Ospreys is jolly unrecognizable now – carpets everywhere, they have removed that gruesome ivy and the garden's been tidied up. And here's a curious thing,' Major Payne went on. 'It turns out that at some point during her third visit, Renshawe became aware of the fact that the woman who had been visiting him was not Beatrice but Ingrid. He recognized her by her birthmark – the blood-red naevus on her palm. He had seen it in the aftermath of the crash – when he went up to Ingrid's car to help her out. It stuck in his memory. He said it had haunted his dreams.'

'Why didn't the silly fellow do something about it?' Lady Grylls cried. 'He should have called the police straight away.'

'He should have but he didn't,' Antonia said. 'He decided it would be right if Ingrid killed him. He *wanted* her to kill him. He had convinced himself that he deserved to die at her hands. As an act of expiation. He was riddled with guilt.'

Lady Grylls sighed. 'How deliciously complicated.'

They then pulled crackers and read the silly jokes inside them.

'*Why was the computer ill? Because he had a virus!*'

'*Why did the monster's eyes turn green? Because he was jealous!* By the way, what happened to Colville?' Lady Grylls asked.

'He crashed his car and died. It happened that same night. No one would ever know for certain now, but there's a suspicion that he might have done it on purpose.' Major Payne stroked his jaw with a thoughtful forefinger. 'The Taj Mahal necklace was found in his pocket, ripped apart. And another curious thing. My tobacco pouch was in his other pocket. He had slashed through it several times with a pocket knife. I wonder why he did that.'

'Do you?' Antonia said.

'You don't mean he thought – that he imagined–' Payne sat up as realization dawned on him. 'Golly. The green-eyed monster, eh?'

'How extraordinary,' Lady Grylls wheezed. 'It's as though I'd known. I mean I've got you a new tobacco pouch, Hughie. That's your Christmas present – I shouldn't have told you. It was *meant* to be a surprise. Oh well, too late now. *Assassins at Ospreys* – wouldn't that make a jolly good title for your next book, my dear?'

'I don't think so,' Antonia said.

Outside it had started snowing.

This Large Print Book, for people
who cannot read normal print,
is published under the auspices of

THE ULVERSCROFT FOUNDATION

... we hope you have enjoyed this book.
Please think for a moment about those
who have worse eyesight than you ...
and are unable to even read or enjoy
Large Print without great difficulty.

You can help them by sending a
donation, large or small, to:

**The Ulverscroft Foundation,
1, The Green, Bradgate Road,
Anstey, Leicestershire, LE7 7FU,
England.**
or request a copy of our brochure for
more details.

The Foundation will use all donations
to assist those people who are visually
impaired and need special attention
with medical research, diagnosis
and treatment.

Thank you very much for your help.